A DEAD SHIP IN THE DEEP BLACK

THE LYRA CYCLE: EPISODE 1

RENE ASTLE

ARMCHAIR ALIEN

Contents

INTO THE BADLANDS

1: HΛRBIN

A PINPOINT NEEDLE OF light caught Harbin Low's attention, stabbing at the headache lodged in his skull. The dockers who used the gangway as a shortcut between the two sides of the Euko Station spaceport were absent. He squinted as he peered out the window that spanned one side of the passageway. It looked out onto the port's solar side, not that he could see the distant sun, even if the piers, buttresses, and barges of the port weren't in the way. The sun and its planets were specks, barely brighter than the rest of the galaxy.

Being on the lowest tier of the backside of the commercial port, the space outside was full of junks and junkers, or large scavengers that couldn't afford the fees higher up. Harbin's lips pulled down. *He* should be further up, enjoying the view of the rippling gate. Even though watching the pleasure yachts and their pampered passengers caused acid to burble in his stomach. He blinked, his mouth pressing into a thin line. He was on *this* catwalk staring out *this* window for a reason: he had a mission.

A brown insect crawled across the green-tinged glass, fluffing its dull casings to reveal gossamer wings and a bright purple abdomen underneath. Harbin reached a finger out towards the insect, then pulled his hand back at the last second — he wasn't sure he wanted to touch an unidentified bug and certainly didn't want to stick his finger in whatever gave the glass its sickly hue. Station windows weren't supposed to be green, but he was in its belly. *Its intestines.* His nose wrinkled, pulling up at his lips. With the inconstant lights flickering in the service corridor, it felt like he was deep under the ocean. Except he wasn't anywhere near an ocean. Or a planet for that matter. The closest object of any size was a dwarf planetoid long ago strip-mined of anything useful.

No, Euko was a third-tier jump gate station on the rim of a third-tier solar system. Harbin had been born on a station much like this one and worked hard to forget it.

His scowl deepened. Stepping towards the glass, he focused his gaze beyond the green coating, instead eying the ships that filled the port. Their blinking lights and docking beacons outshone the stars in the black beyond. And this was just one tier, the lowest, of the massive jump gate port. Glancing up, he saw the bellies of just as many ships above him, moving in and out of the spokes of docks in a mesmerizing dance led by an AI in a server room somewhere.

Any one of them would do. His jaw clenched as he scanned the ships. He didn't know why he was down in the stinking, cold depths waiting for a very particular fish in this sea. But his was not to question why.

"Do you see it yet?" a soft voice beside him said, yanking him out of his musings.

Harbin slid his gaze sidelong. Gar, his contact, peered through the green glass with a smile printed on his face. He frowned at the man's smooth skin and slicked-back hair, at his slightly iridescent suit. This was the man he'd been told to listen to. One who'd never had to stare down death.

Harbin shifted his attention out the window, forcing the frown from his face. "No."

Although he'd tried to ignore the third person on the gangway with them, rounding out their uncomfortable trio, his gaze still flicked to the man's reflection. The third man leaned against the frame at the far end of the glass, watching them with half-closed eyes instead of studying the ships. Harbin shifted away from his cool appraisal. The man ran a hand through his hair, then looked down at his nails and casually flicked open a knife, using it to pick under his fingernails.

The scowl return to Harbin's face, so deep he felt it in his neck, and he turned back to the window. "Why are we after *this* ship? Any of these could do the job."

Gar shrugged. "Why do we do any of the things we do...because *she* says so. And we all know where our salt comes from." The slick man pulled out a handkerchief to dab his dry forehead. "Maybe there's someone on board she wants." He tucked the square of cloth away. "Or someone she wants dead."

"And just how am I supposed to get this particular ship?" Harbin asked as a ship bumped a little too hard into the docking assembly, drawing his attention.

Gar chuckled. "That's not my problem now. It's yours." He lifted a shoulder as his reflection graced Harbin with a serpentine smile. Then he turned away to amble along the gangway, disappearing through the green-hued twilight into the bowels of the station.

The third man shifted from the wall, flicking his blade closed. He stepped towards Harbin with a grin on his face, patting him on the shoulder. Harbin glared at the man's fingers.

"Don't worry. I got your back," the man said, apparently oblivious to Harbin's distaste. "I'll get you what you need off that ship."

Harbin looked at him and considered breaking the man's fingers or punching that handsome face. He sighed and shifted his gaze back to the glass. But *she* wouldn't like that. And Gar was right. Everything Harbin Low did, he did for her.

2: TINK

T HE *Lyra* shuddered as its rear slipped sideways, causing it to bump into something, presumably the pier. Tink patted the engine, grimacing at the greasy fingerprints she left on the gleaming blue housing. "It's okay, girl, you'll get some TLC soon."

She swore the ship hummed in response, and she smiled as she plucked a rag from her pocket and wiped away the grease spots. A hiccough in the fuel manifold drew her attention, barely audible over the other murmurs and whirrs of the engine room. Tipping her head to the side, she heard a faint whine from behind the axial stabilizer. A frown pulled her lips down as she listened. Picking up the torch from her workbench, she tucked it in her mouth then shimmied under the air intake to get at the offending flywheel. Once in place, she flashed the torch up. Two glowing, green eyes peered down at her.

"Grim!" Tink reached an arm between moving bits of engine to grab at the grey cat. He jumped over her hand and fled the way she'd come. Shaking her head in the confined space, she set to adjusting the flywheel, then crawled back out. Grim sat on her workbench, cleaning himself.

"Why did I take you in again?" she asked as she dusted off her jumpsuit. The cat blinked at her, then lifted his leg to scratch at his neck, rattling the bauble on his collar which did nothing to scare bugs away. Tink turned away, pulling out a stethoscope to listen to the engine. Her eyebrows drew together — there was a ping somewhere in her system. The *Lyra* shivered again but didn't bounce.

The ship comms crackled as it came to life, startling her, and causing Grim to hiss.

"I swear, Tink, if you don't get that engine in line, I'll space you," the disembodied voice of Captain Rebeka Mino said.

Tink snorted. "Don't worry." She gave the stabilizer a gentle rub. "She doesn't mean it." With Tink's small frame and knowledge of every nook and cranny of the ship, she knew that even if the captain were serious, her anger would burn out long before she found her. And Tink knew Rebeka Mino — under the hard exterior there was a core of iron that wouldn't do anything to endanger the crew, no matter how angry she was. That included *not* spacing Tink. Besides, the engine wasn't the cause of their current problems; that was Ish's flying.

Another judder shivered through the ship, and a light started blinking on the display to her left. She flicked the light with her finger. "Not again."

She sprinted towards the cargo bay. The docking ring assembly wasn't extending, and one thing a ship in port needed was an airtight seal.

Tink was giving the docking ring control panel a love tap with her wrench when the captain snuck up behind her.

"I swear...." Rebeka started, shaking her newly shaved head. The skin, recently oiled, gleamed under the lights of the cargo bay. Tink couldn't decide if she liked the look or not; it made Rebeka seem fiercer than the crown of silver-lavender curls had.

"You're not going to space me." Tink tucked the wrench into her belt.

"Not what I was going to say." Rebeka looked at the sliver of cold light growing at the top of the gangplank as it lowered into the docking assembly, then sighed with a heave of her shoulders. "One more job and I'm retiring to Avalon."

"Seriously?" Tink had known Rebeka for more than half her life, ever since the older woman had come to work on the ship Tink called home even as a child. There'd been a bit of friction in those early days — Tink looking for a mother figure she'd never really had, Rebeka refusing to play the part — but now Tink couldn't imagine the *Lyra* without her. She arched an eyebrow as high as it would go before continuing. "That dull, backwater planet? You're telling me you're going to become a farmer? Or worse, a farmer's wife?" Tink wrinkled her nose.

Rebeka didn't respond to the jab, keeping her gaze trained on the ramp. "About the next contract...."

"No." Tink shook her head. "He's scum and he can't be trusted."

"Just because he tried to arrange your marriage to that Antillian bugmeal salesperson doesn't mean he's scum." When Tink tipped her head down and arched an eyebrow, Rebeka rolled her eyes and continued. "Okay, he's scum and can't be trusted. But he's well-paying scum, and we need the money." The ship punctuated her words with a groan.

Tink tucked her thumbs in her toolbelt and rested her hands on her hips. "Money doesn't do us any good if Imperial Customs confiscates the ship. Or it's blown up by gangsters, pieces scattered across the galaxy...and us with it."

Rebeka graced her with one of those looks that left Tink unsure of whether she'd won the argument or not, before walking towards the ramp. It was now half-open, revealing more of the spaceport beyond – the same grime and grit of any Bowels. The light here was tinged a shade more towards green than blue. Just past the halfway point, the ramp gave an unhappy squeal. A curse echoed through the empty cargo bay from somewhere behind the large hydraulic hinge.

"When are we going to replace these things?" Ish popped his head up from the far side of the metal strut, his face smudged with grease. The ship's navigator, and her assistant in a pinch, he was also their temporary pilot. He hated the job, and didn't excel at it, as evidenced by the love taps the *Lyra* had given the pier as he docked her. He was most at home guiding the ship through the slipstream. When Tink had watched him at it, his brown skin glowed in the light of his incomprehensible maps of undulating colours.

The fringe of his hair fell in his eyes, and he swept it back with long fingers, smearing more grease across his forehead. Noticing his hands, he wiped them on his white tank top.

"Not until we make some money." The captain's dark brown eyes travelled from him to Tink then back. She made a face at his tank top.

Ish didn't respond. Instead, he stripped off the tank and pulled on a tunic. Scrubbing his face with the tank top, he came to stand beside Tink, placing his hand on her back. "A few days in port might be nice. Maybe we can both find some company." He graced her with a lopsided smile.

The captain frowned. "Be back here at 22:00 Zulu. We're leaving as soon as we can get a contract sorted."

Ish huffed, rolling his eyes. "I need to unwind after all that flying."

"Count me out." Tink put up her hands and stepped back, shaking her head. She knew what kind of fun Ish was looking for, and that they didn't have the same taste in men. He liked the brawny beefcakes he could wrap around his little finger; she liked her men more cerebral. "I need to get some work done."

"That's not what you need." He snorted, then threw his hands up when she made a face. "Fine. I guess I need to have fun enough for the both of us." He waggled his eyebrows at her then strode towards the exit, passing the captain.

Rebeka grabbed his collar, stopping him short. "You're not going anywhere until we interview these new recruits. One of them is the pilot you say we need."

Ish sighed. "You just experienced my docking skills. We *need*." His gaze shifted to the cargo bay door as the ramp hit the pier, giving the ship a jolt. The hatch on the station side slid open, and a smile spread across Ish's face. Knowing Euko Station was a pit at the bottom of a hole, Tink turned to see what had caused the change in expression: a group of men stood at the end of the ramp, with an overly muscled man at the forefront.

"The new recruits." Kandi came to stand beside Tink. Tink glanced at the *Lyra's* security officer-slash-medic who was dressed for port leave. A sleeveless silver halter and matching low-slung pants exposed swaths of golden skin. Her hair, currently an electric shade of pink, was pulled back, away from her high cheekbones. Blades rested against each thigh. Tink's ears still rung from the string of curses Kandi had let out on learning the new stationmaster had banned blasters in the entertainment districts of Euko Station. She struck an imposing figure, standing a good head taller than Tink, which wasn't actually saying much. With her hands on her hips, the muscles in her shoulders and biceps bulged.

"I wonder which one of those fine men is the pilot," Ish said. "Maybe I can test how skilled he is with his hands."

3: ΔLeK

A LEK CRANED HIS NECK as if to crack away a spot of
tension, covering up his actual intention: scan the
spaceport hub and the tier above for danger. Through the glass
that arched over the pier, lights from ships and service tech
floated against the dark space beyond. Like the firebugs that
flitted over the river where he'd spent the happiest days of his
childhood...until his childhood ended in ice and death. A sliver
of ice stabbed at his heart as memories swirled. Frowning at
his lack of attention, he continued his check as he forced
himself to stand easy. Spies, snipers, hunters: they could all
hide amongst the ships and machinery and portside activity.
And then there were the non-human threats. An assassin bot or
kamikaze drone looked a lot like a service automaton until it
blew you up.

He shifted on his feet, as if he were stiff from standing, and
used the movement to get another look at the men waiting in
the hub with him. All male, which surprised him. Only seven
of them in total, for two positions, which surprised him even
more, given the lack of jobs to go around. He was by far the

strongest, not to mention the tallest...though those things wouldn't help him get the job he was here for. After glancing over the others, he turned his gaze to the windows that surrounded the branch of the port they were in, which was a spoke on yet another branch. A twig on a giant metallic and glass tree that led back to the central spire of the space station.

Despite facing the window, he didn't see the space beyond. Instead, he focused on the reflections as he casually pretended to clean under his fingernails. He was the point on a small chevron, and he examined the right wing first.

The man on the far end was obviously a computer tech, even though he wore a pilot's cast-off bolero. But Bolero was almost as tall as he was, usually too tall to be a pilot, and his bony frame and the grey cast to his pale skin spoke of someone who spent too much time surrounded by qubits, strings, vectors and a bunch of other things Alek didn't understand.

Next to Bolero stood Mustache. The man's impressive facial hair was clearly well-cared for. Too well-cared for by someone seeking a position on a cargo ship. Mustache was obviously a pilot, a good head and a half shorter than Alek, and with the slight, permanent sneer common among stick jockeys. Despite the mustache, he looked fourteen. Likely not the most experienced pilot, if that's what the ship was looking for.

Beside him was White Pants. Alek couldn't imagine him as either a pilot or a computer tech, both jobs occasionally requiring one to get dirty. He seemed more interested in Alek than the ships coming in. Alek pulled his shoulders back and flexed his arms, causing the man to look at the window instead of his biceps. Catching his eye in the reflection, Alek quirked an eyebrow. The man winked, then smiled, realizing he wasn't Alek's type, before taking his attentions elsewhere.

The Quaker stood right next to Alek. A shiver passed through the man, and Alek's eyes narrowed as he searched the reflection for the man's bag. Spying it, the case didn't seem to hold any threat, but it was hard to tell without inspecting it. When Quaker shook again and rubbed his nose, realization dawned on Alek: a Stardust addict. Somehow the man had made it through the initial screening, but Alek dismissed him as a threat to both his person and his chances at a job.

He shifted his attention to those on his left and caught the man next to him examining him in the window before snapping his gaze away. Studying the man out of the corner of his eye, Alek wondered what he'd gleaned about him. He eyed the man's reflection in the glass, watching him peer up, mouth agape, at the hundred other branches on the spaceport tree.

Nothing, he decided. *The man learned nothing.* Slightly shorter than Alek, he was a lot fairer, with hair the colour of the sun-kissed wheat that grew beside that river of Alek's childhood memories. Towheaded, his mother would have said, whatever that meant. Though he couldn't tell in the window reflection, in his mind's eye, the man's cheeks and nose were splattered with freckles, unless he'd removed them. The man stretched his arms over his head, the bottom of his shirt lifting, giving Alek a glimpse of the muscles underneath.

Pilot or computer tech? Alek frowned at the fact that he couldn't tell.

The last man was a peacock, both in his dress and his puffed-out chest. The conservatory of his childhood home — not the one by the river — had housed peacocks, cloned from

DNA smuggled from a zoonautical station on some icy moon. He'd tried to like the birds; they tried to attack him at every opportunity.

He glanced at his wrist patch again, making sure he had his new ident memorized. *Alek Wa.* A name he could answer to without too much trouble, closer to his childhood nickname than his recent stage name had been.

Flicking his wrist, he checked the time: the ship was late. Re-focusing his gaze, he looked past the glass at the arriving ships. Their flickering and pulsing lights speckled the black, like stars themselves. One coming in too fast drew his attention. The beaten-up vessel slipped sideways, and he forced away the tension that crept into his muscles as he braced for impact — if the ship took out the hub, bracing himself wouldn't help against the icy darkness of space. Movement caught his eye. The ship shimmied back into his field of vision.

Lyra. Even with the letters chipped and dented, the name was still clear. He swore under his breath, causing the man beside him to glance at him. He shifted away, leaning casually against the post behind him, and nodded at the ship before turning back to the other men. "It looks like that's our ride. At least, it's my ride."

The others turned to the ship, their expressions ranging from worry to hunger to... unreadable, which interested Alek much more. As a judder reverberated through the hub, he shifted his attention back to the ship, or the parts still visible behind the docking assembly, a frown forming on his face before he replaced it with a smile. There were patches of rust on the hull, meaning the little tug was capable of atmo. Yet, it wasn't being docked by the station AI.

He flicked his wrist to bring up messages. Why he needed to hire onto this dinged-up rust bucket, he didn't know. His employers hadn't shared that tidbit of info. But the message was very clear. *Get on the Lyra.*

A flash of something caught his eye two storeys up. A rifle scope on a space station? He squinted but couldn't tell. He breathed deeply, in and out, forcing a calm he didn't feel; even if it was a sniper, they likely wouldn't shoot, since puncturing the window would kill at least six other men, seven counting the customs agent.

The bored agent leaned over his console, tapping at something on his screen. His rumpled uniform had a smattering of white dust on one black lapel, and the brass on his flat cap was unpolished.

Down the long corridor leading back to the central spire, Alek heard rumbling voices and his heartbeat quickened. Whether it was port security barring entry to whoever wanted to use a pulse rifle on a space station or Dominion agents tracking him down, he didn't want to know.

The gate in front of him started to open, and he straightened himself up, getting ready to put on a performance. Luckily, he had a lifetime of experience at being something he wasn't.

4: Rebeka

REBEKA MINO LOOKED AT the tablet in her hand then back at the person in front of her.

"Seriously?" She lifted an eyebrow. His mouth opened, though whether from surprise or as a prelude to protest, she didn't know and didn't care. "No," she said as she held up her free hand, forestalling him. "Go. Just go." She pointed to the corridor leading back to the station. The man at least had the grace to look abashed as he picked up his bag and trundled off, a shiver coursing through him.

"Bleeding Stardust." Turning to the remaining applicants, she frowned. "We may be a jack-of-all, picking up whatever odd jobs come our way, but we still have standards. No active criminals and certainly no Stardust junkies. Anyone else need to leave?" When there was no exodus, she addressed the next person in line.

"Severn Lynch." Surveying his specs on her tablet, she tried to keep the tiredness out of her voice when she asked her first question. "Why should I let you on my ship?" She sighed when she realized she'd failed. There was no answer. She looked up at him to see a lopsided grin on his pretty face, with its perfect teeth, splash of freckles and bright blue eyes. She quelled the urge to punch him.

"You sent all the other computer techs away." He lifted a shoulder in a shrug. "I'm the only one left. Assuming you still need one, it's me or waiting for another batch of applications."

Studying him, she noted the slight tension in his jaw and how his blue eyes were a little too sharp. He was hungry for the job, despite his demeanor. The work history displayed on her tablet looked to be a good fit — middling grades on a Core Tech degree from a licensed academy, systems maintenance on commercial haulers, let go from his last ship when customs impounded it. She pursed her lips, then sighed, pulling her shoulders away from her ears. "Fine. Grab your stuff and stand over there." She indicated the other side of the ramp with a jerk of her head.

Rebeka turned to the last two people. The pilots. She pulled up both sets of specs side-by-side, stabbing her tablet so hard her finger stung. The sooner she got this over with, the sooner she could go to her cabin and have more shots of amber whiskey than were good for her. She sighed. *After I sort out the next contract.*

"Our two pilots. But there can be only one." A smirk tugged at the corners of her mouth but quickly fell, her heart not in it.

"Orion Neill." The small man in front of her gave a sharp nod. He was clearly young, despite the ridiculous mustache, and had the slight frame of a pilot which made him seem even younger. Combined with his baby face, it gave the impression that he'd only flown in sims. "Why should I put my ship in your hands?" she asked, getting to the point without preamble.

When the man spoke, his words were measured and quiet. "I've flown everything from corvettes to cruisers, T-fighters to tankers."

She glanced back at his specs. He didn't lie, unless he'd hacked his record. She fought the frown that tugged at her mouth as she wondered why he was applying for a job on the *Lyra*.

"Never one quite like this before...a jack-of-all scavenger ship." He shifted and Rebeka's gaze returned to his face. His upper lip quirked, then his eyes widened a fraction when he saw her looking. "I like a challenge."

Her lips thinned, and her words had an edge when she spoke. "Looks like you're younger than my ship. Less experienced." She focused on his face then asked her last question. "Why did you leave your last ship?"

"It was all local, core systems, core planets. I want some adventure."

Rebeka's eyes narrowed on him, and he glanced away, before she finally turned to the last person in line. He was taller than her by a good head, and that was saying something. Combined with his broad shoulders and muscular build, he was unusually large for a pilot. Cockpits were small spaces.

"You don't look like a pilot. What have you flown, Alek Wa?" she asked, her eyes squinting. Despite being uncommon, she'd had encounters with others surnamed Wa. Unpleasant encounters. Though he didn't resemble any Wa she knew.

"Not quite so many ships as this fellow." He glanced down at the man beside him. "And never one of this vintage. But I can get you out of any tight spot you find yourself in. Asteroid hopping, atmo skipping, starshotting...I've done it all."

She let her pursed lips tell him what she thought of that then changed tacks. "Why did *you* leave your last employer?"

He was silent for a second, his face tensing. "They wanted me to get modded." His expression flipped, a broad smile on his lips, arms going wide. "Can't improve on perfection."

Rebeka sighed. For a moment, she'd almost had some sympathy for him.

Neill piped up. "What's wrong with being modded? Everyone can use an edge sometimes." The man sneered. "Maybe they thought you needed the help."

Rebeka's gaze slid sideways to re-assess the young man, catching a silver gleam in his right eye she hadn't noticed before. "Wait here." She stepped over to the rest of her paltry crew and leaned in. "So Ish, you've seen the specs...what do you think?"

"Neill," Tink said before Ish had even opened his mouth. "This Wa is a loud-mouth, muscle-bound hotshot."

"Ish?" Rebeka said, ignoring Tink. "You're our backup pilot."

Ish took the tablet and flipped through their specs and test results. Shrugging, he handed it back to her. "Both their in-system skills are better than mine. Wa tested higher?"

"Marginally." Tink nudged him with her elbow. "Are you sure you just don't want that over-muscled man on the bridge beside you?"

Fire lit in Ish's eyes, and his mouth dropped open as he pulled himself up and stepped towards Tink. "I would never risk —"

Tink threw her hands up. "I know. It was a joke."

He crossed his arms over his chest. "A bad one."

"It wasn't funny." Rebeka graced her with her best disappointed look.

At that point, Kandi strode forward from where she'd been polishing her long, whorled blade. "Wa."

"What? Not you too?" Tink brought her hands to her hips.

"You can't accuse me of wanting him on the ship because he's beautiful, even though objectively he is. He's not my type." She tucked a loose fuchsia strand behind her ear. "We could use a bit of extra muscle."

"So, two against two," Tink said. "Captain wins."

Rebeka glanced at her. "Captain wins." Shifting around, she spoke so the two men could hear her. "Wa, go stand with Lynch. Sorry, Neill, not today." She ignored Tink's huffs, staring at the man as he peered at her for a second, a spark blazing in his eyes, before he hefted his bag and stalked off down the corridor.

Turning back to the ship, her lips tingled, anticipating the glass of whiskey waiting for her. Kandi and Ish looked at her with hopeful expressions. "Go. But be back by 22:00 Zulu. We're leaving before the rush." Ish moaned but ran after Kandi, who was already striding down the passageway. Even though her blasters were safely on the ship, the two perfectly legal blades strapped to her thighs were hopefully enough to protect them both in the Bowels of Euko Station.

The eyes of the two new recruits followed the pair. "Not you two. You need to get familiar with the *Lyra*. Tink, if you will. I'll be in my cabin." Rebeka didn't stick around. Instead, she headed back into the ship. A shadow emerged from a dark corner of the cargo bay, and green eyes peered at her. She knelt down to scritch between the cat's ears, which he deigned to tolerate.

"R&R will have to wait, Grim." Her shoulders slumped as she realized she couldn't relax with a book and a glass of whiskey yet. She had a contract to arrange.

5: Tink

"THAT'S ALL YOU HAVE?" Tink eyed the bag slung over Alek's shoulder as they navigated the narrow passageway.

She glanced past the pilot to the hovering trunks that dutifully trailed Severn down the corridor, bumping into walls and posts now and then.

Alek followed her gaze then turned back to grace her with a lazy smile and a lop-sided shrug. "I travel light. Besides, I don't imagine there's a lot of extra room on a ship like this."

Tink's eyes narrowed as she stared at the passageway in front of her. "A ship like this?" she said, keeping her voice flat.

"Built for function." He was so close behind her the words whispered over the nape of her neck, raising the fine hairs. "Not beauty."

Tink stopped short at that response, causing him to bump into her, a little harder than she'd expected. She started to fall forward but his strong arm around her waist stopped her and pulled her back against his torso. He smelled like...clean. Not engine grease. Extricating herself from his grasp, she turned to glare at him. "Watch where you're going."

"Sorry." His smile said he wasn't.

Tink scowled and then turned back to her tour. "Common room – galley's in there." She waved her hand at the door, before taking a hard right. "Passenger quarters." She waved at a door on her left. "Though it's mostly storage. We don't get many fares."

"Crew quarters." She indicated the long, narrow hall in front of them.

"You're not upset at not getting time off like the others?" Severn asked, as Alek muscled past her.

"No, I'd rather be on the ship." Tink shook her head and stuck her thumbs in her belt loops, before turning away. "Bridge is at the end, as is the captain's room, which connects to her ready room and through that the bridge."

"And where do you sleep?" Alek's lopsided smile returned, along with a quirk of his eyebrow.

Over Alek's shoulder, Severn rolled his eyes, and Tink had to stifle a smile lest Alek think it was for him. "I basically live in the engine room. But you'll sometimes find me there." She waved at a door near the far end, not quite across from Rebeka's. "That's Ish." She motioned to the one beside hers. "And Kandi across from him."

"And whose is that?" Severn nodded at the one on the far side of hers.

"More storage." Her gaze lingered on the door to the room that had been her uncle's, her lips pulling into a frown. "And these two are yours."

"Arm wrestle you for first pick?" Alek flexed the muscles in his biceps.

Tink ignored him, instead heading back to the stairs they'd come up. "If you want to personalize, that's on you. For now, drop your bags, and I'll show you the rest of the ship."

"This is the engine room." Tink swept an arm around the space filled with ancient machinery and pet projects, then turned to watch the new recruits. Her uncle always said you could judge a person by how they responded to an engine room.

"Obviously." Alek arched an eyebrow as he scanned the space.

"Wow, is that a Takeshi Blue?" Severn strode over to the gleaming housing of the impulse engine. "I thought these were all in museums."

Tink joined him, running her fingertips along the surface. "Nope, this one is lovingly cared for and purrs like a kitten...most of the time." A pathetic mew from someplace behind the engine punctuated her words. "Hera wept! Cat, where have you gotten yourself this time?" She leaned past Alek to grab a torch from amongst the bits and bobs of various projects scattered across her workbench.

She stopped short when she realized he held something in his hand. "Excuse me," she said, her voice sharp as she reached for the trinket.

"This is the Argos." Alek pulled away as he turned the delicate model of the legendary interstellar sailing ship over in his large hands.

"Yes, it is. And it's mine." She plucked it from his grasp with her long fingers, frowning at the grease on her hands, and placed it in its home on the bench. Her cheeks flushed as his blue eyes studied her. Unnaturally blue, almost the colour of the Takeshi's housing. With a huff of breath, she picked up the torch and turned back to the machinery. "And this is the slip drive." She patted another casing. "Neither of you should ever need to worry about that," she added, hoping they wouldn't ask for any details.

"This little thing?" Alek said. "This punches a hole in space?"

Tink's lips pressed together. "It's not so much that it's punching the hole as pulling us through a hole that exists, and then it lets us move through the stream once we're in it. At least that's what Ish says." Another meow, more insistent this time, rescued her from more questions. She dropped to her knees to scoot past the slip drive. "Argh, good-for-nothing stray. Do you expect me to always be there to rescue you?" She opened an access panel that led to a power conduit and shone the torch into the dark space. The light caught the large motes of dust that rained down. A pair of green eyes flashed back at her. "How the hell did you even get in there? It's dangerous."

Severn crouched behind her. "Can I help?" he asked, pushing his long fringe out of his blue eyes — a calm blue, like the skies of Solace.

Tink shook her head. "Only room for one of us in there." He stood and shifted back, leaving her space to move. Laying the torch on the floor, she shimmied towards the cat. As she caught a bit of fur at the scruff of his neck, Grim began to purr and she prodded him closer. Hefting him into the crook of one arm, she crawled back into the engine room. "I see you're putting on the pounds." As if on cue, the cat opened his mouth, and Tink caught sight of an iridescent bit of shell and legs that still twitched. "Must be all the bugs you're catching. You're not the scrawny creature that ambled onto the ship when we docked at Mantadae Gate." The grey cat, made greyer by the dust, peered at her with his green eyes and mewed as his purr revved up a notch. She blew a strand of wayward hair out of her face, picked up the torch and stood.

Both men looked at her in silence. Maybe they thought she was a little unhinged. But she was okay with that. Life was simpler when people stayed at arms' distance. Her gaze flicked to Severn, and her cheeks grew hot again. *Well, not always.* She squared her shoulders and strode over to them. Alek reached out to stroke the cat's head. At that, Grim hissed and twenty sharp points dug into the flesh of her shoulder as he used it to launch himself down the passageway towards the generator.

"I guess he doesn't like us," Alek said, with a lopsided grin.

Tink stifled the frown that threatened to pull her face down — she was pretty sure which one of them the cat didn't like. Instead, she followed Grim down the corridor that was, as always, bathed in green light.

Glancing over her shoulder, she saw Alek stooping so he wouldn't hit his head in the low passageway. "These are the algae tanks." She ran her fingers over them as she walked down the passage. Severn followed her lead. Sweat started to bead on her upper lip in the warm corridor. Sometimes, after hours spent hunched over her workbench, she came and sat with her back against the tanks and let the warmth seep in, relaxing her muscles. "These pipes lead to the algal converter, turning green goop into all the energy a starship needs." She stepped into the room that housed the algal converter and fuel generator — though 'room' was being generous. Nook more like.

"All of it?" Severn leaned over her shoulder, his torso pressing against her back. She shifted to face him, in time to see him sweep away a lock of hair that had fallen in front of his eyes, tucking it behind his ear. "Life support and all?"

Tink tried to take a deep breath in the confined space. "Well, almost. The slip drive has its own fuel source." Tink frowned; she didn't trust the black-box magic that powered the slip drive. She shook her head and shifted to her tiptoes, peering over his shoulder at Alek, who was still at the far end of the corridor, leaning toward one of the tanks, gazing into its depths. Raising her voice, she spoke. "I do have other things to do, if you could join the tour."

He looked at her with a slight grin and ambled towards them. "Sorry, I thought you two were getting acquainted." He flashed his eyes to Severn before returning to her. "I'll try to keep up," he said as he squeezed his tall, muscled frame into the small space behind her.

Even without him touching her, Tink could feel the heat radiating from his torso, over and above the warmth of the tanks. Feeling a little woozy, she tried to take a deep breath. The air in the room was stifling. Despite being used to working in cramped spaces, a wave of claustrophobia washed over her. She shook her head and lay her hand on the bright green housing in front of her. "This is Mean Green, the chloroplast converter."

"The what?" Severn asked.

"The green goop machine." Alek's breath whispered over her ear as he leaned in to see in the tight space. "Hmm."

"Amazing, isn't it?"

"Huh?" He turned his head towards her, his lips inches from her eyes.

"How a small colony of single-celled organisms can grow to power a starship."

"Oh yeah. Amazing. But this colony is going to have some problems soon." Alek nodded towards the left side of the converter.

Tink followed his gaze. "What do you mean?"

"Your nutrient intake manifold is, I'd say, 80% clogged."

She leaned forward, squinting at the indicated part, and snapped back to look at him, her mouth opening and closing like a fish. "But..." She didn't know what to say: he was right. Her neck flushed as his unsettling blue eyes locked onto hers. The heat crept into her cheeks...the ship might be old, but she kept it running spick-and-span.

"We should finish the tour so you can get on that." A smile sparkled in his eyes. Her lips pressed tightly together to keep her from saying what she was thinking. Instead, she stalked back down the corridor to trudge back upstairs.

She'd managed to suppress the flush by the time they got to the closet-sized, two storey room that held the central processors for all the ship's systems. Turning to Severn, she graced him with her biggest grin.

"This'll be your home on the ship, I suppose." She shrugged a shoulder. "It's small."

"Cozy," he said, his hand light on her elbow as he stepped past her into the nook. Then he stopped, his smile faltering. "You have a CASS-ANDRA?" His tone mixed awe and dread in equal measure.

Alek stepped up beside her and gave a long whistle. "I thought they were all decommissioned after...well, you know." His voice was quiet.

"That wasn't the AI's fault. It was the people who didn't listen to her." Tink lifted her chin. Her uncle always said this AI was the most sophisticated one ever made. "We call her Cass."

"Yes, Tink?" a voice said from overhead, causing both men to jump in their skins a little.

Tink smiled. "Nothing, Cass. We just have a couple of new crew. Introduce yourselves."

"Severn Lynch, computer tech." Severn slid his gaze sideways to eye her. "I guess we'll be working closely together."

"Alek Wa, pilot."

"Nice to meet you, Severn, Alek. Please let me know if I can be of any assistance." The voice went quiet.

"Tour's almost done." Tink stepped back and jerked her chin over her shoulder. "Just the bridge."

"I'll stay here if you don't mind," Severn said, lifting one corner of his lips. "Get to know Cass."

Tink and Alek were left alone to walk the short distance to the bridge. Of course, Alek couldn't do it in peace.

"So, you're a Tinker. I would have expected a...bigger ship to have snapped you up." When Tink didn't respond, he seemed compelled to continue. "Unless you're not a very good Tinker."

She spun her head to scowl at him. When she saw his smile, she pressed her lips together. No need to add fuel to his teasing.

As they entered the bridge, the captain came out of her ready room, and Tink let out a sigh of relief. Her babysitting duties were almost over. She went to stand beside Rebeka as they both watched Alek fold his long, muscled limbs like origami into the pilot's chair.

"Wow," the captain said, before taking a sip of amber whiskey. "That's surprising."

Tink didn't say anything, but she had to agree. It was as if the seat was made for him.

6: Rebeka

E VEN THOUGH THE WINDOW of the common room overlooked the cargo bay, Rebeka Mino wasn't seeing the space below, empty and ready to carry ore when they reached their destination — Tartarus, a paltry pit mine of a moon in the middle of the Badlands. Instead, she examined her reflection as she ran a hand over her newly shaved head. She'd forgotten about the old wound on the left side of her scalp, even though she'd had close-cropped hair in the past. Dropping her arm, she turned her attention to the small crew reflected in the glass. Too small, even for a snug ship like the *Lyra*, but they were all the ship could afford. A burly stevedore to lade the ore would be nice. Rebeka sighed.

Kandi's hands moved with purpose, her eyes intent, as she reassembled the blaster she'd just finished cleaning. Ish sat beside her, tossing deep-fried crickets in the air and catching them in his mouth. In between bugs, he regaled Kandi with one of the derring-do legends from his home world. Tink pretended to read something on her tablet but glanced at Rebeka's back every few seconds, all while stroking the cat in her lap when he pushed his head into her hand. Grim's green eyes stared at Rebeka in the reflection.

Their two new recruits sat on the other side of the table. Severn repeatedly lifted his gaze from his tablet to scan the crew, clearly trying to find an in. Meanwhile, Alek leaned back in his chair, eyes closed and boots on the table. Rebeka watched his chest rise and fall for a few seconds. He was doing a poor job of feigning sleep.

Tink let out a fake cough into her elbow, and Rebeka's gaze flashed to her reflection before glancing down at her coffee. She clutched the mug tightly, letting the warmth seep into her fingers, and sighed. None of them would like what she was about to tell them.

She turned to the common room — combined mess, galley and rec room — and joined them at the table, spinning the chair around so she could lean her arms on top of the backrest. Before she said anything, she looked at each of them in turn, coming at last to the two new crew. Severn's eyes were focused on her. As were Alek's, open now, though he copped a casual posture, with his hands behind his head and his feet still on the table. Rebeka frowned.

"Boots off my table." He looked as if he was going to say something, but sat up straight instead, dropping his feet to the floor. Rebeka glanced sidelong at Tink. "I've found us a contract, ferrying a load of zinc ore from Tartarus to Nyx," she said, getting it out in a rush. But before she'd even finished, the complaints began.

"But I thought —" Tink started, but Rebeka silenced her with a sharp look. Tink was the only one who knew about the other contract that had been on the table.

"But nothing." Rebeka grimaced as Tink suppressed the smile that crept into the corner of her lips. "Contracts are thin at the moment. Sometimes we have to work for our supper."

"It'd just be nice to have something a little special for supper," Ish said. "Bugs are getting old." He looked at the bowl of crickets with less enthusiasm than before.

"Something a little less back-breaking for my first job would've been nice." Severn glanced around at the others with a half smile. "Ease into things."

Looking for validation, Rebeka thought. *Why do the Adonises always need validation?*

"How about something a bit less dirty?" Alek tipped forward to slap the computer tech on the back. The tech scowled at him.

"You're welcome to leave, if our honest work is not to your liking." She locked eyes with Alek.

"No, no he's not." Ish shook his head, shifting his gaze between the pilot and her. She kept staring at Alek, ignoring Ish's protest, until the man looked away.

"Nah, wouldn't miss it for the world, dodging asteroids and ne'er-do-wells through the badlands." He grinned his lopsided grin, revealing perfect teeth, and got up from the table. "Besides, you'll need me in the cockpit to steady the ship during loading."

"No," Tink said, standing as well, cat in her arms. "Even if we can't land, the ship has servos. Cass can handle it. As Kandi said, we can use a little extra muscle." She punched him on the arm then strode out of the room. Rebeka frowned as she watched Alek watch Tink leave.

Then he turned back to the room. "Who's hungry? I make a mean custard bug scramble."

Rebeka's stomach growled in response, despite herself.

7: Alek

ALEK FOLDED HIMSELF INTO the pilot's chair and ran his fingers over the controls in front of him. Despite the ship's age, the stick moved smoothly, without hiccoughs in any direction. He tapped on the reverse thrusters and the engine hummed — purred — in response. It seemed as eager as he was to leave the station behind.

Too many people here who might know me. Who might let the cat out of the bag...if they don't kill me first. As if on cue, the grey cat — Grim, Tink had called him — ambled through the bridge, sniffing at his leg before jumping on top of the console above Kandi's Tac station.

The *Lyra* had a small crew. They could all fit on the bridge, though the captain and the Tinker were absent. How Tink ended up on a ship like this was an enigma, given the Tinkers' legendary mastery over anything mechanical. The Dominion tended to snap up the ones they hadn't imprisoned or caused to disappear. There were so few left, they were almost mythical creatures. *Focus now, ponder later*, he thought as the navigator, Ish, slid into the seat beside him. Ish cast a long look his way, letting his eyes travel over Alek's muscled arms. Alek pretended not to notice.

"So, what's the hold up?" he asked instead, a jovial grin on his face.

Ish glanced at the viewscreen then back. "Waiting for clearance. Apparently, Customs doesn't believe the cargo bay is empty." He checked over the panel in front of him and, with a flick of his fingers, pulled up a holoscreen. "Captain's down there trying to convince them."

"Is it empty?" Alek asked, quirking up an eyebrow.

Ish leaned in and chuckled. "The cargo bay is."

Alek smiled at his insinuation that somewhere the ship carried something not quite legal, even though concern at getting caught niggled at his stomach.

Plucking at a point on his holoscreen, Ish canted his head, then poked another spot while tipping his head the other way. Alek mimicked the movement and for a second swore he heard a sound, then realized it was just a change in the hum from the stick he still held. Letting go, he turned to Ish, who had a far away look in his eyes.

"What are you doing?"

Ish blinked a few times before his eyes focused on Alek. "Finding slip points." His voice was smoother, deeper than it had been earlier.

"Ah, right." Alek directed his gaze at his console but was drawn back to the holoscreen and its multihued ripples and undulating lines. "I thought we were going through the gate." He looked askance at the display.

"We are. This is...professional curiosity." Ish peered at him, the corners of his eyes crinkling. "You have no idea, do you, about the stream?"

"I...." Alek considered blustering his way out of appearing ignorant, but his knowledge was so abysmal he realized it would have the opposite effect. "I have an idea. But not a very good one."

"There are layers to the universe."

"Like a cake."

Ish blinked. "No, not like a cake." He curled his legs up, bringing his feet under him, and leaned forward. He hovered one hand over the other. "Some astrophysicists say the layers are entirely different universes."

Alek dipped his chin. "I've heard the theory. It doesn't help me so much with fact."

Ish looked away, his mouth opening, his eyes squinting at the gate shimmering on the viewscreen. When he turned back to Alek, his face was serious. "Have you ever swum in the ocean where there's a riptide? Or in a fast-flowing river?" Ish's hands moved in time with his words, his fingers pulling at invisible threads. Alek nodded slowly, thinking of the family vacation spot when he was young: the wide, frigid river that appeared serene but could sweep a person away before she could shout for help.

Ish continued, his eyes becoming unfocused for a second before returning to Alek's face. "The surface looks calm, just like the rest of the water. But you hit that flow and...whoosh." He clapped one palm against the other before swiping the top hand away. "You're pulled along faster than you think possible. That's the slipstream. And the deeper you go, the faster it is." Ish canted his head sideways. "But also more dangerous."

"So, what's a 'slip point'? I mean, I know it's where we enter the stream but...."

The navigator took Alek's hand and, turning it over so the palm was up, examined the lines criss-crossing it. Tracing one line with his finger, he continued. "Like an ocean, there are rivers and channels. And ripples." His finger stopped. "And at the ripples, well, imagine the river again, frozen over." Alek squinted, trying to keep up with the shifting analogies. The lion tattoo on the man's wrist twitched, and Ish continued. "There are eddies, places where the ice is thinner, where it's easier to fall through. That's a slip point."

"So, we're falling into the slipstream?"

"I...." Ish's head tipped sideways as he continued to examine Alek's hand, his nose scrunching up as he ran a finger back along the line. "Kind of." His hazel eyes peered at Alek through thick lashes.

"I'm straight, fyi," Alek said.

Ish lifted his head, cheeks flushed. He sighed, returning the smile. "You always are." Letting go of Alek's hand, he straightened in his chair, then glanced back with a raised eyebrow. "Not even bi-curious?"

Alek smiled and shook his head. "Not anymore."

"Can't blame a guy for trying though, can you?" Ish grinned and turned back to his holoscreen.

"No, I'll never blame a guy for trying." Alek rechecked the ship specs, before glancing at Ish and the tattoo again. "Sekmeti, eh? Is that why you left Mintarae?" He nodded at the tattoo he'd glimpsed while Ish was playing with his hand. "I heard they're...severe."

The navigator's fingers stopped moving, and the smile that had been lifting the corners of his lips disappeared. "No." He opened and closed his mouth as if to say more. Just then the comms crackled to life, saving Alek from having to make an awkward apology. He shouldn't have pried, being all too familiar with the skeletons people kept inside. He had plenty of his own secrets to clutch close.

"We've finally been given the OK to leave." Captain Mino's voice betrayed more than a hint of irritation. "Let's get out of here before they change their minds."

Alek nudged the stick forward, gently feeding the engine a little juice. There was a slight judder on the left side, and he made a mental note to tell Tink. For the time being, he compensated and headed for the exit, happy to put the spaceport behind him.

8: Rebeka

R EBEKA FROWNED AT THE viewscreen, which displayed the gate undulating in vibrant shades of blue, pink and green. It also showed the long line of ships waiting to pass through: they were going to idle for a while yet.

"Why are we waiting at the gate if we have the slip drive?" Alek asked. Rebeka put down the coffee she'd brought for him, placing it far from his jostling knee.

"If we did that, we'd miss out on this marvel of astrophysics and the monumental feats of engineering graciously provided by the Dominion." Rebeka placed Ish's cha far away from his twitching fingers. "Besides, the fuel for the slip drive is more expensive. So, unless you want to pay for it out of your cheque...."

"I don't imagine my pay cheque is going to be large enough for this coffee." He lifted the mug then took a sip. "Thanks."

Ish leaned close to Alek. "The gates are cheaper, despite the toll."

"Despite the piece of your soul you pay the Dominion." Kandi stood in the doorway, staring at the quicksilver ripples in the gate, her own mug clutched in her hands. When she continued, her light tone belied her near-treasonous words. "Security and convenience in exchange for freedom." She glanced at Alek and Ish then turned around and left.

"Don't mind her," Rebeka said. "She has a rocky history with the Secretariat of Interplanetary Peace and Stability."

"Don't we all," Alek said, his voice flat.

Rebekah glanced sideways at him, but he was focused on the screen in front of them. With barely a flicker of movement, he directed the ship forward. She returned her gaze to the gate as they moved a couple of lengths closer. "And what's your history with SIPS?"

There was silence for a few seconds before he answered. "I was a rebellious teenager. That led to some run-ins with the Local. My grandmother was happy to have me spend a few nights in the cells, hoping it would set me on the straight and narrow."

"Did it?" Rebeka took a sip of her coffee.

Alek turned around and graced her with a lopsided grin. "You'd have to ask her."

Rebeka noticed the smile didn't reach his eyes, but she let it slide, as he turned back to his controls and slid the ship another few spaces forward. "Alek Wa," she said quietly to herself, but the tensing of his jaw muscles indicated he'd heard her, and her emphasis on his family name. The name was one of the handful typically used by the countless *unofficial* royal offspring. She rarely saw a Wa with eyes that blue, but the black hair and sharp cheekbones fit...that was a story she'd have to puzzle out another day. Today, she had a different question. "Why so antsy to get through the gate?"

His head jerked, but he didn't turn around. "Just keen to get started."

"Aren't we all." She peered at the back of his head.

"Keen to start hauling zinc?"

Rebeka's head turned at the new voice: Severn had silently slipped onto the bridge and stood where Kandi had.

"Don't sneak up on a person like that." She took another sip of her coffee, staring at him over the rim of her mug.

"What, it could get me killed?" His laugh died before he finished speaking.

"Yes." Rebeka stared at him, letting that sink in. He shifted from one foot to the other under her gaze.

He broke first, his eyes flicking to the gate. "I'll try to remember that, Captain." He slid past her and went to sit at the Ops console beside Kandi's empty Tac station. He leaned towards Ish.

"Seems like we're all keen to get to the system on the far side of that gate."

"And start slipping to the Badlands," Ish said, his words infused with his broad smile.

9: TINK

TINK UNFOLDED HERSELF FROM the hunched-over crouch in which she'd spent much of the last few days. The wait to get through the gate had been interminable, accompanied by one final harassment from Customs to confirm their flag and their paid-up port fees. The authorities had finally allowed them to pop through to Vulcan V, the main gate near the Badlands.

Then there'd been a series of slow slips, since Ish hadn't wanted to go far into the slipstream. There were monsters in the deep, he said. Tink laughed to herself, pressing her hands into her sacrum and arching her back. Navigators certainly had superstitions about the stream.

First, she'd passed the time doing tweaks and optimizations and rechecks on the engines. Then she'd wiled away the slips inspecting and optimizing the algal converter and fuel generator to fix the issue with the intake manifold Alek had pointed out.

They'd finally made it to Vulcan V, near the border of Dominion space. But the *Lyra* still had a ways to go on impulse...you didn't just pop out of the stream into the heart of the Badlands. Not unless you wanted an asteroid-sized hole in your ship. And the asteroids and failed planetary debris weren't even the biggest danger. That honour went to the zealots and wannabe gangsters and broken prospectors — people full of fanaticism or with nothing left to lose. The only reason any ships came at all were those few prospectors who weren't broke. The ones who'd struck the motherlode and built pockets of opulence amongst the wrecks and the ruins.

Tink had some sympathy for the wrecks and the ruins, being a member of an outcast caste, a vilified people. But that didn't mean she wanted to be in the Badlands or agreed with the captain for taking the contract without consulting the crew.

And now she'd run out of things to occupy her hands and mind, which was why she was in the cargo bay checking their tie-downs and jacks. For a second time. Tink started to lower into a crouch to test them again, but her back decided otherwise. She rubbed at the spot where the lightning bolt of pain had originated.

Squinting at the tie-down at her feet, she realized the night lighting had cycled in, cueing her to sleep. The others were probably all in their rooms, except for Alek, who was on watch on the bridge. But she wasn't tired. Glancing around again, Tink stripped off her boots and jumpsuit, leaving her clad in a tank top and shorts. She shivered, but knew she'd warm up soon enough.

She jogged barefoot in circles around the cargo bay, her soft footfalls barely making a sound, using crates and stairs and winches as a makeshift obstacle course. Once she'd built up a sweat, she did a few stretches then started on the forms of the martial art Kandi had taught her, moving fluidly from one to the next, imagining an opponent in front of her. It was when she was in Crane Catches Fish that she caught a flicker of movement in the shadows. She froze, her head down with one hand stuck out towards the floor, the other leg stretched out, toe touching the ground for counterbalance, butt in the air. She hadn't heard anyone coming down the metal stairs.

A grey form coalesced out of the darkness. Tink exhaled in a smooth flow as Grim came padding across the floor. She held her position so she could scritch his chin. He rubbed his jaw along her standing leg, then turned to look at her as if she were crazy for her current contortion.

"Don't judge. You're not *my* cat, you know? You're a stray. As soon as we find you a good home, you're out of here." The cat merruped. "No, a ship is no place for a cat." He brushed his chin against her face this time, leaving behind a tickle of fur. She sneezed but managed to hold her pose.

"Triton style works better if you have a sparring partner."

Tink almost toppled over in her hurry to stand upright. "Severn." She brought a hand to her chest and swallowed. "What are you doing here?"

He shrugged, tipping his head towards the lifted shoulder. Most of him was in the shadow of the stairs, only his face and shoulders illuminated. "I couldn't sleep. Thought exercise might help." He nodded at her, and his hair glinted gold where the dim lights caught it. "Looks like you had the same idea."

Tink half nodded, half shrugged, hoping he couldn't see her cheeks flush in the twilit space as she leaned against the container holding the emergency response kit. When he stepped out of the shadows to join her, she took the water he offered. In the light, she saw that, below the white T-shirt, he wore a pair of loose pants covered in cartoon bunnies. She couldn't catch the giggle before it escaped.

He smiled back at her, lifting an eyebrow. "They're my sister's favourite animal." The smile slipped from his face. "Or they were."

Tink's stomach dropped with a thud. "I'm sorry. Is she ...? No, it's none of my business."

"No, it's okay. She's passed. I just forget sometimes. But at least I'll always have the bunnies." The one corner of his lips lifted again, causing dimples to surface, and he bumped his shoulder into hers. "Come on, are we going to spar or what? Bet you galley duty for a week that I can pin you in 5."

Her cheeks reddened again as the image of him pinning her crept into her head, though this time, a touch of pique that he thought he could best her so quickly added fuel to the flush.

"You're on." She shifted, getting lighter on her toes and lowering her centre of gravity. She watched him do the same, rocking back and forth as he circled, trying the snake charmer on her. Tink was having none of it. Rebeka had trained her for years, then Kandi had taken over, and she'd learned not to be fooled by distraction techniques.

Tink almost had him after the first takedown. Hers: she'd swiped his feet out from under him with River Flows, then gotten on top of him...or tried to. He kicked his feet over his head, popping up from the backwards somersault into a stance resembling Awoken Bear.

At Two, he tried to use his bulk to knock her off her feet, but she was small and wiry. He needed more than brute force, and she squirmed out of his grasp. She smiled that his skin was already sweat-slicked, making it easier for her to slip away. Then her cheeks flushed, and she swallowed as she turned to see he'd taken off his T-shirt. Well-defined muscles carved his torso and etched his abdomen, disappearing below his bunny pyjama pants.

For Three, she used her smaller stature to her advantage — well, more his assumption of superiority based on strength — as she ducked under the arm he obviously intended to clothesline her with. She sent her foot into the back of his knee in a rough approximation of Tree Falls. But the move left her sprawled on the ground, and he recovered much quicker than she hoped.

So, at Four, he was on top of her, and clearly thought he had her pinned; she could see it in his face. But, apparently, his teacher hadn't taught him Otter Twists. She bucked her hips, and while he laughed, she sent her elbow into his solar plexus and drove her knee between his legs, catching her foot behind his knee. When she twisted, it threw him off balance. At the last minute, she turned Otter Twists into Crane Breaks Wing, sitting on his back, his arm torqued behind him.

She leaned over to whisper in his ear, her breath a little ragged. "Pinned in five."

"That's okay," he said. "I'm happy to cook for a month if it means being where I am right now." He shifted beneath her. "Though I don't imagine anyone else would like me to."

"Ahem."

Tink sprang up, fists fighting ready, and her cheeks flushed again when she found Alek at the bottom of the stairs. Her hands lowered a fraction as he stepped forward, a smirk on his face.

"Aren't you supposed to be on bridge duty?" Her hands dropped to her hips.

"Kandi took over." His gaze slid to Severn before returning to her. "Aren't you two supposed to be in bed?"

Tink glared at him for a few moments before going to collect her jumpsuit. "Yeah, I am. You two have fun." She took the stairs two at a time. "Jackass," she muttered, not caring if he heard.

10: Tink

"**M**EASURE TWICE, LOAD ONCE," Tink muttered as she wiped sweat from her forehead with a grimy hand, then gave the hoist another whack with the sledgehammer. Finally, a clunk and a sad whirr rewarded her efforts, and the winch started reeling in the cable snaked across the cargo bay floor. The space was empty, and would stay that way, given that the tentacles now strapped the cargo snug against the belly of the *Lyra*.

Everything would have gone a lot smoother if they'd been able to stow the crates in the cargo bay. "But no, off-gassing is dangerous." Tink wrinkled her nose. And they wouldn't even get paid more, since it was an all-in job. The ship gave a slight shiver, as if disgruntled at the containers of zinc strapped to its underside. But that small tremble was enough to stop the winch.

"Argh!" Tink tried to pick up the small sledgehammer, but her arms were too tired after shifting crates of ore into the cargo hold. Then out of the hold again when Cass complained that the beaten-up crates were spewing something toxic, confirming Tink's suspicion that they held more than zinc. Which wouldn't have been such a problem if the load hadn't been twice the size advertised. So, onto flats it went, to be strapped underneath the ship.

Which is why she was surrounded by unused cable. But the heavy lifting was done, and the ship was on its way to the nearest slip point. All that remained was to tidy up the snaking mess. She inched the sledgehammer closer, but then gave up as a muscle in her back twinged.

"Can I help?" Severn stood at the bottom of the stairs, hands in his pockets, looking exceptionally clean for someone who'd just been hauling the same ore she had. When he came to stand beside her, the scent of resinous soap wafted in the air.

"You've had a shower." Tink sighed again, then breathed in deeply, leaning a few mils closer.

Severn shrugged. "I think most of us have. If I had realized...." He cast his gaze around the chaos. Instead of continuing, he picked up the sledge. "I should hit here?" He indicated the spot where the paint had chipped away.

"That obvious?" Tink flashed him a smile.

He returned her smile with a grin, then sent the hammer toward the crank. When metal hit metal, the *Lyra* shuddered. Severn stopped and stepped back, his mouth dropping open. "I...."

"That wasn't you." Tink spun around, as if the source was in the cargo bay, even though it clearly wasn't. "Something just hit the ship." As she finished speaking, the alarm sounded. With klaxons blaring and red lights strobing around her, she sprinted for the stairs without looking to see if he followed.

Just as she arrived at the bridge, out of breath, hands on her knees, another impact threw her against the doorjamb. "What the hell is going on? Have we been caught in a gravity well?"

Rebeka jerked her head sideways, the move half negative, half indicating the viewscreen. Tink turned her attention to the screen, and her mouth gaped open.

"What the...." Tink stopped when she saw the colours on the side of their attacker's ship. Her hands clenched into fists. "Pirates. How dare they! And why are they attacking *us*?"

"Because we're hauling 35 tonnes of something that's not just zinc ore," the captain said. Although her tone was even, Tink saw the tic in her jaw.

"I can't slip yet." Ish's voice was tight when he spoke. "Closest point is 754 kiloklicks away."

"10 minutes at present speed." Alek punched a finger at a flashing light on the console in front of him.

"So go faster!" Tink grabbed the railing behind the cockpit, her knuckles white with tension.

"I'm going as fast as I can." Nonetheless, he shifted the stick. The ship whined. "Unless you can get that engine to give me more juice."

"Shields are failing," Kandi said. "I can get us EMP but that leaves us vulnerable too until we can reset. Or I can prime the depth charges."

"But the kick from those might push us even further from the slip point." Ish's fingers flew over the holoscreen. "Recalculating. Looking for another slip. Come on, Cass, help me out here."

Cass' calm voice filled the space. "The next slip point is 670 kiloklicks away. 9 minutes at present speed."

"That's not the help I needed, Cass."

"I'm sorry, Ishmael." Cass' voice stuttered as another blast hit the ship, and Tink nearly toppled over the railing.

"Shields at 15%." Kandi didn't turn from her station as her fingers flew over her display. "Targeting solution in 5...4...."

"I can lose them and hide us in the asteroids." Alek's voice was disturbingly calm.

"Those asteroids will tear us apart without shields." Tink glared at him.

"Kandi said our shields are at 15."

Rebeka barely glanced at her before turning back to him. "Do it."

"Captain!" Tink turned to Rebeka as acid burned in her stomach.

"Yes, I am the captain." Her lips pressed together, then she breathed in and out slowly through her nostrils. "The blasts from that ship *will* kill us. The asteroids *might*. I'll take those odds right now."

"Strap in," Alek said.

"Sit down and buckle up, Tink," the captain said.

Tink debated being willful but changed her mind at the look on Rebeka's face. She sat and strapped herself into the normally unused Second's seat beside the captain. She was glad she did. She barely had the buckle closed when Alek pulled them into a spin that caused the ship to groan and her stomach to flip. Even without the bulk cinched to its hull, the manoeuvre would have made the ship unhappy. It also exposed their back end to the pirates for a few long seconds before he headed straight towards a large asteroid.

It had been thirty minutes since anything shot at them, and Tink's stomach had finally descended from her throat. That meant she could focus on how on edge her nerves were.

Despite being a spacer most of her life, it was still eerie to float through space, through a field of ship-sized asteroids, passing them like ghosts. The lights were dim to conserve power, the main engine was off, and the ship silent except for the occasional hum of a low-impulse correction. She knew every burp and sneeze of this ship when it was running at full capacity. It was the symphony of her life, and it was gone.

Alek made another minor correction, and the ship purred as it shifted slightly to avoid an incoming chunk of interplanetary debris. She hated to admit it, but he seemed to know a thing or two, using the gentlest nudges needed to keep them from crashing into rock.

"Any sign?" Rebeka whispered. They all whispered, the few times they spoke, even though it wasn't necessary.

Kandi shook her head. "Nothing." Yellow lights flashed on the display in front of her, interspersed by the occasional red of an asteroid getting a little too close for comfort.

"Shields?"

"25 percent."

"That's all?" The captain's voice got louder before dropping again. "Let me know when we're at 50."

"You can't be thinking of going out there again?" Severn paused his pacing back and forth behind Tink and the captain.

They were all there now, crammed onto the bridge. Tink had remained in her occasional seat on the bridge since there was no help she could give in the engine room and, for once, she didn't want to be alone. Even the cat was there, perched on the ledge that ran around the room, eying them as if his predicament were their fault.

"We should wait here until we starve?" Rebeka peered at Severn, who opened his mouth to say something as he stepped past Tink and took a seat at the Ops station beside Kandi, but Rebeka forestalled him. "Or until the cavalry shows up?" His mouth snapped shut at that. "No, at 50 percent maybe we can stick our noses out."

Another red blip appeared on Kandi's display, but this time an audible proximity alert accompanied it.

"Ship ho." Even Cass' voice coming from the ship comms seemed to be a whisper.

"Jacks!" Kandi and Alek said simultaneously.

"I don't suppose you can fly us out of this, hot shot?" the captain asked.

"Not likely." Severn squinted at the display in front of him. "We've been tagged." He pulled a copy of what he was looking at onto a corner of the viewscreen so everyone could see, while shifting and magnifying a section.

"When did they have a chance to spike us?" Ish asked.

"Maybe when flyboy showed them our butt." Severn pulled the display off the viewscreen and started tapping something out at his console.

Tink glanced at Alek — he didn't say anything, but his face darkened as he glared at Severn.

Severn flipped through lines of code on his display. "I think I can get rid of it, but..." His lips scrunched.

"But what?" Tink said. Getting up, she went to stand beside him, hovering in the doorway of the bridge. "If you can get rid of it, get rid of it."

"I need to tweak Cass' logic gates...during an engagement."

Cass' brain. Despite her flippant dismissal of his reservations about Cass, she knew the CASS-ANDRA's reputation. And, even for her, the idea of messing with the guts of the AI caused a flutter in her stomach. A shudder coursed through the ship as a blast hit it. Tink clutched the door frame to keep upright.

"Do it." Rebeka sounded calm, but Tink caught the twitch of her fingers as she clenched her armrests, before she forced them to relax.

Severn ran out, pushing past Tink as he headed towards the computer cupboard to do the captain's bidding. Tink thought about joining him, but realized she'd be even more useless there than she was on the bridge.

"Asteroid passing through." Two red lights flashed on Kandi's screen and the proximity sirens blared.

"It's fine," Alek said, even though the chunk of rock loomed large in the viewscreen.

"Get ready to fly us out of here as soon as he deals with that tag...and Cass, can you shut off the bloody sirens?" Cass didn't answer, but the sirens stopped. As they did, another blast shot past their starboard side.

Tink sidled up to the captain, keeping her eye on Alek, who focused intently on the pilot's console. "Do you think maybe we should let Ish—" She hoped her whisper was quiet enough that only the captain heard.

"No." Rebeka glanced at her. "I don't. Whether or not he opened us up to be tagged, I imagine he wants out of this alive as much as you do."

"Slip point detected dead ahead," Ish said, his voice bright.

"Will it take us where we want to go?" Tink asked.

"Away from here, yeah." Ish tugged at strands of light in his holoscreen, causing them to ripple and glow in a mesmerizing dance.

"Priming slip drive." Alek punched a button and swiped his palm across his console. The ship whined, but soon it became the purr of a ship ready to run.

The captain sat back in her chair, punching a button beside her. "How's —"

"Tag disabled." Severn's voice, high pitched through the comms, replied before she even finished speaking.

Rebeka drummed the armrest as she spoke. "Take us out of here, flyboy."

Alek shifted in his chair, the only sign that he was doing as asked, but the ship responded. So did the red lights on Kandi's display.

"You might want to sit down." Alek didn't turn as he spoke. Again, Tink debated staying on her feet out of spite, but decided it wasn't worth the cracked ribs or worse. She sat down in her seat and strapped in just as they emerged from behind the asteroid. The proximity alerts started again, faster this time. And Tink saw why. They were about to shave the belly of the pirate ship. Better than the sides, which bristled with pulse cannons, but still too close. Alek pushed them forward at full speed. Tink closed her eyes and tucked her hands under her knees to keep from clutching the seat.

She braced for impact...5...4...3...2.... Nothing. She opened her eyes, but only saw empty space ahead. But Kandi's face was still grim, imbued with green from the light of her display. Tink saw the red blob of the other ship close behind.

The *Lyra's* backend slid sideways as Alek flew around an asteroid at full speed.

"Slip point in 2 minutes." Ish's fingers plucked at his holoscreen. "We might pull some of these rocks in with us."

"Is that bad?" Alek asked, not taking his eyes off his display.

"Yes." Ish continued tweaking the slip point calculations, or whatever it was he did with those ripples and wavy lines.

"The stream speeds them along, same as us," Tink said, letting Ish focus. "But with the wrinkles and eddies, we don't know where. We don't know how fast." The ship screamed and listed as another jolt hit them, and Tink pressed a palm to her thigh.

"What was that?" the captain asked.

With a sick feeling in her stomach, Tink realized what had caused such a howl. "The cargo." She pulled over her display and flicked through to find the tentacle controls. "They hit the cargo." She stabbed at the disconnect button with her index finger. A grinding sound was followed by a thunk. "Zeus' bollocks!"

"What?" Rebeka glanced at her as Tink struggled to unbuckle her strap.

"The cargo has shifted, causing us to be unbalanced," Cass' calm voice added.

"The disconnect isn't responding." Finally getting herself unstrapped, Tink took off at a run towards the cargo bay. She heard Ish yelling at her as she fled along the corridor towards the stairs: slip point in 60. Tink wasn't a navigator, but she was pretty sure entering the slipstream with unhinged cargo was dangerous for ship and crew.

Her heart pounded in her ears as she sped passed Severn on his way back from the computer cupboard, spanner already in her hand. She barely spared him a glance as she continued headlong, almost throwing herself down the stairs. It was only when she got to the cargo bay that she realized he'd followed her.

"Hit the emergency disconnects," she shouted, running to the first one. It was a big red button he was unlikely to miss. She swerved right to slam her palm into the first one. She dared a small smile at the clunk of the tentacle disengaging from the cargo. Another thunk followed seconds later. Glancing over her shoulder, she saw he'd done the same on his side and was heading to the second one. She sprinted to the last one on the right and punched it with her fist.

Nothing.

"15 seconds to slip." The ship groaned, and a metallic clang reverberated through the cargo bay.

"What are you doing down there, Tink?" Alek's voice said, followed by a curse as the ship swerved, even more unbalanced now that one tentacle connected the cargo to the hull.

She hit the button again with the same result. She lifted her leg, intent on kicking the thing when Severn appeared beside her, hammer in hand. He swung it at the disconnect. Nothing happened for a second, during which she heard every beat of her heart. Then there was a clunk as the last tentacle let go, and the ship shimmied before finding its line again.

"Slipping."

Tink collapsed against a pylon, welcoming the nausea she always felt in the stream. Severn slid down beside her, hands on his knees. Then he made a sound. It took her a second to realize he was laughing. She turned to see a relieved smile on his face and couldn't help joining him.

Then she stopped as his lips pressed against hers.

11: HΛRBIN

HARBIN LOW'S EYES WERE closed, and his fingertips rested on the rail of opalescent milled plex in front of him. A coil of pleasure swirled around the base of his spine. He stood on the bridge of the *Argent*. He'd never commanded a brand-new ship before. And it was Barracuda class, amongst the sleekest and fastest vessels in the armada. His eyes opened a sliver as he smiled at the thought, running his fingers along the rail, shiny and smudge-free.

Monitoring the encounter between pirates and prey from a wise distance, his ship hadn't made a sound beyond the quiet hum of a predator running silent. And he'd already seen the ship's shroud in action when he was introduced to it. A shudder passed through him, recalling the moment. The *Argent* had been nose-to-nose with a weapon-studded ship primed to fire. Then the space in the viewscreen had shimmered, the only sign that the *Argent* had become invisible to the other ship.

A cough disturbed his silence, and he glared at his Second.

Delphi Liet was clearly worried. The tell was when she rubbed the scar that ran down the left side of her face. She glanced between him, her display and the viewscreen. "They're at the slip point." Her voice was a hoarse whisper.

Harbin turned his attention to the main screen, which displayed a fractured vision from the various stealth probes they'd deployed around the asteroid field. The probes didn't have any shroud tech, but they scanned as just lumps of metal. He watched as the ship dropped its lopsided cargo, then blinked out.

He gave no orders as he watched the pirates swooping in to collect their prize. They'd only agreed to help agents of the Dominion because of the cadmium smuggled in with the zinc ore. Well, that and the *Argent's* pulse cannons. Casting his gaze around the bridge, he saw her nervousness reflected in the fidgeting and sideways glances of the rest of the bridge crew.

Good, it keeps them battle ready. But Harbin himself remained calm as their prey disappeared. His pulse ticked steady in his neck. He tipped his head sideways, his eyebrows finally pulling together in some show of emotion. It was strange. It wasn't due to the bots designed to keep him level and clear headed. This was all natural, a combo of years of strict training and a youth spent surviving.

The *Argent* hadn't been seen. His new ship had performed as per spec, shrouding them in a cloth of stars, the fabric of space itself, and scrambling their signature so they appeared like just another asteroid to any scanners.

"Should we follow?" Liet asked, tapping out a herky-jerky rhythm with her foot. Her worried tell had shifted to the one that said she was ready for battle. His mouth pressed into a line, wondering how she won at cards as often as she did.

Regardless, she was a blood-thirsty one. It was one of the reasons he'd fought to have her assigned to his new crew.

"It's the slipstream," the navigator on duty said. "At best, we can *try* to follow."

"No need." Harbin waved his hand, then stepped back and sat down in his captain's chair, still smelling like the factory.

"But if we don't follow, we'll lose them." Liet's fingers hovered over her console. "The tag is gone."

"But the *tagger* is still onboard."

12: Alek

"**S**HOULD OUR ONLY ENGINEER really be outside doing repairs?" Severn's voice sounded hollow over the comms. Alek scowled. He would've shut the comms off, but they were his only link to the ship...and the bubble of life inside.

"What about your only pilot?" he said as he watched Tink crab walk along the hull beside him.

Kandi's voice replaced Severn's. "If you want to be the one left in here with her, while someone else goes and messes with her ship, be my guest," she answered, ignoring Alek's comment entirely. "In that scenario, I'd rather be out there with nothing between me and cold, empty death but a thin spacesuit."

Alek couldn't say he agreed with her. He'd rather deal with a hellacious Tink than be spacewalking. He swallowed the lump in his throat and focused on the hull of the ship to combat the nausea that always threatened whenever he had to be out surrounded by the endless vacuum.

"Haha. Very funny." Tink caught up to him, and he could see her eyes roll behind her faceplate. Her helmet light illuminated her face, a beacon in the blackness. He hadn't noticed the freckles scattered like stars across her cheeks before. She flashed him a half grimace, half smile as she responded to their two minders. "Would you pay attention to our vitals, please?"

"We've been paying attention to your vitals for an hour," Kandi said. "I'm bored."

"What, you've cleaned *all* your weapons already?" Tink responded, shuffling closer, forcing Alek to edge further along the jackline.

"'Haha' back at you." Kandi's words were flat.

"Yes, she has," Severn said. "Are you almost done? You must be getting cold."

"It's starting to seep through, yeah." Alek flexed the fingers of one hand, keeping hold of the jackline with the other.

Tink crept closer to him. "Cass, are we almost done?"

"The sensors indicate one more stress point." Cass' voice was calm, as always. "I can't determine the extent. It might be fine if you postpone fixing it, or it might be where the ship breaks apart."

"Great." Alek smiled at Tink, who actually smiled back, causing the corners of her eyes to crinkle.

"The panel is five metres to your right," the AI said.

Tink sidled over until she was nestled beside him.

"So why aren't the bots doing this?" he asked, making the mistake of glancing over her shoulder at the empty black beyond the tail. A bit of bile rose in his throat. He swallowed; if there was one rule of spacewalking, it was don't vomit. He forced his eyes back to her face.

Her suit shifted. He imagined her shrugging a shoulder. Even in a helmet, a wayward curl had escaped the cap and was plastered to her cheek.

"They're broken. I haven't gotten around to..." She stopped. "I need parts to fix them, and we hired you all instead of getting them."

"Oh." He glanced down at his gloved hand, the one gripping the jackline. "Sorry."

"We needed a pilot." Her shoulder shifted again, then her leg. She threw it over his thigh, jostling him and testing his hold on the line. "Excuse me," she said as their helmets bumped. Her brown eyes met his.

"Nothing to excuse." He gave a lopsided grin. He thought about saying she could wrap her legs around him anytime, just to drive home the sexist boar persona, but the words stuck in his throat.

"No, I need to get around you. Panel's on your other side."

"Oh right." He shifted, letting her crawl over him, feeding her safety line out. As she got to work on the patch, the line in his hand caught his attention. He glanced at her, so focused on her task. Their only engineer. The only one who understood the inner workings of the defense systems, of their few weapons. He looked back at the line and frowned.

"Okay, that should do it," she said. "Cass?"

"Sensors indicate the panel is sealed."

Alek watched as Tink crab walked back to him, one hand resting on the hull of the ship, rather than the jackline, while the other tucked a tool in her belt. The ship lurched, the line jerking.

"Cass?" Alek hated that his voice was pitched higher than normal. "Kandi?"

"Ish?" Tink said, her voice normal as she continued towards him.

"Just a pocket of dirty space," Ish said from the bridge. "Nothing to worry about. Correcting now."

The ship shifted again, and Tink with it. Her boot slipped on the thin lip of metal they'd been following around the hull.

"Whoa," she said with a laugh, her arms going wide. Alek lunged out to grab her. His fingers barely caught around her tool belt.

"Jacks!" He hauled her back towards him, wrapping his free arm tight around her waist, while the other gripped the jackline so tight his fingers went numb. Her helmet bumped his again.

"What?" A big grin formed dimples on her cheeks. "You big scaredy cat. It's fine. My safety line would have stopped me."

He swallowed, taking her hand and placing it on the jackline. His hand free again, he pulled her safety line. "No, I don't think it would have." He lifted the frayed end to where she could see it in her visor's field of view.

The grin froze on her face, then fell. "It wasn't like that during the pre-walk checks." Her eyes glanced up to meet his.

"No, it wasn't."

13: Rebeka

"UGH! WHAT IS THIS?" Rebeka said, peering into the mug Tink had brought her. "I said coffee."

Tink shrugged, one-shouldered since her other arm held the cat. "Maker's on the fritz, so you get cha." She slumped into the chair on the far side of the captain's desk.

Rebeka grimaced then took another sip as she scrolled through the feed on her tablet. It didn't taste so bad now that she knew what was in it.

"Still nothing?" Tink asked.

Rebeka shook her head and slurped the cha as she continued to flip through the feeds. Her stomach burned. She blamed the acid in the drink and put it down.

"We *are* out in the Badlands," Tink said. "They're sparse and, more often than not, only barter."

"It'd be nice to have something that would at least pay wages. Fund some repairs when we get back to port. You can't do that with animal feed or arts and crafts." Rebeka glanced at Tink. "How is the ship, by the way?"

Tink shrugged, jostling Grim again. "Okay. It'll get us back to port. It might complain the whole way and hold a grudge, but it'll do it."

"So, Muscles was useful after all?"

Rebeka chuckled and picked up her mug again to hide her smile at the face Tink pulled.

Instead of answering, Tink went on about the ship. "It could use a bit more TLC when we're in dock, to make sure our patch jobs hold. Which leads us back to needing a contract. But contracts are thin. Unless you're in the Badlands, as we are, and then they're mythical or...."

"Slog work for criminals or bare rock homesteaders who pay in animal feed." Rebeka let her grumpiness out. "Or they don't pay at all."

"Not all of them are like that." Tink raised an eyebrow at her, and Rebeka tipped her head in acknowledgement. "What was it your predecessor used to say? Space takes all sorts, and there's a place for all of them."

Rebeka scoffed. "He also said space is a big place — easy to get lost in and never be found...."

"Especially in the Badlands," Tink said, joining in with a smile on her face. "It's why many folks come here...to not be found." Tink came to stand beside her, peering over her shoulder at the feed she flicked through. The listings convulsed; with only one ancient ansible feeding the entire area, the Connect was spotty. "Hmmm. You're right. Not much." She stepped back. "Here, you need this more than I do."

Before Rebeka knew it, a cat was dumped in her lap. "Huh?" she said, pulling back to look at the cat that stared at her with equal suspicion in his green eyes. She turned to Tink. "Really, the cat?"

"Trust me. There are studies."

"Cats bring contracts?" She arched an eyebrow at Grim. "Are you magical?" The cat merruped in response.

"No." Tink rolled her eyes. "Stroking them relieves stress."

Rebeka looked at the cat again. The cat peered at her. She was sure they both thought this was a bad idea. But she turned back to the screen, laying her hand on the cat's head. With her other hand, she flicked through the feed again. Looking for...*that*.

She paused. "What about this?"

"I don't know. You're the captain."

"Yes, I am. Doesn't mean I don't want your opinion."

Tink leaned over her shoulder again, biting her lip as she scanned the details. "Looks fine enough," she said, standing up. "Seems legit? Something the ship can manage, and it's not as dirty — or as dangerous — as the last job."

Rebeka tapped the ad to reply. Just as her finger hit the screen, a thump travelled from her feet through her thighs and into her chest. A split-second later, the sirens sounded, and twenty sharp points dug into her flesh as the cat launched himself into a skitter across the floor.

"What now?" Tink said, the words coming out in a groan. Without waiting for an answer, she took off sprinting. The thump had definitely come from below. The engine room, Tink's domain. Still, Rebeka downed the last of the cha and followed at a slower pace.

14: Tink

TINK DASHED HERSELF AROUND the captain's chair and fled the bridge, then chastised herself for not checking system diagnostics before leaving. It would have at least given her an idea of what the problem was. But when her ship needed her, she listened. She debated stopping to check the console outside the door, but as she got closer, the screen flickered and dimmed. Something was very wrong.

Racking her brain for possibilities, she turned into the central corridor at a run, ricocheting off the far wall and bumping right into Severn, who was coming out of his room. She pushed past him, ignoring the question written on his face, and flew towards the stairs down to the engine room.

"Cass, what's wrong?" She could barely hear Cass' reply over the sounds of sirens, but she caught the worrisome stutter.

"Theeere's a pro...problem with the algal conversion sysss....tem." As Tink swerved into the corridor of algae tanks, she came face to face with the problem. Or knees to floor, as she slipped in water slick with green goo.

Tink shook her head. "Cass, shut off the alarms." Cass didn't answer, and the sirens kept up their caterwaul. But underneath the wail, she heard the timbre of running water. Examining the tanks, the ones nearest her were fine, still full of water and bright green algae. But it was only a matter of time until they followed the others further along: the level in those tanks was dropping, losing algae and the aerated, nutrient-rich water the plants needed to live.

Her knee throbbed and her feet continued trying to slide out from under her as she scrabbled along the aisle towards the nearest safety valve. Cursing whoever had designed the ship, she made a mental note to replace the tile in the algae corridor with the same honeycomb grating as in the engine room.

"What should I do?" a voice behind her said as a strong hand gripped her elbow and hauled her up against a bare chest. An unruly lock of hair fell across her face, and she tucked it behind her ear with a slime-coated hand. Looking up, she saw Alek's expression was relaxed despite the water that gushed into the corridor.

"Shut off the valves between the tanks." Tink shouted to be heard over the sounds of sirens, burbling water and Cass' stuttering pronouncements. She pointed to the red valve handle. "We need to protect what algae we have left until we figure out the problem."

She turned away, going to the next one on the right side, hoping he would follow her lead on the left. She got the next two valves shut, but she slipped again, ending up on her knees. *It's too far*, she thought as she watched the water levels fall.

Unless... She threw herself headlong, sliding through the goo. When she grasped at the piping running along the bottom of the tanks to stop herself, her hand slipped. She slid too far. Reaching out in a last-ditch grab, relief coursed through her as she felt metal in her fingers. Holding tight, she pulled herself back and turned the valve as quickly as she could.

With a final glug, the flow of algae and mineral-rich water slowed to a trickle then stopped. Strands of wet hair clung to Tink's face as she tried to tuck them behind her ear. Giving up, she traced the lines from the tank to the algal converter, her fingers catching on filaments of algae. Under the flickering overhead lights, which were not considered essential in an emergency, her eyes scanned every well-known inch, trying to figure out what had gone wrong. When she reached the connection to the converter, she squinted. The gasket pushed out from the joint. She frowned at a bulge in the pipe. Pipes didn't blow in *her* engine. And she'd checked over the whole thing when she'd replaced the manifold.

"What happened?" Alek asked from just over her shoulder, his warm breath whispering in her ear.

Tink didn't look at him, but instead tipped her head sideways. "I...don't know." Her teeth chattered as she spoke despite being drenched in warm, briny water. Leaning forward to peer at the joint, she probed it with a finger, then pulled back to clutch her arms around her torso as a shiver passed through her. She glanced at Alek. His pyjama pants clung to him, as soaked as her own clothes, while he stood barefoot beside her. But he seemed fine. His arms rested at his sides rather than being wrapped around himself, even though he didn't appear to have an ounce of body fat to keep him warm. She shivered again. "Can you get the tigger from the main engine room?" she asked.

He took off at a jog, his feet kicking up little splashes. Tink frowned — he had no trouble staying upright, and he was gone before she could tell him what a tigger was. Her shoulders slumped, and she turned back to the converter...she'd tell him it was the spot welder when he came back empty-handed. She peered at the connections, still baffled. As she poked at the pipe again, she noticed the tips of her fingers had gone white.

Shock. She forced herself to breathe deeply, in and out, and reminded herself that the water was warm. She was warm. There was still algae in the tanks. Before long, splashes coming back down the corridor announced Alek's return.

He handed her the spot welder. She looked at it then at him. "You know what a tigger is?"

He paused, pulling back a bit. "My sister liked to repair old vehicles."

"Hmm, don't we all?" Tink turned away, all her focus on patching the joint and getting the ship operational. Just as she finished the patch, blowing on it to cool the adhesive, the lights went out. There was silence in the dark for a terrifying handful of seconds. Another quiver passed through her as a chill settled under her skin despite standing in warm, salty water — the cold of being dead in deep space. Then the emergency lights kicked in.

Tink glanced up at Alek. With the planes of his face highlighted in red, he looked like one of those masked monsters from Goru theatre, silent and demonic.

Taking a deep breath before her teeth chattered again, she held out her hand. "We should find the captain."

"Why did the pipe blow?" the captain asked, grasping the back of the chair, her knuckles white. They'd all gathered in the common room for a debriefing. Tink shivered from cold this time — the shock had worn off but the water soaking her clothes had started to cool. Alek stood beside her, leaning on the counter. She inched closer, grateful for the heat radiating from him.

"I don't know." Tink's voice was quiet as she examined the pattern of droplets on the floor. Alek shifted, and she felt his hand sliding along the counter behind her. She kept looking down, running her wet shoe through a small puddle. Strands of limp curls fell in front of her face.

"And why don't we have lights?" Kandi's face appeared diabolic in the red glow of the emergency lighting.

"It's a non-essential system." Alek's tone was smooth but serious. Tink glanced at him, surprised by him speaking so knowledgeably, and without derision, about her ship. "Main lights shut down to conserve power until the generator is at baseline capacity again. You might have noticed the drop in temperature. Unless you're a Siriun muskokan, you'll want to layer up for a while."

"But we have power on the bridge," Ish said, then lifted his mug. "And coffee."

"Coffee is essential," Rebeka said, grasping her own mug more tightly. "Especially in times of trouble." She took a sip then continued, turning to Tink. "So how long until we're at baseline capacity?"

Tink shrugged, glancing around at the faces of her crewmates. "I don't know. 5 days, maybe 10." Rebeka peered at her, a frown pulling at the corners of her lips. Tink dropped her gaze to the floor, eyebrows pulling together. "It's just a patch job. Assuming it doesn't blow again...." She lifted a shoulder. "It depends how much algae we lost. How quickly we can regenerate."

"There must be some way to get it to grow more quickly." There was an edge to Severn's voice. She tipped her head to look at him, lifting just her eyes. "What does it need to regenerate?" he asked, his voice low, as he came to stand beside her.

On her other side, Alek's arms came to cross over his chest. "Time."

"No, not necessarily." Tink tipped her head the other way. "Usually, the generator is a closed system, needing very little to keep it ticking along. But..." She bit her lip and glanced at Rebeka, knowing the captain wouldn't like the idea that she'd come up with. *But the captain is a pragmatist.*

Tink stood up taller and turned her gaze fully to Rebeka. "The algal converter is running on emergency rations as well, right? Low heat, low light." She stepped over to the table and put down her mug, still full of now-cold coffee. "But the optimal conditions for it are light and warmth and mineral water." She picked up two more cups and placed them beside her own.

"So?" Rebeka asked, her eyes narrowing.

"So, if we shunt more power to it, it can regenerate more quickly."

"But we have no more power to shunt to it. Not without pulling power from something else." Ish drew swirls of spilled coffee across the table. "And there's nothing left to pull power from." His fingers stopped and his head jerked up as he looked her in the eyes. "No."

"What?" Alek stepped up beside her again.

"She wants to shunt power from life support." Ish didn't take his eyes off her when he spoke.

"I didn't say...." But Tink stopped. It *was* what she'd been thinking. "It's the only constant that uses enough power to make a difference."

"No." Rebeka stepped forward.

"It would only be for a bit, to get it—"

"No, we're *not* shunting power from life support. Even if we have to wait 10 days."

Tink slumped back against the counter, and Severn wrapped an arm around her shoulders.

He leaned close, his breath whispering over her ear as he spoke. "You know, and I know, that the biophilic system on the ship has failsafes. You've engineered it to." His shoulder shrugged. "But that's not enough for everyone."

Rebeka gave Tink an indecipherable look before turning to the others. "Kandi, Ish, see if there's anywhere else we can conserve power. Severn, work with Cass to find any bit of efficiency." Her gaze returned to Tink and Alek. "You two, go take a shower."

"But we need to save the warm water for the algae tanks."

"No, we don't," Rebeka and Alek said in unison. Tink started to protest, then threw up her hands and trudged towards the showers, leaving just as the captain added, "Meet back here at 16:30 Zulu for another briefing."

The patter of falling water tickled Tink's eardrums, and steam filled her nostrils. Despite knowing water was in short supply, and the power to heat it even shorter, she relished every precious second, determined to max out her allotment. The warm water pelted the tension from her shoulders and washed away the anger, leaving behind only frustration. Not for the first time, she thanked the stars the ship was old enough that it had traditional water showers, rather than sonic ones. Besides the fact that she never felt fully clean after coming out of a sonic, there was something about hot water that washed away more than sweat and grime. Since most of the water was reclaimed for use in the algal tanks, there'd never been a strong reason to convert.

However, showers were carefully timed. Out of the corner of her eye, she saw a yellow light flick to red: the warning that her allotment was almost up. She sighed and ran her fingers through her tangle of hair one last time. The red counter ticked down to nothing. And reset to green. She frowned and tapped the lights. Then a slow smile lifted her cheeks — the captain must have overridden the limit, giving her extra time. Nonetheless, she turned the water off. She was clean enough. They needed the power, and she had work to do if she hoped to get the algal converter running at full capacity again asap.

She stepped out of the shower into the small cubicle, lit by a single light dimmed to emergency levels. A weight dropped in her gut as she cast her gaze around, then she closed her eyes and groaned, rubbing her hands over her face. She'd come straight to the shower without stopping for a change of clothes. She opened her eyes to peer sidelong at the jumpsuit she'd been wearing, still soaked with now cold water — sticky, mineral-rich and full of algae. Her nose wrinkled and her skin crawled. Squeezing water out of her hair, she debated her options. There was no way she was putting that jumpsuit on again until it was washed. She'd rather streak through the ship. Her lips pursed as she pulled a bath sheet from the shelf. Wrapping the long cloth around her, she hoped everyone else was occupied.

Tink opened the door of the shower cubicle to step into the main room. And bumped into Alek, his hair wet, dressed in a fresh pair of scrubs and a clean tank, a towel around his neck. She stepped back, her eyes widening. The emergency lights cast him in a crimson halo, highlighting incongruous flecks of red in his black hair that she hadn't noticed before. Sparks of red glinted in his eyes.

He gave her a lopsided smile as he held out the clean jumpsuit folded in his hands. "I hope you don't mind. I noticed you came straight here." She glanced up at him, her mouth opening at the thought of him in her quarters. "Don't worry. Kandi retrieved it."

She swallowed and took the jumpsuit from him. "Thanks." He nodded and turned around. She hesitated for a moment then unwrapped the bath sheet. "The captain didn't extend your shower ration?"

"She did. I didn't think it was fair to use it." He ruffled his hair dry with his towel, and Tink watched the muscles of his shoulders and upper back flex and contract under the grey tank.

"Done," she said, zipping up the front of the jumpsuit. He turned around, and his eyes focused on hers. She looked away, her cheeks flushing. Tilting her head to squeeze some water out of her curls, she blew at a strand stuck to her face, trying to dislodge it without letting go of the towel she was using to dry her hair. She froze as Alek's fingers brushed her cheek, tucking the curl behind her ear.

"I like that you've kept your freckles."

Tink's stomach somersaulted, and she focused on squeezing water out of her hair, though there was little left. Squashing the flutter in her gut, she frowned. "What's it to you?"

He shrugged. "It's just nice to see people being real." He threw his towel in the cleaner, and she sent hers after it. "I told the captain that I'd cook up a meal for everyone, if you want to help. I think we need some sustenance."

Tink was about to protest that they couldn't spare the power, then her stomach grumbled. Her mouth salivated at the thought of another one of his custard bug scrambles. "If you want anyone to eat it, you shouldn't let me anywhere near it." She gave him a small smile, and he responded with a chuckle.

"Fair enough." His eyes lingered on her face for a few seconds, then he turned towards the door.

Tink's stomach twittered again. "But I am pretty hungry." She inhaled sharply as she reached for her soiled jumpsuit, tossing it in the cleaner with the towels as she followed him out. "I can keep you company."

15: Alek

ALEK'S FINGERS TAPPED AT his console as his blood pulsed a tattoo in his neck. They were back at Euko Station. He glared at the utilitarian spaceport, even though the sight of it meant an end to the past 5 days of ever-increasing snipping between the crew. They'd argued over everything from the low thermostat setpoint to the angry hue of the emergency lights to the cold subsistence rations. Beside him, Ish sucked — loudly — on a packet of jujuberry nutrient goo that smelled like vomit. Alek shot a look his way, and the sucking became quieter. He breathed in, forcing his shoulders to relax. Ish was pale, and there was a slight tremble in the hand that held the goo packet. Alek reminded himself that the navigator needed the energy to recover from the drain of slipping.

Alek turned back to the port, weighing the odds that someone he didn't want to see lurked in Euko's shadowy corridors, waiting to pounce on him when his guard was down. He huffed. *I just can't let my guard down.*

"I'm not rehashing this debate, Tink," the captain's voice boomed from the corridor, shortly followed by the person herself. She stalked into her ready room and closed the door without so much as getting a status update. The windows of the room were clear, however — the shading ability being one of the things turned off to conserve power — and he watched her scowl at her desk.

"But—" Tink came onto the bridge and stopped short, blinking. Glancing around, she stomped over to the door to the ready room and opened it without knocking, slamming it behind her.

"What do you think that's about?" Ish asked before taking a long draw of his goo and turning his chair to face the spectacle.

Alek shifted to face Ish, glancing sidelong at the other two behind the window. "I imagine the same thing it's been about for the past 5 days: getting the money to fix the ship." He inched his chair further around, squinting in an attempt to read their lips, but Tink faced away from him, so he only got half the conversation. "Something about a contract. The captain plans to take it. And I guess Tink isn't happy about it, if she's arguing with the captain."

"Mmm, they do that all the time. It's like they're an old married couple."

Alek glanced at him. "I hope my marriage isn't like that."

"You're married?" Ish lifted his eyebrows, his focus fixed on Alek as he finished his goo.

The captain opened the door and strode out, saving Alek from answering the question. Tink trailed Rebeka, almost stepping on her heels.

"But—" Tink said.

"No more buts." Rebeka turned to her. "We're taking the contract." Alek breathed an internal sigh of relief. Maybe they'd leave port before they even docked. He'd get a reprieve from facing his handlers, and the power behind them...the unknown person who'd sent him on this errand.

"But the ship can't handle it." Tink's hands were on her hips. "My patch job won't hold. We need a new converter. Or a full refurb, which needs components and tools I don't have." Her chin lifted and her eyes gleamed. "And time."

"That's why we're taking it. The contractor will pay an advance — an interest-free loan — and has arranged to have the repairs greenlit." Rebeka mimicked the engineer's posture, while at the same time Tink's shoulders sagged. "Prepare to be boarded."

Alek's stomach twisted at the sound of that, even though he knew she meant boarded by repair crews. Then he leaned forward, elbows on his knees, as he mulled over what Rebeka had actually said. That was quite the deposit for a little jack-of-all ship like the *Lyra*. Through narrowed eyes, he watched Tink's mouth open, but nothing came out. However, a war clearly raged behind her fiery eyes.

"Fine." She stomped off the bridge, as Rebeka sequestered herself in her ready room again. Ish made a face then slouched in his seat and closed his eyes.

Alek turned back to the viewscreen, eyeing the station again as he considered what the contract the captain had found might be. And who was behind it.

16: Rebeka

REBEKA STOPPED AGAIN BUT couldn't keep her foot from tapping. She glanced over her shoulder. Alek was struggling to keep up, despite her shorter stride. Her lips twisted in a grimace...she was working out some of her vexation by getting her heart rate up, but his long legs should have been able to out-pace her. She'd brought him along for muscle, to carry either the gift she was picking up or the tool Tink swore she needed back to the ship — something called an industrial chain ratchet.

At least that's what Rebeka told herself. If she were honest, she could easily carry them both, but she wanted backup in the narrow lanes of the Bowels. Every station had similar levels down below — and it was down, even though there was no *down* in space. Whatever the name on the map said, they were all called the Bowels by residents and spacers alike, a term likely coming as much from the foul miasma that hung in the lanes and the unidentified, viscous liquid that tended to drip from the pipes overhead as from its location in the belly of the station.

Her eyes narrowed as Alek came towards her. She tipped her head sideways, homing in on his legs. He straightened up and walked more purposefully, perhaps noticing her scrutiny, but she could have sworn he had a slight hitch in his step. *Maybe I should have brought Severn instead of sending him with Kandi and Ish on the resupply run.*

A flicker of movement behind him drew her attention. Spying the soundless urchin, she opened her mouth to give warning, but was stopped short.

"Touch it and I'll blast your fingers off," Alek said without turning around, grasping the small hand that reached for his weapon. The blaster Kandi had lent him only after stern exhortations to bring it back in better shape than he got it. The child's eyes went wide as he dragged them forward. Almost imperceptibly, he bumped his wrist to theirs. Rebeka's eyebrows pulled together. "Go and don't come back," he said as the kid pulled their wrist back, looking at their patch with a confused look on their face.

"You shouldn't give the street rats anything," Rebeka said as he caught up with her, no sign of a limp in his step. "You just encourage them."

He shrugged a shoulder. "My chits, my choice."

Rebeka didn't say anything more, instead focusing on checking the doorways and alley entries as they descended further. The lights became more sparse and less bright. The shadows deepened and the reek grew.

"How far down are we going?" he asked, his voice low. Out of the corner of her eye, she saw him performing the same scans of their environment she was.

"Scared of the dark?" she scoffed, glancing at him. Her eyes flicked left at a scratching up ahead and a sense of shadows gathering behind them. Rebeka lowered her voice. "You might want to get your weapon out."

"You think things are about to get kinetic, Captain?"

Her eyes narrowed at the use of *kinetic*, a term she hadn't heard since her days in the Legion. Though she was glad to see him pull out the blaster.

Rebeka heard the whine of the borrowed gun powering up and a soft click as he checked his charge. *My new pilot knows a thing or two about weapons. Good to know.* She readied her own blaster. *Wonder if he learned that from the same place he picked up military slang.*

"You didn't answer my question." He shifted around so his back was to hers. "How far?"

"We're already there." She glanced left, and the door beside them opened, casting a green halo that was soon blocked by a large man.

"Mino!" His voice boomed, echoing down the lane.

"Arjen, your timing is impeccable." Rebeka lowered her weapon a few degrees but didn't holster it.

"Come, come." Arjen's voice turned sharp as he continued. "Scat! Shoo!" There was a skittering as the shadows hurried to do his bidding. "Good for nothing guttersnipes," he mumbled.

Rebeka snorted, knowing Arjen fed and clothed many of those 'guttersnipes', then she shifted, stepping towards the door. She sensed stillness behind her. Glancing over her shoulder, she beckoned to Alek, whose eyebrows drew tightly together while his lips pulled into a severe frown.

They got safely back to the ship, the riff raff no longer bothering them after seeing who they'd visited. No one who knew him messed with Arjen, despite his resemblance to a teddy bear. Back aboard the *Lyra*, Rebeka decided she'd rather be back in the Bowels: the ship had descended into chaos. Tink was still grumping and grimacing at having someone else, let alone a crew of someone elses, touching her engine.

Kandi returned shortly after they did, with a chest full of charges for blasters, large and small, as well as pulse rifles. Alek started to help Kandi stow those safely. Instead Rebeka conscripted them both into getting the canister she'd picked up from Arjen secreted away: a gift for Tink that it would be better if the Engineering Guild, whose members currently crawled all over the ship, didn't know about. They didn't take kindly to unauthorized plasma boosters on impulse engines.

They'd just finished hiding it away when laughter travelled up the gangway, followed by the clomp of boots and the rattle of wheels. Severn and Ish had returned with food. Real food to replace what had gone off in the chiller when the power was down as well as a restock of the nutrient packs and unflavoured bug bars they'd had to resort to. Despite being sweaty from lugging the heavy cart around, they wore smiles that made her happy.

Rebeka's lips lifted in response, but that was tempered by the hand Severn laid on Ish's back. *It's probably just friendly.* She forced the smile back to her face. *The last thing I need is a lover's tiff on the ship. Let alone a love triangle*, she thought as she followed Severn's gaze as Tink stomped into the cargo bay, coming right towards her.

"Do you know what they're doing?" She waved some widget in Rebeka's face. An algal tech in his green coveralls and green-tinged skin trailed Tink, his shoulders slumping as he sighed.

"Fixing the algal generator," Rebeka said with a slight shake of her head. "As contracted."

"I need..." The man reached for the widget, but he was even shorter than Tink.

"They're unhooking my juice box from the impulse jumper!"

"It's against regulations!" The man shot Rebeka a pleading look.

Pulling herself up tall and drawing her shoulders back into her power stance, she turned to Tink. "Give the man his widget back." She used her most authoritative voice, and almost smiled to see the man inch away.

Tink blew a lock of hair from her face. "It's not—"

"I don't care what it is. Give it back. The sooner they're done, the sooner they're off the ship." She stared hard at Tink, giving her head a slow nod. Tink started to open her mouth, then snapped it shut, perhaps reading the subtext: the sooner you can reconnect things.

Tink looked askance at the man, but in the end held out the tool for him to take.

"And the sooner we get out of here, the better," Rebeka said.

"Hail Hecate to that," Alek added, quietly enough he might not have meant it to be heard.

17: Tink

TINK WAS RESIGNED. DESPITE all sense, they'd agreed to the contract from Ellis: rescue two packages from a ship adrift. One was a small container holding an experiment of the Dominion Science Council, the second a crate of well-aged Asterian wine that was precious to the noble requesting the salvage. After they retrieved those packages, they could do whatever they wanted with the wreck: salvage rights were theirs.

She sat hunched at the table in the common room, having left her self-imposed exile in the engine room after they rose out of the slipstream. Now that they were inside the target system's asteroid belt, Severn was on watch as Cass took over piloting while Alek got some rest. However, what Alek was doing didn't seem very restful to her. The repetitive thwap-thwap-pow coming from the other side of the common room would be almost hypnotic if it weren't so irritating. She watched him flick the paddle, the muscles in his forearms contracting as he returned Ish's volley. She sighed and huffed, blowing a curl out from in front of her eyes. He smiled when he scored a point against Ish, and a dimple formed on his cheek. Her eyebrows pulled together as she turned her attention to the starburst she was working on and tried to focus. The thing was tiny, and the springs, gears and pinions were blurry despite the goggles. She took care to avoid the charge; it wouldn't do to blind her crewmates in an explosion of light.

At Kandi's laugh, she lifted her head and strained her neck, cracking out a spot of tension. Kandi stood over Ish's shoulder, giving encouragement with an smile on a face more accustomed to being fierce. Tink squinted at Alek and Ish, and the game they played. She grimaced. She'd never mastered Kora, with its paddles and balls — she didn't have the necessary coordination. She watched as Ish's hand flicked and Alek's forearm twitched. The pilot's powerful build gave him little advantage in this game of reflex. Even so, judging by the grin that crinkled the corners of his eyes — and the look of concentration on Ish's — Alek didn't seem to be doing too badly. She dropped her eyes to examine her starburst again, a frown on her lips.

A half minute later, she glanced over at the captain, who sat beside her in companionable silence, the traitorous Grim in her lap, purring away. She was ostensibly reading something on her tablet, but Tink saw her glance at the game, a small smile tugging at the corners of her mouth.

The thwap-thwap ended with a hurrah. *Ish's voice.* Tink looked up with a smile to congratulate her friend, only to see Alek patting Ish on the back. "Rematch?"

Ish beamed back at him. Tink felt a jolt as she realized her friend was almost as tall as Alek.

"Next time," Ish said, running a hand through his hair, glancing at the clock. "I should get cleaned up." He looked back at Alek, who'd lifted his shirt to wipe a sheen of sweat off his face, revealing toned abs. "So should you," Ish continued. "We're nearing our destination." He snatched up the tunic he'd divested when they started playing and left the room.

Alek, on the other hand, filled a glass with water and came to join her and Rebeka, flipping the chair around to sit in it backwards. Tink grimaced at Kandi when she mimicked him. Kandi pulled a face in return, and Tink pretended to be absorbed by her starburst.

Rebeka lifted her head. "You *are* needed on the bridge, pilot." But her light tone took any command out of those words.

"Why?" Tink scoffed, examining a spring. "So he can hotshot us into the sun?" Silence fell, and she looked up to see the cause. They all stared at her, even the cat. Kandi's eyes narrowed and her arms crossed over her chest, while Rebeka's lips pressed together, and Grim's ears flicked. But Alek's expression was unfathomable. Tink shifted in the chair that had become suddenly uncomfortable.

"Why don't you like me?" he asked, turning the glass around in his hand. He gazed at her with that inscrutable look in his storm-blue eyes, not breaking away.

Tink peered at the half-finished starburst, then forced herself to meet his eyes again. "It's not that I don't like you. I don't like you taking risks with my ship."

"*Your* ship?" he said, raising an eyebrow.

"All engineers see the ship as theirs." Rebeka's tone ended the brewing argument before it began. Then she stood up, unceremoniously dislodging the now disgruntled cat. "But Ish is right. We should all get ready to work."

"Aye aye, Captain." Alek stood up and gave her a mock salute before heading for the door. Rebeka graced him with a half-frown that was almost the same as a smile.

"Oh, that kind of thing will get you killed," Kandi said with that same easy smile that unsettled Tink, pushing him ahead. She stopped at the door and gave a stage whisper over her shoulder. "I think he likes you." Her laugh at Tink's grimace was full-throated. Tink's heart lifted to see her friends so happy. Then it crashed again. *How can they excuse Alek's behaviour?* She sighed as the cat jumped into her lap and started kneading.

Rebeka turned to the coffee machine to refill her mug then started for the door.

"Maybe we can get a new pilot at the next port," Tink said, looking down at the cat, which peered at her with his green eyes.

"No." Rebeka's voice brooked no argument.

"But we'll pass a port while slipping back." Tink looked at her, hoping her face conveyed worry for the ship and its crew, not antipathy towards Alek. Because it wasn't that she disliked him; she just disliked his flying and his mannerisms...the impact he had on *her* friends and the bundle of nerves in her abdomen since he'd come on board.

"We're not breaking in a new pilot mid-job." Rebeka's voice softened. "Besides, the next port *is* where we drop off the cargo, and he may not want to stay on with you being such a grumpus." She headed out the door and down the corridor to the bridge.

"But..." Tink dropped the cat, who chirruped his disgust, to run after Rebeka, who was already halfway to the bridge.

Arriving at the bridge, Rebeka became Captain again. "Where's the target?"

"Coordinates are just the other side of this moon." Alek looked between his display and the viewscreen, which was filled with an opalescent green orb. Ish leaned over and read off some numbers, his voice too low for Tink to hear. Alek gave a sharp nod, then the ship banked as he shifted its trajectory.

"Not getting any signals," Kandi said, the seriousness back in her expression. Severn sat at the station beside her, scrolling through the sensor readings.

Tink leaned towards the captain. "We could pop back to the last gate..."

"No," Rebeka said, lacing the word with more sharpness than a single word should have. The captain didn't even glance at her, instead keeping her focus on the viewscreen where something large had appeared now that the moon was at the edge of their field of view. Much too massive to be some minor noble's pleasure craft. Tink's stomach felt like tiger ants gnawed at it.

The bridge went silent as everyone tried to process the scene in front of them. Tink's mouth dropped open. But it was Alek who said what she was thinking.

"What the hell is that?"

18: Rebeka

F OR A LONG SECOND, Rebeka stared at the monster that hung in their viewscreen. A heavy silence blanketed the bridge, and a worm of worry gnawed at her stomach.

It was a ship...a very big ship covered in craters and scorch marks. Her eyes narrowed, thinking of what it meant for her crew. Even with its registration burnt, she knew exactly what class of ship it was, though she didn't know that anyone else would.

"A Leviathan." Kandi's voice was full of awe. Or dread. Rebeka couldn't tell which, but looking at the faces of the others, it seemed like they'd all heard of the largest class of ship in the Dominion's fleet. And the second most fearsome.

"That's what they sent us to retrieve?" Ish said, almost in a whisper.

"Not retrieve. Scavenge." There was an icy edge to Tink's voice that Rebeka rarely heard. Looking at the engineer, she saw Tink's focus was on the ship, instead of casting a judgmental eye on her for taking the contract. "You don't *salvage* a Leviathan."

"They don't expect it back." Ish's voice raised at the end, though he knew as well as anyone their contract stated they could do what they would with the ship as long as they brought back two packages: one, the results of an experiment, and the other, ludicrously expensive alcohol belonging to a member of the royal family.

Rebeka gasped quietly, but it was enough in the hushed ship to cause the others to look her way. She coughed into her sleeve to cover it. She'd just realized a nuance in the phrasing used during the contract negotiations. *Royal* family...not the wide network of noble relatives and pretenders that constituted the much larger *Imperial* family. Someone amongst the Emperor's closest kin wanted something on that ship. And there was no way the *Lyra* was getting out of this with the ship as salvage. She'd be happy if they got out of it alive. The creature in her stomach turned to acid as it wormed through her intestines. A shiver crawled down her spine.

"What do you think happened to it?" Severn asked. Rebeka looked at him sidelong as he glanced around the room. "Asteroids?"

"Space gas?" Ish offered hopefully. But it was clear this was no asteroid, no pocket of space gas. She'd seen ships with wounds like this before, floating dead in the vast battlegrounds in front of the Hauer Gate.

"No, those are scorch marks." Kandi stood up and walked closer to the viewscreen. "Cass, zoom in 200 percent. Here." She lifted her index finger to the screen.

"EMP?" Rebeka said, even though she knew it was wrong even as she spoke. A Leviathan would have countermeasures to protect it from any electromagnetic pulse, at least anything a non-Legion ship would have.

Kandi shook her head, pointing a finger at a couple of spots on the hull. "That...and that, look like pulse cannons."

"Should I take us closer?" Alek asked, his voice even, though she noted the tension in the muscles of his neck, and his shoulder blades pulled tight together.

"Take us around." Rebeka stepped past Alek and Ish to join Kandi as the *Lyra's* nose canted downward, and the ship rolled a few degrees to starboard.

"And that —" Kandi stopped short as they came around the far side of the ship, lit by the weak sun. "That's from a plasma torpedo. I don't know what this is." She ran her fingers over the display, following the massive wound in the ship's side. Rebeka's lips twisted at there being a weapon Kandi didn't know.

"What have we gotten ourselves into this time?" Tink stepped up beside her, no hint of recrimination in her voice, only worry. Worry that Rebeka understood but couldn't let herself voice. Instead, she rubbed the web of flesh between thumb and index finger on her left hand.

"Pirates?" Ish said, an equal mixture of dread and respect in his voice.

"Rebels?" Severn added.

"Coup between imperial factions?" Tink suggested.

Rebeka frowned, not sure which of those she'd prefer. "Now, we have no idea what happened here. All we know is that we signed on to do a job. And we always do our best to deliver." She stepped back from the viewscreen. "Tink, can the *Lyra* tow that thing, if needed?"

"Seriously?" Tink grimaced when Rebeka nodded. She blinked. "I thought the plan was to get it up and running, and fly it out of here?"

Rebeka scowled at the scene outside once more before finally turning away. "It is but plans change. I want to know our options."

"With my tweaks to the refurbed algal generator and the plasma booster you picked up, we have lots of power, as long as we keep it away from any larger gravity wells." Tink rubbed her nose, a sign she was deep in specs. "It'll max out the length of the tentacles, but I think we can make it work."

But Ish shook his head.

"Spit it out, Ish." Rebeka crossed her arms over her chest as she peered at the navigator.

He turned from the viewscreen, his fingers tapping on his console. "We can't slip towing something that large."

"We won't." She turned to Tink. "Go over there. See what shape it's in. Try to get it running. Take Alek with you."

"But—" Her hands started to rise to her hips.

Rebeka huffed out her nose, and Tink went silent. "Take him." She knew she won when Tink's arms dropped to her side.

"And me." Kandi arched an eyebrow. "As you say, we have no idea what happened here."

Rebeka's eyes narrowed, then she nodded, once. "And Kandi."

Come the Leviathan

19: TINK

"I KNEW THIS CONTRACT was a bad idea," Tink whispered to herself, her voice sounding flat inside the helmet of her suit. Somehow that knowledge didn't make her feel triumphant. She yanked her foot up against the pull of magnetism and took another step forward, metal reverberating as her grav boot snapped back to the floor. Besides being dead in the water, the ship was deserted. It had that empty, hollow feeling that a ship without a crew had. The few times she'd experienced it, it felt like ants crawled under her skin.

Shifting the pulse rifle she'd reluctantly agreed to carry, she nudged a piece of mottled debris out of the way, stirring up some of the red flakes that hung suspended without gravity to pull them down. *Hmmph, rust on a ship like this. I don't feel so bad about the* Lyra.

The ship was dark except for sweeps from their scopes and the glow from their helmets. Although there was residual atmosphere trapped inside, the tests on its breathability came back inconclusive. So they kept their helmets on, much to Alek's chagrin and Tink's amusement. Up ahead, Kandi led the way, methodically sweeping her light around the space. Next in line was Alek, with Tink's toolbox strapped to his back, moving his gun in arcs to sight the ceiling, even though there was nothing up there besides more dust, rust, and shrapnel. Behind her, Severn brought up the rear, his light flashing at her feet every now and then. Back on the *Lyra*, he'd grudgingly mentioned that it might be useful having a computer tech in case they needed to crack the system. But they needed to get power to the system before they could do that.

Lost in thought, Tink bumped into Alek. "Oomph. Why did you stop?" she said over comms as she brought her hands up. She grabbed hold of his bicep to keep herself from falling back.

"Kandi told me to." Tink craned to look around him, still holding his arm, to where Kandi glared at them from behind her faceplate.

"I also told you to be quiet." Her sigh was audible in Tink's ear.

"There's no one here," she replied. Even though it was barely more than a whisper, her words echoed in her helmet.

"You don't know that." Kandi's helmeted head shifted as her eyes continued to scan the corridor.

Tink made a face, then realized Kandi could see her expression as well as she could see Kandi's. "Yes, I do, and so do you."

"We still need to check." Kandi turned to face the corridor again.

"So why are we stopping then?" Tink shrugged the heavy rifle up. Then, realizing the point had risen at the same time, shifted again to aim the barrel down.

"It's a really big ship." Kandi's torso twisted left then right. That's when Tink realized they were at a crossroads — she hadn't noticed the branches of the other corridor in the dim light. "I think we need to split up," Kandi added. She didn't sound enthused by the idea, but then the helmet comms flattened everyone's voices. "My guess is bridge, ops and officers' quarters are down there." She pointed left with her rifle. "Severn and I will go that way. Alek and Tink, you go the other. Find the engine room if you can. Maybe we can still power this behemoth up."

"Leviathan," Tink said.

Kandi's eyebrow arched, but she continued her instructions. "More importantly, look for these packages. That's what we're being paid to retrieve."

Tink tried to nod, but it was lost in her helmet. "Yes sir," she said instead, attempting to bring some levity to lift the heavy mood, but it fell flat.

"Yes sir," Alek echoed, his tone serious.

"Normally I'd say maintain radio silence but, in this case, keep comms open. And feel free to chatter away. Quietly." With that, she headed left, motioning for Severn to follow her. He glanced at Tink as he passed, his face grim, then his eyes flicked to Alek before he followed Kandi.

Tink turned to go after Alek, who'd already started down the right branch, when she heard a sound, a ting-ting-ting like a small hammer hitting metal. She stopped, surprised she could hear anything in the minimal atmo. She tipped her head, glancing at Alek as he started back towards her, a question on his face. She shook her head, silencing him, and angled her head the other way. "Do you hear..." Kandi's voice crackled in her helmet, interrupting her. Alek winced, obviously hearing the same thing.

"Second thought — we stick together." The words were high-pitched over the comms. "Come here, will you?"

Tink's lifting eyebrow was mimicked by Alek's as she looked at him in question. Leaving the question unasked, she turned back to join the other two, Alek following her. The corridor was dark, except for her helmet light and scope, the latter of which she kept lowered for fear of shooting one of her crewmates by accident. Particles of ice and rust glinted against the midnight blue, drifting in the eddies caused by their passing. Eventually, she saw green light spilling from a doorway. It silhouetted the two figures in atmo suits. Kandi and Severn stood side-by-side facing the room, the light beyond casting their lumpy shadows against the far wall of the corridor. Coming up beside Severn, she looked around him to Kandi.

"What's up?" she asked as she sensed Alek stop close behind her. She winced when she felt his hands on her shoulders and was about to snap at him when his gentle pressure turned her to face the doorway. "Oh."

"Yeah, oh," he said. Inside the room, bodies hung suspended in the air, like puppets without a string. Some motion of the limited air maybe, or of the ship itself, caused a few of them to move, as if they were floating in an unseen ocean. Tink startled, jumping back into Alek, as one drifted right past the door, its one eye wide and mouth agape. Flecks of rust covered the man's neck and uniform.

"Not rust," she said, glancing at her gloves speckled with red.

"Not rust," Kandi repeated, stepping into the room.

"What are you doing?" Severn reached an arm out to stop her.

She turned to him, her eyes sharp and her lips thin under her faceplate. "Change of plans," she said, turning to Tink and Alek as she hoisted her rifle to her shoulder. "We find the packages. We get the hell out of here." With no argument from anyone, she continued, glancing at Tink. "We'll tow the ship, since Tink says we can." She started into the room again.

"Wait." Tink reached out this time.

Kandi looked at her and blinked. "I'd like to get this over with...stat."

"Me too. And there might be a faster way." She eyed the room for a second, then turned away. "One that doesn't involve wading through room after room of dead bodies."

"You think there's more?" Severn asked, his tone flat.

"Why wouldn't there be? This is a huge ship." Tink waved her free hand. "The plasma torpedo might have caused catastrophic systems failure. There might be a whole shipful of dead crew floating around."

Kandi peered at her, eyes narrowing. "Some of these people weren't killed by whatever happened to the ship."

"What do you mean?" Tink wiggled her toes in her boots to combat the icy chill seeping into her feet and her fingers.

Kandi's eyes slid sideways towards the room. "Some of those injuries were caused by close quarters blaster fire."

"Oh." She glanced back the way they'd come, into darkness. "Mutiny?"

"Or the rebels boarded them." Severn cast his scope along the corridor.

"Someone looking for the same thing we are," Alek added, and Kandi nodded.

"So, faster way it is." Tink turned to Alek, noticing the grim expression on the cocky pilot's face. "Give me the pack." Slowly, he did as she asked and lowered it to the floor.

She undid the latch and opened the lid. "Our contact specifically asked if we had a biodynamic stasis coupler."

"Okay?" Kandi's voice rose at the end, turning it from statement to question.

"What are you thinking?" Severn crouched beside her.

"If the experiment is biological — " she pulled a small box out of the pack "— I might be able to tweak my bosch sensor to find it."

"Even in containment?" He peered at her, a half-smile on his face.

"I am a Tinker, aren't I?" She grinned and nodded. Then she looked back at her tools, her grin turning to a grimace. "Or I could just scan for a backup battery in use."

A heavy thud shook the ship, and Tink swayed in her grav boots. Severn stopped at the front of their line. She continued to sweep the large space with her scanner. Its green light pulsed at infuriatingly regular intervals, even though the cavernous room was empty so far.

"What was that?" Severn asked, his voice tight.

"Tentacles." Kandi stepped past Tink to stand beside him. "I let the captain know what we found. She agrees with the plan to get the packages and get out. Her and Ish are getting ready to tow." She walked back to Tink. "Anything?"

"Shhh!" The scanner had blipped red instead of flashing green. "Step back."

Kandi scowled at her but did as asked. "Rebeka says if we don't find these things by the time they're done, we go back."

"But...." Alek and Severn said at the same time.

"We can tow the ship and figure out what to do from there."

"Would you all be quiet?" Tink let her voice rise. The scanner flashed red again. But faster now, she was sure of it. She turned in a slow circle, the pulse rifle hanging loose from the strap at the crook of her elbow. She was beginning to think she'd imagined it when the scanner light turned red and stayed there, blinking at an even tempo. She glanced up, almost expecting a crimson-eyed monster to lunge out of the shadows. Walking towards whatever had gotten the scanner excited, she held the instrument as steady as she could in her shaking hand, a light from over her shoulder sweeping the darkness in front of her. A bulky presence stepped up beside her, and she glanced over to see Alek, whose eyes shifted from the scanner to her when she moved. After a few seconds, they were joined by Severn and Kandi, and they all moved forward as a four-person phalanx.

Slowly a grey bulk formed out of the darkness in front of them. The scanner light stopped blinking, staying solid red. Tink's eyes narrowed.

"Bleeding Hades, a wall." Severn stepped forward, rapping on it with the tip of his rifle. He started to follow the wall to his right. "So close yet so far."

"You sure it's straight ahead?" Kandi asked, peering at the scanner then at the wall.

Tink nodded. "Yes." She felt another tentacle latch onto the ship.

"Jacks." Severn's curse echoed in her helmet. Kandi swung her light around to find him rubbing his knee. "Huh, we're in the engine room," he said, standing up straight. "And would you look at that." His scope lifted to illuminate something in front of him. "They have the same algal generator your little ship does."

Tink scowled at the reference to her *little* ship, despite the fact that it was true — they had the same generator.

"Must be a backup," Severn continued. "No way could a Mean Green provide enough juice for a ship this large." He smiled at her through his face plate. "One of these tanks only hold 500 gills."

Tink started to smile back then remembered he'd insulted her ship. She turned back to the wall where Alek stood, running his hand over it.

She gasped. With a flick of his fingers, the wall slid open. Silence hung between them for a few long moments.

"How did you know there was a door?" Kandi asked, nudging him out of the way as she brought her rifle back up to her shoulder and swept an arc of light through the small space that had been revealed.

"And how did you know how to open it?" Severn rejoined them, and Tink noticed his rifle barrel had come up a few inches. Alek just shrugged, a movement that was also accompanied by bringing his rifle to his shoulder.

Tink eyed him, her lips tense and her eyebrows pulling together. Then she turned towards the room. "More importantly, how did it open without power anywhere else in the ship?"

"Failsafe?" Kandi's voice crackled in her helmet. "But I think we've found the packages." Tink muscled her way past the bristling men.

Sure enough, two crates filled the tiny room, one smaller, one larger, both a dull grey where their scopes passed. Lights flickered weakly on their lids, indicating some status Tink couldn't puzzle out in the moment, but there was a hesitancy to the flickers, especially on the large crate. It looked like its backup battery was running low. But that was the aged wine; however precious, the alcohol wasn't her main concern. No, her focus was on the smaller one...it and the experiment it contained. Tink scanned its surface, running her fingers and then her biosensor along joins and hinges, making sure it was still intact. She didn't want to bring an active biohazard back to their ship.

"Good?" Kandi came up beside her.

"Seems so." Tink nodded. "Yes." Another tremble reverberated through the Leviathan. After travelling along the metal and up her legs, it didn't feel like a tentacle attaching.

Kandi hoisted her rifle, slinging the strap over her shoulder. "Good. Let's get these moving and get back to the *Lyra* posthaste." No one argued.

20: Rebeka

REBEKA GLARED AT THE crates the crew had brought back from the Leviathan. The packages sat in front of her as she stood in the cargo bay with her arms crossed over her chest. One hand at her throat while her thumb stroked the artery. She dropped that hand to the lid of the smaller crate — the one with the biohazard symbol on it. "You've connected the power?"

Tink grunted from the other side. Rebeka took that as a yes, since it was a change from the swearing of the past ten minutes.

"What the hell kind of contract is this?" Kandi said, stalking towards her, her muscled limbs bare. She was clad, like the rest of the recovery crew, in her skivvies. Her usually bronze skin was ashen from the decontamination process. Rebeka snorted at the irony of sending them through the decon unit when they'd brought a biohazard onboard. But it was a contained biohazard. Unlike whatever might have been floating around that ship. It wasn't just the blood from the victims she was worried about. Bioweapons were illegal for all but select members of the Legion's Fifth Echelon divisions — the best of the best. But that didn't mean others couldn't get their hands on them.

"A fool's errand," Alek said, running his hands through his temporarily grey hair, dislodging some of the decon powder.

"Stop that. You're getting dust on everything." Tink popped up from behind the unit. "Especially me." She ran her hands along her arms and over her tank top, then checked something on her tablet. "All systems seem to be functioning within spec." She scowled at Alek. "Unless dust gets into the biocon unit." Alek opened his mouth as if to say something, but instead he stopped, crossing his arms over his chest as Tink disappeared behind the crate. The puckered scar that crossed his right pectoral writhed with his movement.

"What about this one?" He poked the larger crate with his toe. "Shouldn't it be jacked in?"

"Getting to it." The bulk of the crate muffled Tink's voice.

Rebeka grunted. "If their precious alcohol isn't in ideal conditions for a few minutes, it'll still get you drunk."

"An awful fancy biocon unit for alcohol." Alek's forehead furrowed as his lips pulled down in a frown. "Even if it is from a now-decimated planet."

"Stasis, not biocon," Tink said as she stood up. "And by all indicators, it's running fine." Just then, the crate emitted a whine. "Well, fine enough. It might have been jostled about a bit during the attack."

"Which leads me back to my question," Kandi said. "Not rhetorical: what kind of shit have we gotten ourselves into?" Instead of looking at Rebeka, Kandi focused on strapping her weapons belt around her hips, striking a very odd figure in her underwear. And it was not something she usually did onboard the *Lyra*, but Rebeka couldn't blame her. "We're supposed to believe we can legally salvage a Leviathan? The powers-that-be are okay with that? I call —"

"The rebels," Severn said, as he strode over to them from the decon unit, tucking his hands into the sleeves of his shirt.

"What do you mean?" Even to herself, Rebeka's voice seemed sharp, but she hoped it came across as just a captain debriefing her crew.

He looked up, then pulled the shirt over his head and down, though not before Rebeka noted the white striations of old scars criss-crossing his muscled torso.

Shirt on, he continued. "You saw the marks on that ship." He nodded towards Tink, Alek and Kandi. "And we can all attest that the dead wore Legion Special Forces uniforms."

"Appearances can be deceiving," Alek said.

"But not a Leviathan, floating dead in space." Severn took a step closer, and Tink grimaced, caught between the two men.

"We don't know what attacked them." Alek pulled his shoulders back as Severn stepped closer to Tink. "For all we know, it's some internal power struggle amongst the royal houses." Alek stepped back and shrugged. "Sorry," he said, looking down at Tink before turning to Rebeka. "But they happen all the time. We just don't hear about them."

"If we don't hear about them, then how do *you* know?" Kandi shifted to stand beside him, placing her hands on the larger of the two crates.

"How do you *not* know?" Rebeka said. "Despite what Alek says, we see it all the time. One week the Taxarchon is from

Clan Koning, the next it's Clan Erregina. Only the Emperor stays the same."

"So, what do we do now?" Alek asked, glancing up from the crate.

"We find somewhere to stash the Leviathan, then we deliver the packages and complete this contract." She nodded once and dropped her hands to her side. "But first we get away from here. Everyone, get some rest. You need it." She returned to Alek. "Except you. I need you flying this ship instead of Ish."

"Aye aye, Captain." Alek gave her a salute, crisp despite his teasing tone.

21: Alek

T HE LIGHTS HAD CYCLED toward night, dim and blue, and the *Lyra* was quiet. Alek cocked his head, surprised how quickly he'd become used to the whirrs and chirps of the ship.

With everyone else asleep, he was supposed to be on the bridge. Instead, he stood in the cargo bay staring at the crates as he replayed the events of their sojourn on the Leviathan on a mental loop. Something in the fractured images niggled at the base of his brain. It was like watching old vids corrupted with age, with little tics in the movement. But he couldn't pinpoint what was causing the glitch.

A moth fluttered in his gut as he ran his fingers lightly over the top of the crate, hardly daring to touch it. The metal was cold, but then the cargo bay was an icebox. Three lights blinked in sequence on the grey surface, extra bright in the darkness of the hold. He heard a thud and spun his head to look over his shoulder. *Nothing.* No one else haunted the large space. Probably no one else on the ship was even awake. Then a flicker caught the corner of his eye. He squinted at the window into the common room, but there was no one there.

"Seriously, getting scared by bogeymen," he said, turning back to the boxes. Their lights dimmed momentarily, as if there was a dip in the power.

"You're an adult. Don't let your imagination run away with you." He took a deep breath and leaned over the status panel. Then jumped back as a form flew towards him from the other side of the crate. With a soft thump, Grim landed on top of the box and chirruped at him. "Bleeding Hades, cat." He stepped back to the package, scritching the cat's chin before running a hand along his arched back. "Don't go sneaking up on people like that. You're liable to get yourself shot." The cat merely pressed his head into Alek's hand and purred.

Scooping up the cat, he loped towards the stairs leading to the bridge. He spared a last glance at their cargo, wondering what his minders expected him to do. But when he arrived at the stairs, he decided not to go up. Instead, his head tipped to the side as he looked down the corridor that led to the engine. He hadn't been that way since the converter joint blew. After glancing over his shoulder, he headed down the hall past the engine room. The green light from the algal tanks soon enveloped him, causing him to shiver despite the heat they radiated.

He ran the fingertips of his free hand over the warm tanks and continued towards the repaired generator. Tink had insisted the converter be replaced with the same model as the old one, so it seemed almost the same. A ting sounded behind him. This time he didn't let himself get spooked and took another step closer.

"What are you doing down here?"

Alek stopped, a point of ice blooming between his shoulder blades at Severn's voice. Slowly, he turned around. "I could ask the same of you."

"I followed a shadowy figure down a corridor to our fuel source. You were here first." Severn grabbed a pipe overhead and did a lazy pull-up, all while continuing to stare at him. "Shouldn't you be on the bridge?" he asked.

Alek frowned as Severn lowered himself down — the computer tech had muscles. "Shouldn't you be asleep?"

"Couldn't sleep."

"So, you thought you'd come to the engine to exercise?" Alek kept his voice dripping with disdain.

"Need to do something to keep occupied." Severn reached the bottom of another pull-up. "Otherwise, my mind makes up all sorts of shit."

Alek frowned at Severn. But the man was right: he should be on the bridge. They were nearing the asteroid field they'd travelled through on their way to the wreck. The captain hoped to find somewhere there to hide the ship.

"Well, I just came down to keep Grim from getting into something he shouldn't." The cat purred double-time against his chest. "Catch you later."

Alek shrugged past Severn, his heart brightening as the smug smile slipped from the man's face. Then his heart fell again. Severn wasn't the one who'd been sent aboard the *Lyra* with a mission. He was, and he wasn't sure he believed in that mission anymore. "But what I believe doesn't matter," he whispered to himself as he jogged up the stairs to the upper level, releasing Grim at the top.

22: Rebeka

*S*ILENCE. Except for the hum of the ship, the bridge was quiet. Rebeka hadn't expected chitchat, but she'd expected at least a little interaction. Even the cat didn't make a sound as he glared at them from his high perch, his tail flicking back and forth. In her experience, silence on the bridge was a bad sign. "Alek, status."

"We're nearing the asteroid belt. We should enter in 15 minutes." He stayed focused on his display and didn't elaborate.

"And...."

"And?" He half turned his head. "The Leviathan is making the *Lyra* harder to handle. This ship was never meant to haul something that large. It makes us bulky and a bigger target for a chunk of rock."

"I thought you were a hotshot who could fly me out of anything." Rebeka tried — and failed — to lighten the mood, though she noticed a smirk on the sliver of Alek's profile visible to her.

"We need to drop it before we slip." Ish squinted at her, as if expecting her to protest.

"I know." She grasped the rail in front of her. "But we can't slip until we're away from those gas giants on the other side of the belt regardless. We can drop the ship on one of the rocky moons circling the largest one."

Ish took a sharp breath in, opening his mouth then snapping it shut.

"Spit it out." She leaned on the rail, peering down at him.

"If we head tangential to the plane of the system once we're inside the outer edge of the asteroids, we can slip before we reach the gas giants."

"An in-system slip?" Tink said, raising an eyebrow. Rebeka understood her question: in-system slip points were rare, and where they existed, they were rarely used. The gravity wells from any suns and large planets caused weird distortions in the slipstream, or so they'd lectured in *Intro to Astrodynamics*. But Ish was the expert on all things stream.

He gave a sharp nod, his fingers twitching on his knees. "There's a solitary slip point. I noticed it on the way in."

"A single slip point so close in?" Rebeka asked. "Isn't that unusual?" The slide of Ish's eyes sideways confirmed her understanding: it was. "Do you know anything about it?"

"Cass and I are working on it."

"Humph." Rebeka had nearly abandoned ship when she'd learned the *Lyra's* AI was a CASS-ANDRA model. But, over the years, the AI hadn't given any reason for her to suspect it of being faulty. At least, not until recently. She turned to Severn. "And how is Cass?"

He flicked his gaze up before looking back down at the tablet in his hands. "Seems to be running fine. But..." He stopped.

"But nothing," Tink said. "Cass is fine. Now the generator on the other —"

Rebeka held up a hand, silencing Tink. "But what?" She gestured at Severn to continue.

"She's right. I just worry." He tapped his tablet with his thumb. "But everything is in spec."

Rebeka didn't like *in spec*. During her years as a soldier, she'd come to trust gut over spec any day. But she shifted her attention to Tink anyway. "What about the generator?"

"I'm still trying to get the new converter in sync with the ship."

"But it's working?" Rebeka sighed, rolling her shoulders then pulling them down, away from her ears.

"Yes, but —"

"But it's *in spec*?" Rebeka threw Severn's words back at Tink, arching an eyebrow, and the engineer graced her with a grimace. "I'll be in my ready room. Don't bother me unless the ship is on fire. Or the corpses on the Leviathan reanimate and want to board the *Lyra*." Her second attempt at humour fell as flat as the first, mirroring her mood. She conceded defeat and trudged into her so-called ready room, which also served as her office and extra storage. She closed the door, but not before a grey streak flew past her to take up residence on her desk. "Grim."

All she wanted to do was curl up with a glass of whiskey and a good story. But she had business to attend to first. When she shooed Grim off her desk, he jumped into her lap and started kneading. She frowned at him but nonetheless stroked his back with one hand as she pulled up the holodisplay with the other. She opened an encrypted channel.

"Connect me to Ellis." The screen flickered as the signal hopped from ansible to ansible before landing on the desk of some pretty young thing. The man couldn't have been over twenty, with a fake smile and dimples to match. She spared a fleeting thought at what else about him was fake. It was strange how Ellis surrounded himself with people so young and beautiful; given all the expense he put in to making *himself* younger and more beautiful, she expected his vanity would make him hire toothless, wrinkled harpies. Rebeka had been acquainted with Ellis for too long to be fooled by the surgery and the bots.

"I need to speak to Ellis."

"He is unavailable at the moment," pretty young thing said, his voice betraying the fact that he was actually as young as he seemed.

"Tell Ellis if he doesn't get on the line right now, I'll drive this Levia— " Pretty young thing disappeared in a blink to be replaced by Ellis' too smooth face and too slick hair. Rebeka's lip curled. "I think I liked the other view better."

"So do I, my dear." Ellis formed his lips into a plastic smile. "What's the urgency?"

"I think you know bloody well what the emergency is. I have a Leviathan full of ...." Her voice dropped even though the signal was encrypted. "Full of dead bodies strapped to my ship." Ellis' lips formed into a circle, feigning shock. Too bad for him, he wasn't a very good actor — he couldn't make his eyes lie. And the surgeries and nanites left him with little expressive range.

"Captain Mino, I'm appalled."

"What the hell is going on?"

"I have no idea. And frankly, I'm shocked that you and your crew would participate in such nefarious activity, despite being rascals and rogues."

"Activity you contracted us for, Ellis."

"I had no knowledge of what was at the site. I'm just the broker."

"Bullshit, Ellis. You wouldn't broker a deal for your mother without knowing all the details."

"That's because my mother is a degenerate criminal. Now, if I were in your place, I would have left that ship where I found it and contacted the authorities immediately."

"You'd never leave a chance for profit floating in space."

"But I'm not you. Now, if you have nothing else, it is very late here, and I need my beauty sleep."

"I want to know what you've gotten me into, Ellis, and who I'm going to find knocking on my door." Rebeka leaned into the holoscreen. "And don't forget I have a fully functional Leviathan at my disposal."

"But I was —" His eyes narrowed, barely perceptible crow's feet appearing at the corners.

"You were told it wasn't working?" Rebeka smirked as his lip twitched. "You forget, my engineer is a Tinker. Maybe if you hadn't been so focused on arranging her marriage to an Antillian bugmeal salesperson." She stabbed the button to disconnect, causing her finger to smart.

As she shook the pain out, a yellow light flashed on her desk. The refurbished generator. She glanced out the window to see Tink sprint out of view. "Maybe Tink was right," she said to Grim, who'd jumped back up on the desk. "About a lot of things."

The cat merruped, peering at her with his green eyes.

23: Tink

T HE NEW CONVERTER GLEAMED, out of place amongst the old generator that surrounded it. A transient desire to take a grinder to it and scuff it up flitted through Tink's mind, but the thought caused a stab of pain to her heart. Instead, she got comfortable. Squatting in front of the generator, she examined the numbers on the sensor display as she tweaked each setting. The aeration and mineral ratios were still off, even though the algae seemed happy. Another engineer would probably be fine with it. But she wasn't just any engineer. When she canted her head, she swore she heard a hiccough in the system.

With a scowl imprinted on her face, she glanced up at the connector that had blown on the old converter. She couldn't understand how it had failed. The previous piping had been in good condition, as good as the new stuff that invasive tech crew had used. She checked the lines religiously — this ship was her soul. There was a reason her uncle had nicknamed her Tink - she loved the Tinker ethos as a child. A life spent surrounded by machines as much as people, tending, tweaking, inventing until they died. It was an idea based on a big kernel of truth. Whether by nature or nurture, even planet-dwelling Tinkers tended to tinker, not that there were a lot of them. Tink looked up at the lights overhead and blinked back tears. Not that there were a lot of her people left at all.

Wiping her nose on a rag, she turned back to testing Mean Green, with its new converter. She glanced sidelong at the faulty connection point that had caused it all, fuzzy in the corner of her vision. In the blurriness, there was something strange where the converter met the generator. A slight difference in the luminosity of the metal. She leaned closer, still not looking at it straight on. There was definitely something there. She turned her head to peer at the joint, then flipped her goggles down to examine it in different spectrums.

"Bleeding Hades." Her skin flushed, starting at her neck before creeping into her cheeks. She flipped the goggles back up and looked again. There was a hairline scratch that hadn't been there the last time she'd done a stress check.

"Whatcha looking at?"

Tink fell back onto her butt, one hand coming to her torso to keep her heart from beating out her chest. "Don't sneak up on a person like that." She twisted to glare at Severn.

"Sorry." He smiled in return, reaching out with one of the mugs of coffee he held, offering it to her. "But I didn't sneak. You were just so focused." His smile grew, and a dimple formed on the left cheek, then he took a sip of his own coffee. Tink's frown softened, and she drank from her mug to cover it as Severn continued. "Better I tap you on the shoulder, and have you flail your arms, knocking the coffee I brought you all over your machinery?" He held out a hand to help her up. "I don't think you'd appreciate that."

She stared at his hand then took it, giving him a half smile. "Maybe try singing."

He laughed, and she joined him. "I'm trying *not* to scare you, remember? I can only warble Manchean ballads. Maybe I can whistle though." Stepping up beside her, he nodded at the generator. "Something definitely had you captivated. If only you'd look at other things that way." His voice dropped lower.

She almost asked what other things. But seeing the quirk of his eyebrow, she knew exactly what he meant. She shifted, giving him room to get closer in the small space. As she stared at the generator, she breathed in his scent: spice and citrus and something floral. "I think..." She shivered at the thought she hadn't spoken aloud yet. "I think someone tampered with the converter." Tink sighed at the relief of sharing the idea, then a worm of worry gnawed at her gut: Severn could be the saboteur.

"What? No!" He brought an arm around her shoulder, and her muscles tensed for a second, then she breathed in, letting the weight and warmth comfort her.

"That's what caused it to blow." She turned to look at him, heat in her cheeks again. His face was a mask of disbelief, and concern filled his pale blue eyes. "I know my machines. It's the only explanation that makes sense. I just didn't want to believe it."

"Because it had to be one of the crew." His hand ran down her arm, coming to rest at her elbow. "Any idea who?"

She shook her head, bringing her mug up between them. "No. It can't be Ish. We've been friends forever. The captain...no, she wouldn't do anything to harm the ship or the crew." Her shoulders sagged. "I can't believe any of them would."

"I hate to say it, but you have two new crew on board." He grimaced, taking another sip of his coffee. "Not saying it was me, but you don't know me or Alek all that well. Though, really, do we know what anyone would do if the right pressure were applied?" He looked at the generator, but his gaze wasn't focused.

Tink raised an eyebrow. "Do you know enough about an algal converter to sabotage it in such a way that it keeps the crew alive and the ship limping but in dire need of repairs?"

He shrugged. "There is the Connect. You can find anything there."

"In a way that's not immediately obvious to the engineer that works on it every day?"

Looking into his mug, Severn opened his mouth then closed it, his teeth clinking together. Tink watched his lips move back and forth. She was about to tell him to spill when he said, "I did see Alek down here the other day." He glanced back at her, the skin around his eyes tight. "It was after it blew, but there was no reason for him to be here."

"How dare someone mess with my ship!" She almost threw her wrench down. Instead, she slipped it into her belt. "That's it. He has to explain himself." She spun on her heels, intending to stalk down the corridor, but Severn's hand grasped her wrist, stalling her. She scowled at him but let herself be stopped. His fingers loosened around her wrist but didn't let go.

"What?" The word came out short and sharp. A lock of hair had escaped from her scarf and fell in front of her eyes, coming to tickle her nose.

"It's my word against his." He glanced down the corridor before looking back at her, his blue eyes locking onto hers. He reached out, hesitant at first, and tucked the wayward strand of hair behind her ear. Tink felt herself flush again, but not from anger this time.

"So?" She looked down into her own mug, which she held between them.

"If you haven't noticed, he's ingratiated himself pretty firmly with the rest of the crew."

"Hmmph." Tink gulped down the dregs of her coffee. "Even the captain's defending him."

Severn bobbed his head. "Maybe we should watch him. Gather evidence. *Then* take it to the captain."

Tink sighed. She could see the wisdom of watching and waiting, and not confronting Alek on her own. "I'm no sleuth. In case you haven't noticed, I have no subtlety." She flicked her gaze up to his. "But you could watch him for me."

His blue eyes lit up with sparks of electricity. "I'll be a spy. For you." His voice was low and rough, and his fingers traced her jaw to her chin. The breath caught in Tink's throat, and her pulse beat double-time in her neck. Sucking in a lungful of warm air, she rose on her tiptoes to plant her lips on his. She decided she could get used to this as she felt him smile against her mouth, apparently not noticing he'd sloshed coffee all over the floor.

Pulling away, she glanced down before looking back at him. "You're making a mess of my engine."

"I promise I'll clean it up." He peered down at the spilt coffee before returning his gaze to her. "After I kiss you again."

Tink arched an eyebrow. "I'm pretty sure *I* kissed you."

Severn didn't reply. Instead, he leaned forward, reaching his free hand to the side of her face, and pressed his lips to hers.

24: HARBIN

THE *Argent* quivered, the only indication of a piece of space debris hitting its shields. A minuscule tremble travelled through Harbin's legs and up his spine. But the impact hadn't caused his shiver — the new ship had the latest deflection tech, as well as the most cutting-edge weapons and a new-fangled shroud fresh from the Dominion Science Council. No, it was the icy void of deep space that seeped into his bones no matter how warm the ship.

His skin crawled, though he couldn't tell whether that was from the sonic showers or the conversation he knew awaited him. A light blinked on his wrist, and the pit of dread grew in his stomach. He watched the sequence and sighed, gently tapping the patch to send back a response: *Waiting.*

"I'll be in my ready room." Without another word, he left the captain's chair and went into said room. He tapped the panel by the door to lock it. The window was clear, letting him observe his bridge crew...and letting them observe him. He touched the panel again, and the glass fogged.

The room was small, almost claustrophobic. But then the Barracuda class ships were small. Sleek. Like the predator they were named for, ready to strike at the slightest ripple, able to cut through space and atmo alike as if it were a knife. Harbin had seen a barracuda on a school trip to a zoonautical archive on Cetus. He was more impressed with his new ship than he had been by the fish.

And this ship was new, not just new to him. This was a double-edged sword. It had the latest tech and high-yield weaponry, and its shielding and stealth capabilities were galaxy-class. But he didn't know what it was capable of in a dogfight. More importantly, with his promotion, he'd been given a new crew, and he didn't know what they were capable of. Or where their loyalties lay. Delphi, his second, was the only member of his old crew he'd been allowed to bring over.

The lights blinked on his wrist again, a slightly different sequence. *Coast clear*. Running his fingertips along the edge of his desk, he marvelled at the elegance that hid the tech. The top was a deep blue plex with holo emitters and haptic sensors embedded in the surface. He sat down and tapped to bring up the holoscreen. Even though there was no video, it was still easier than trying to communicate with his informant via wrist patch.

Pawn to Rook. The holoscreen oscillated with the vibrations of his informant's voice.

"Rook here. Status?"

We have the Lev...ship.

"Obviously. What about the packages?"

*The packages...*there was a pause.... *Packages are secure.*

"The Queen wants the package in her hands asap. Can you deliver?" Harbin waited for an answer. He was about to speak again when the screen flickered.

No. Not right now. I'm not secure.

"She —"

The screen pulsed then went silent, without even the static of space. Harbin's fingers rapped the desk, waiting to see if it would reconnect. Being embedded on the *Lyra* meant the informant controlled the flow of all communications, which Harbin conceded was wise if frustrating. When nothing happened for a minute, he tapped in a series of numbers and blinked as the ident beam scanned his eye, checking his code.

"I hate this clandestine bullshit." He stabbed the desktop with his finger to connect. "Rook to Knight."

These codenames told him exactly where he was in the hierarchy. And it wasn't very high. He drummed his fingers on the plex as he waited for the Connect signal to pass from ansible to ansible. The screen remained blank, and he wondered if one of the ansibles had been attacked again. It happened sometimes when the rebels were trying to raise a ruckus. He checked the connection code again...he'd entered it correctly. He was reaching out to disconnect when the screen finally flashed to life, presenting him with a smooth face, slick hair and sickening grin.

"Harbin, my dear." The smile fell away. "What's new?"

"My friend's friends have picked up the wreck. More information on delivery is pending."

"What? Why pending?"

Harbin weighed his words. Even though the line should be encrypted, it still went through ship comms, through the

Guilds' ansibles, through the Dominion's gates. "Communication is intermittent. Informant is not secure. So, more information is pending."

His contact shifted, leaning so far he disappeared off-screen. The lack of even static told Harbin the signal had been muted while the man had a side conversation.

The man's face came into view again. "New orders. Get the package. Kill everyone onboard the *Lyra*."

"What about Pawn?"

"Sometimes sacrifices must be made." The screen blinked out, the connection cut.

"Kill him too then." Harbin Low stared into the deep blue plex where the overhead lights caught imperfections and ripples buried beneath the surface as he pondered his next move.

25: TINK

T INK FROWNED FROM WHERE she sat in the captain's chair glaring at Alek's back. The muscles of his shoulders shifted as he nudged the ship onto a slight course correction.

"Captain." Cass' tone, usually calm, held an edge, almost human.

Tink glanced to the far end of the ready room, at the door that led into the captain's cabin. It remained closed.

"Pilot Wa," Cass said.

"Yeah, Cass?"

"I'm sensing..." There was a pause that worried Tink. She'd fought the loudest to keep the Cass AI after the incident 12 years ago, despite being only a teenager, arguing that it wasn't *this* AI's fault. She really hoped the Cass onboard the *Lyra* wasn't glitching out on them. "...an anomaly."

"An anomaly?" Alek said, glancing up. "Can you be more specific?"

Tink watched him out of the corner of her eye as she leaned back in the chair, crossing her arms over her chest. Changing her mind, she stood up, intent on knocking on Rebeka's door.

The two of them needed to talk, regardless of any anomalies. Time to wake the captain up — she'd had enough beauty sleep.

"An anomaly. To starboard. It's like...an empty spot in the sensor readings."

"An empty spot?" Tink paused then turned around, her head tipping sideways. "Are you feeling okay, Cass?"

"I don't feel, Tink, but yes, systems are running a-okay."

"Can you describe the empty spot?" Ish glanced from Alek to her. "Maybe it's just a slip point?"

"It is not a slip point. But thank you for your suggestion. It is...empty. The stars that were there are not there anymore." Cass' voice stopped.

"What —" Tink began, intent on asking the others what they thought the problem might be, but Cass interrupted her.

"And it's moving. Heading our way."

"The empty spot is moving?" Alek asked.

"Yes."

Tink loomed over Alek's shoulder. "Kandi, can you confirm?"

"I'm looking, but I'm not an AI."

"Look faster."

"There seems to be a lot of chatter out here."

Tink spun around to see the captain pulling on her jacket. "You're awake."

"I am now. What's up?"

"Cass has detected...an anomaly."

"An anomaly." Rebeka raised an eyebrow. "Cass-related anomalies concern me." She turned to Kandi. "Shields up?"

Kandi nodded, looking at her sidelong. "Of course." Her tone was razor-sharp.

Rebeka's lips pressed together, then she shifted her attention from Kandi to the rest of them. "Any more information?"

"There's a —" Kandi started to answer, but the ship rocked sideways before she could finish.

Tink found herself thrown into Alek's lap with his arms wrapped around her. She flailed, struggling to get up. "Let me go."

"I'm not the one who fell onto you." He lifted his hands, palms out. She crawled off him, only to have to grab his shoulders to stay upright as the ship bucked again.

"Status," Rebeka said, sitting down. "And Tink, get yourself buckled in." For once, Tink did as she was told without argument, using the railing to pull herself to her occasional seat beside the captain.

"The anomaly." Kandi looked up from her display. "It's shooting at us."

Tink watched Rebeka's jaw clench and her eyes narrow. "What is it?" she asked, her voice quiet as a thread of fear wound its way around her abdomen.

"It was hypothetical." The captain spoke in a hoarse whisper. "A myth of starstruck spacers."

"What?" Tink swallowed against the lump in her throat.

"A shroud. They're warping space, wrapping it around themselves."

"Who? Pirates?" Tink glanced at the others and saw they were equally horrified by the prospect of pirates that could hide themselves until the last second. Everyone except Alek, who just looked angry.

Rebeka shook her head. "Even the richest pirates don't have that kind of tech."

There was a hush on the bridge. That only left three options: the Guilds, the Cartels or the Dominion. None of those were comforting thoughts, even if the thing weren't shooting at them.

Rebeka's voice broke the silence. "Fly boy, can you get us out of here?"

"I can try."

"You said you could get my ship out of any spot it found itself in."

He turned to his console. "You didn't say there'd be a whale of a vessel strapped to my belly."

The ship banked as he touched the controls, but Tink felt its struggle as it towed the bulky Leviathan, either under-driving or over-compensating. The ship whined as they were hit again.

Tink started to unbuckle. "I should get down to the engines."

"Sit down, Tink." Rebeka didn't look at her, but Tink heard the conviction in her voice and re-did her buckle. In the next second, she was glad she had as the ship shuddered again.

"Miscreants! Hitting my ship." Tink's cheeks flushed, her head spun, and her palms started to sweat.

"That one hit the Leviathan." Kandi turned around. A thought began to form in Tink's brain, but Kandi beat her to it. "If they're after the Leviathan, maybe we should disengage."

Tink heard the captain breathe in slowly and huff the air out quickly. "Do it."

"I've got it." Tink pulled up the retractable console at her seat and accessed the tether controls, hoping they behaved this time. "Releasing tentacles." One of the tethers blinked red. It wasn't releasing, and they were travelling at evasion speeds. "Jacks!" She punched it again, knowing there wasn't time to get down to the cargo bay before the off-balance load caused damage. "Third time's a charm." She hit it so hard her finger stung. After a split second, the light shifted to green. The ship lurched forward as the tethers released their load.

"Okay, heading into the asteroids."

"The tethers are still reeling in," Tink said, her voice sharper than intended.

"Better the tethers are damaged than us." Alek didn't look at her, all his focus on the console in front of him.

"Kandi, what's the status of the anomaly?" Rebeka asked.

"The anomaly is holding position," Cass' voice answered.

"Not quite," Kandi said. "A small runner's broken off from the anomaly."

"Not shrouded?" Tink asked, though she could see the blip on the viewscreen plain enough.

"Nope, clear as crystal. It's heading for the Leviathan."

Another hush fell over the bridge, once again broken by the captain. "And the anomaly?"

Kandi flicked her fingers on her display. "It's headed our way."

"Prep decoy charges," Rebeka said, and Kandi nodded, her fingers already moving.

"Tentacles in," Tink said, turning back to her display as another blast rocked the ship's measly defenses. They were a hauler, a small-job salvager. Their weapons and shields were meant for repelling pirates, who tended to give up if they deemed the cost outweighed the gain.

"Those aren't warning shots, Captain. And they're not EMP charges." Kandi craned her head around. "They're shooting to kill."

The *Lyra* banked again, followed by a bob and a swerve. Then it plummeted. Sometimes artificial gravity had its downsides, and for Tink this was one of them. Bile burned in her throat.

"What are you doing...trying to crash us into an asteroid?" Her cheeks were hot.

"If I can make it look like that..." Alek twitched the stick again, and the ship yawed. A gargantuan mass of rock filled the viewscreen, and Tink let out an *eep* despite herself. She didn't feel so bad when she glanced sideways and saw Rebeka's fingers clutching her armrests, tendons taut.

"Decoys ready." Kandi's fingers flicked over her console as she peered at her overhead display.

"Releasing now." The captain tapped the display beside her as something pinged off their port side.

"That was an asteroid!" Tink shouted.

"It was a pebble." Alek pulled harder on the stick, hugging the asteroid that filled their viewscreen. There was a crash and bang from somewhere inside the ship, and Tink started to comment. But her mouth hung open, no sound coming out as a lump formed in her chest. Her eyes went wide for a second as she stared at the viewscreen. Then she shut them as tight as she could, tucked her chin to her knees and threw her hands over her head as they headed straight for the large asteroid.

The cargo bay had a muffled quality, though every thud and groan caused Tink to wince. She didn't trust the hollow in the asteroid Alek had flown them into anymore than she trusted the cock-sure pilot with his winsome smile. A clunk sounded from above, and Tink frowned. The flatness of the sound unnerved her, reminding her of the lifeless Leviathan. It didn't help that the lights were dim, in night mode, part of the effort to conserve power and minimize their signature. Not quite as dark as the dead ship...but near as.

Tink threw another kick at Kandi, who dodged it with ease, swatting Tink's leg with her padded hand a little harder than was necessary.

"Focus." Kandi's hushed voice still cut through the heavy air. "Or else what's the point?"

"That *is* the point." Tink brought her attention back to Kandi, lifting her gloved fists in front of her chin. "To distract me. And you." Tweaking and building all alone in her engine room hadn't been enough to stave off the heebie-jeebies.

Kandi's eyes narrowed, then she gave a sharp nod. "One more time?" She lifted her padded hands and forearms back up for Tink to take a swing at.

Tink swung at her with a right cross, hitting the pads with a satisfying thwack, before driving her opposite leg towards Kandi's other side. She shifted to get ready for the next sequence when a muted ping sounded by the staircase. Tink glanced over to see Alek descending, but a second later found herself flat on her back. She swivelled her head back to glare at Kandi. "Hey!"

"Pay attention. An opponent won't let you look away without paying for it."

She frowned at Alek, angry at him for distracting her. When he sat down at the bottom of the stairs, her frown deepened. "What do you want?"

"Can't a person watch?" He leaned back, resting his elbows on the stair behind him, a cockeyed smile on his face.

"Of course," Kandi said. "You might learn a thing or two."

He arched an eyebrow. "I might at that."

"Maybe you two should spar," Tink said, trying to take off her gloves.

"No, no, no." Kandi bobbed in time with her words. "Then how would we distract you?"

Alek is distraction enough. Tink blinked, disgruntled by that unbidden thought. She turned her gaze to the floor as her cheeks flushed. Thankfully, she was saved by the lights. In that moment, they flickered again, as they had intermittently since the last attack.

"I should get back on that." She seriously attacked her gloves this time, but they fought back, resisting her attempts to remove them. Then, somewhere in the belly of the ship, a clunk sounded as the asteroid shifted. The lights went out entirely. Kandi swore. Even the curse was muted. Tink paused her efforts to get her gloves off, waiting for the emergency lights to kick in.

"At least we still have gravity," Alek's voice said, annoyingly calm. "And life support." The seconds ticked away without the lights coming on.

"This is not good." In the dark, Tink attacked her gloves with her teeth, finally able to pull them off her sweaty fingers. Then, as suddenly as they went out, the lights came up again, a blinding bright white before dimming to dull twilight. The floor tilted once more, following the turn of the asteroid.

"You couldn't have landed us in —" She was stopped by another sound, much closer by this time, a tearing like...fabric ripping. She glanced to her right, then charged into Kandi, throwing her back onto the cargo bay floor as the smaller of the two crates from the Leviathan — still large enough to cave a person's skull in — slid across the floor.

The biocon unit. A jolt of adrenaline punched her heart at the thought of what might be unleashed if it busted.

She landed on top of Kandi with an *oomph* and braced herself for the bang of the crate against the stairs...a sound loud enough that their pursuer's sensors might pick it up. But the crash never came. She rolled over and popped up facing the stairs. Alek had his hands against the crate, feet braced against the bottom step. The muscles of his arms and torso strained, and his neck and jaw were rigid with the effort of holding the crate. Tink's mouth dropped open, then the asteroid shifted again, and she had to step back quickly to keep from falling. The crate slid back to its starting point, grating against the metal floor with an unpleasant screech.

Alek grimaced and craned his neck, rubbing his left thumb on an old scar on his right forearm as he stepped towards the unit. Tink sprinted to get another set of tie-downs. As she ran back to Alek, her steps faltered. A jagged crack ran down the side of the biocon unit.

"Cass, seal the cargo bay!" She crossed the last few strides to the crate and handed Alek one of the straps. As he cinched his strap into the anchor ring on the floor, he looked at her over the crate, a question written on his face.

"The biocon crate. It's broken." Her sweaty hands slipped on the winch, and she wiped them, one at a time, on her tank top, before she was able to tighten the tie-down.

Kandi went over to the crate and unhooked the latch.

"What are you doing?" Tink grabbed her hand.

"If it's going to kill us, we're probably dead already. I want to see the cause of my death." She finished unhooking the latch. "Aren't you a little curious?"

"No."

Kandi shrugged and hefted the lid up. "Well, maybe they packed an antidote." Turning back to the crate, she peered inside. A few seconds later, she started laughing. Her laugh grew, becoming so strong her eyes teared up as she draped herself over the open lid. Tink and Alek both stepped away. "It's..." Kandi stopped to catch her breath, pushing herself up and wiping her eyes. "It's fireweed," she managed before she was taken by another fit of laughter.

Tink kept her distance. "What's a fireweed?"

Kandi took a few gulping breaths before she was finally able to string more than a few words together. "If you're stressed or can't sleep, you can make a tea out of it. And the people of Hadrian's Drift use it in love potions. Apparently stokes the libido."

"So, it's not going to kill us?" Alek took a cautious step forward.

"Not unless you feed it to Tink to make her moon over you. And then it'll be her that kills you when she comes down from her love high." Kandi collapsed into another laughing fit, though Tink didn't see what was so funny.

26: Rebeka

"WHAT THE BLEEDING BARNACLES?" Rebeka's voice was low, her throat tight, as she glared down at the dim cargo bay through the common room window. Below, the busted crate sat with its lid open, revealing its innocuous contents. *A relatively common plant, Kandi says.* She shivered. *A weed.* Breathing out, her breath misted the air. They were still running quiet and conserving power, which meant the life support systems were in Basic mode, not Comfort, and certainly far from Luxe. Mug of coffee clutched in icy fingers, she turned back to the common room, where the crew had assembled. Even Grim sat perched over the galley cupboards. "Are you sure you brought back the right package?"

Tink nodded slowly and opened her mouth, but it was Kandi that responded. "They were the only two things with power in that whole ship. Locked in that secret room." She popped out the charge canister in her blaster, then checked the sights. "Those are the packages. We have to acknowledge they sent us after a bloody weed."

"Maybe there's something special about it," Ish offered, spinning his full cup of cha on the table. Steam rose in the chilly air, but the aroma of spice did little to cover the reek of fear. "Maybe they've bred it. Or engineered it." He cocked an eyebrow as he spoke, but he continued to stare into his cha. "For all we know, they've made it emit poison instead of oxygen."

Kandi shook her head. "No, I ran it through the multi-analyzer in the medbay. It's plain, old fireweed."

"Why would someone attack a ship for that?" Tink said. "Why attack us?"

Severn stepped from the corner to stand over Ish's shoulder. Placing his hands on the back of the chair, he leaned forward. "Maybe the rebels didn't know what was in the crate?"

"The rebels?" Rebeka said, pausing as the lights flickered, browning out before coming back up. She glanced up at the ceiling, as if that would make a difference, then returned her attention to Severn. "Why do you say that?"

"Who else could it be?" He joined her at the window overlooking the cargo bay. "Who else would dare attack a Leviathan?"

"The rebels *wouldn't* dare attack a Leviathan." Tink came to stand at Rebeka's other side, arms over her chest.

Alek wedged himself between her and Tink, his fingers wrapped around a mug of coffee. When she glanced at his face, his jaw twitched with tension. "It could have been an imperial faction."

Severn scoffed. "What faction would attack a Leviathan? The owners of that ship are the emperor's own, or someone very close to him. If any other imperial house attacked it, they'd be executed faster than anyone else."

"Well, if it was the rebels, maybe we should find them," Alek said. "I bet they're in the vicinity." He took a sip of his coffee, his eyes narrowing further as he watched Severn. Rebeka kept watching him. His lips twitched, then he continued. "Sell them the package. Maybe that ship that's been taking shots at us would go after them instead." Rebeka's lips pursed, though she couldn't say it was a bad thought.

"Unless that ship *is* the rebels," Ish said, his cha still untouched.

"It wasn't the rebels that attacked us." Kandi placed her blaster on the table, then joined them at the window, leaving Ish alone. "The tech that ship had? The firepower? No way. That's Legion."

"Well, someone was willing to pay us a lot of money to get their weed back to them." Rebeka sighed, scowling at the package and definitely not looking at Tink, who'd been right about not accepting the contract...Ellis was a slick, sneaky weasel. "We need to get the packages to the contact asap then get the hell out of this contract."

"Um, I hate to point out that the ship is still damaged," Tink said, the lights browning out to punctuate her words. "Lights are intermittent. Life support is on rations." She turned to Ish. "Are we even capable of slipping?"

Before he could answer, the lights blacked out again — even the emergency lights — but this time they didn't come back up right away. Somewhere to her left, Tink groaned. In the darkness, a thunk echoed from the cargo bay.

"Kandi, does this weed of yours walk?" Alek's voice drifted through the pitch black.

"It's not my...." The lights came up before Kandi finished. "Uh oh."

Four heads swivelled to look at what had caught her attention, while the sound of Ish flinging himself around the table to join them at the window filled the silent room.

Rebeka froze, her brain tripping over itself trying to digest what she was seeing. A slush churned through her abdomen. The thunk had been the other crate unlocking — perhaps caused by some failsafe opening the outer lid when the power became too unstable — and revealing its contents. It wasn't some rich noble's precious alcohol.

There was a boy in the box.

27: Tink

Tink RUBBED HER NOSE as she peered at the package. Another box sat nestled within the outer crate. Lights blinked on its status panel, set a thumb's width below the small plex window that showed the boy's face.

The boy appeared to be sleeping except for the blue cast to the skin. Tink tore her gaze away and ran the scope around the edges of the inner box, assiduously avoiding looking at the face again.

"So?" Rebeka hovered over her shoulder like an exam proctor.

"So what?" Tink straightened up, which forced the captain to step back. She blinked as she glanced from Rebeka to Kandi, who stood with her blaster at the ready. "I can't see anything." She shook her head, and her gaze caught the others. They stood by the stairs, keeping their distance as ordered. Tink flipped her goggles down, and their shapes went watery with the new lens. Turning toward the crate again, she flicked through settings to check if anything lit up her sensors. "It's just a biostasis box in a crate."

"With a boy in it." Rebeka huffed behind her, not quite close enough to breathe down her neck. "No reason it opened?"

UV...nothing. "Oh yes, that's easy."

"Okay, care to share?"

Infrared...nothing. "The power crapped out."

"But it was unpowered on the trip from the Leviathan to here." Kandi shifted, and Tink glanced up to see their heatmap silhouettes before returning her attention to the box.

Chromatograph. Nothing. "I'm guessing that ship was frigid enough, dark enough, airless enough. Here it needed more power to maintain stasis conditions." She shivered. The cargo bay of the *Lyra* on energy rations was a cold place, which made her think of how icy stasis would be. And there'd been studies suggesting those in stasis weren't entirely unaware. One of the reasons it was illegal except for incorrigible criminals and traitors to the Dominion. Or those who'd crossed the Cartels, which didn't care if it was illegal.

"Stasis conditions?" Kandi asked, bringing Tink back to task.

Rather than answering, Tink flipped the lens again. *Spectro.* "Whoa."

"What?" Rebeka asked, coming forward again.

Tink swallowed then lifted her goggles up and took a big step back. "Um."

She looked from Rebeka and Kandi to the others, who'd all crept forward, despite the captain's orders to keep their distance. Ish led the pack and stood beside the captain, who glanced over her shoulder but didn't send him back.

Lifting his gaze to Tink, he said, "He's just a kid." His jaw clenched tight, strangling the words. He jerked his chin towards the boy. "Did you see the bruise?"

They all leaned a bit closer as Ish wiped the window off with his sleeve.

"It might only be a shadow," Tink said, her voice low as she took Ish's hand, pulling it away. When his eyes met hers, she caught a glimpse of the shadows in his past. The bruises he'd suffered when his father tried to form him into the leader he wanted his son to become.

"If he was put in stasis beaten up..." Alek started.

"We don't know what happened." Rebeka cut Alek off.

"But to put a child in stasis —" Tink pressed the idea. "He can't be a criminal. And how would a kid cross a cartel?"

"We don't know what happened." Severn repeated the captain's words without taking his eyes off the boy, his expression flat.

"No," the captain said. "We just need to decide what to do."

"What were you whoa-ing about?" Alek asked. Tink startled to find him standing right beside her. She inched closer, relishing the modicum of extra heat that radiated from him.

She scanned the faces of her crewmates, twisting her lips before answering. "There's some kick-ass dampening field on this thing."

INSIDE THE BOX

28: Rebeka

REBEKA GLANCED SHARPLY AT Tink. A dampening field wasn't meant to keep things *out*. She looked back at the face framed by the small window and swallowed, wishing she had some coffee. Or something stronger.

Alek craned his neck, his eyes narrowing as he peered at the square of plex. "Huh, I wonder what else is in the box with him then, to warrant such a dampening field. That's not cheap tech."

Rebeka rolled her shoulders to mask the shiver that passed through her, while Tink took a step back from the crate and clutched her arms around herself, rubbing them with her hands.

"I should get back to work on the power system repairs." Tink inched further away. "Life Support needs more juice if we want to shift to Comfort again." She started to turn towards the stairs, but Rebeka grabbed her arm.

"No, I need you to keep examining the box."

Tink opened her mouth as if to protest. Instead, she huffed and went back to inspecting the crate.

"What about the boy?" Kandi asked, tugging at the end of her pink ponytail.

"What about him?"

"Should I examine the boy? He's a living being after all."

Rebeka's lips pursed as she fought the frown that pulled at them. "No, we'd have to unseal the stasis unit to examine him. I'm not prepared to do that."

Alek stopped examining the face in the window, and his head popped up. "Do we even know he's alive?"

"The box thinks he's alive." Ish stabbed a finger at the lights on the lid of the unit.

Severn grabbed his hand and pulled it away. "Don't touch that, you might —"

"What, wake up a child?" Ish jerked his hand free and jabbed the lights again. They flickered in response. Severn's hand reached towards Ish's again as a frown settled on his face.

"Enough," Rebeka said, using her best captain's voice, which was very similar to her upset parent voice, though she hadn't used the latter in years.

Ish and Severn stopped bickering, turning their scowls on her instead. She needed to get them out of their current snafu before tempers tore the crew apart.

"Squabbling won't help." Rebeka turned back to Kandi and added, "Check what you can without cracking it open."

Kandi pressed her lips into a thin line but joined Tink in leaning over the crate without saying anything.

"What will help is getting rid of that box." Severn nodded at the crate.

Rebeka couldn't argue, but she preferred not to be a dictatorial leader — she tried to consult her team before she gave them orders. "We need to decide what to do." She kept her voice even and strong. "Options?"

"Hand him over to the rebels," Alek said. Again, Rebeka found she didn't entirely disagree with the sentiment, even if the idea came from the rash pilot. If the rebels had attacked the Leviathan, they had more firepower — and more chutzpah — than she thought. Certainly more than the *Lyra* and her crew.

"No." Ish's hazel eyes flashed to Alek as his cheeks reddened. His jaw clenched before he spoke again. "We have no idea what they intend to do with him."

Kandi looked up from the box, her face grim and her voice quiet. "We don't know what the empire plans to do with him either."

"Space him," Tink said, her face hidden by the crate.

"That's not funny, Tink." Ish stuffed his hands into his sweater sleeves as Tink popped her head up, flipping her goggles off her face.

Rebeka shot the engineer a sharp glance. "You're not serious?" She switched her tone to disappointed parent, hoping Tink's words were some horrible attempt at levity gone wrong.

Tink shifted her gaze from Ish to her, rolling her eyes. "Of course not," she said in a tone that wasn't entirely convincing. Rebeka pressed her lips together to keep from snipping. Tink looked away and continued. "But we need to get him off this ship." She waved her scanner at the crate. "Besides the fact that he's probably illegal —"

"I think we can definitely consider him contraband," Alek said.

Tink glanced at him then continued. "Not exactly what I meant, but sure. The ship can't take many more beatings, and I suspect our pursuers are going to keep coming until whoever they are gets what they want. We can't just give them a weed...I think we all know that's not what they want. If they want the kid, let's see what they'll offer for him."

"He's a human being." Ish waved his hand at the stasis unit, drawing Rebeka's attention to the lights and their flashing cycle, reminiscent of dancing firebugs. Their pinpoints of fiery light stabbed at her retinas, needling the headache that threatened to form.

"We don't actually know that," Tink said, her voice quiet. "Despite the Centauri Convention."

"Bollocks to the Dominion's rules!" Ish pulled his left hand out of his sleeve to cut through the air.

Rebeka had never seen the navigator so worked up. "You mean...?" She returned her gaze to Tink before switching her attention to the lights. Bots were one thing, mods too. But wholesale engineering of lifeforms had been severely restricted by the Centauri Convention after the destruction of Eris; though there were still reports of super soldiers going berserk every few years.

The lights finished their dance and went out. Rebeka tipped her head sideways. Then jumped back, her heart pounding, as the boy's eyes opened, his mouth agape in a silent scream.

Rebeka breathed long and slow to get her heartbeat back to normal, then turned to Kandi, who gawped at the box along with everyone else. "Kandi, get your med kit. I think you need to examine the kid after all."

Kandi glanced up at her, blinking rapidly before her eyebrows twitched as she finally processed what Rebeka had said. She gave a sharp nod, then turned to do as asked.

"Alek, grab a stun gun from the weapons cupboard." At his frown, she continued. "Just in case. Severn, get some blankets. He'll be cold and in shock." The two men left, while her, Tink and Ish stood sentry around the box. And the boy it held.

29: HARBIN

THE HOLOSCREEN IN FRONT of Harbin Low remained dark but the voice was clear.

"The package is broken." The informant paused. "And the boy is awake."

Harbin swallowed. "And?"

Silence filled the ready room for a long moment. Those few seconds stretched and warped like time in the deepest layers of the slipstream. Harbin had the same pit in his stomach that he always felt in the stream — whenever he slipped into it, a part of him feared he'd never surface again. But he wasn't in the stream — he was in the here and now waiting for a response. He wondered if the mole had heard him. There was a crackle as the transmission picked up again.

"And nothing. He's somewhat unresponsive."

"That's...unfortunate." Harbin frowned, thinking of the latest plan to punch a hole in the *Lyra*'s side, causing a sudden loss of atmo but leaving the stasis unit intact. But now, that would kill the boy as well, and *his* death was not part of the plan.

"Not necessarily," the mole continued, unaware of Harbin's thoughts of death that included him. "If the boy is terrified, one might be able to lead him along with something familiar. Like dangling a toy in front of a child, or jewels in front of a noble."

"Do you have something familiar to use as a lure?" Harbin's ire started to creep up his neck. He wanted to get this mission over with, and blasting open the *Lyra* had been his best shot.

"I...have to go." The mole's voice dropped to a whisper.

Harbin heard when the line blinked out, leaving nothing but the silence of space. He sat back in his chair and glared out at the bridge. So far, his promotion had involved a wild goose chase, a red herring, and a game of cat and mouse where the mouse didn't realize it was being chased. At least he'd gotten the *Argent* out of it. He ran a hand along the finely milled plex surface of the desk.

A light flashed under the plex. *A call from an ansible. Long distance.* He sighed and tapped the light once. The flashing changed. Red-red-blue. *Gar's call sign.* Harbin squinted sidelong at the blinking. It was if they knew when a call with the mole had just ended. He sat up straighter as the flash became more insistent, his eyes scanning the ready room of his new ship. He wondered how many bugs they'd planted in its rooms and corridors, and chastised himself for not wondering sooner.

Harbin tugged his sleeves down then stabbed the light, bringing up the holoscreen again. This time it displayed the person on the other end. Noting the lines on Gar's usually smooth face, Harbin smiled. At least he wasn't the only one suffering.

"Gar," Harbin said, tipping back in his chair again, feigning casualness since he never let himself relax in Gar's company. "What can I do for you?"

"An update, as always. Our Archon is on tenterhooks." Gar glanced at the shadows over his shoulder. "What news do you have?"

"I imagine you know the latest." Harbin was pleased with how even he kept his voice.

"Pawn cannot contact us. The long-range signal from the *Lyra* would be detected."

"But the *Lyra* wouldn't detect whatever was sent by your little critters on *this* ship, not unless they were looking for it."

Gar frowned, causing more lines to form around his mouth.

"Just tell me the state of things in your own words," a voice said from the shadows behind Gar. Almost too low to be a woman's. Nonetheless, Harbin knew exactly who the voice belonged to even before the shape formed out of the darkness.

"Archon." He sat up straight again and nodded sharply.

Halcyon Koning placed a bony hand on Gar's shoulder, and Harbin almost felt sympathy for the man. That was until she trained her eyes on him through the vastness of space. Even though he'd been born on Saxemunde Station, with glacial Celadon IX wandering through the viewports, he always forgot how cold blue could be until she pinned him with her gaze. Icy and sharp.

"Enough with the obsequiousness. Update."

"The *Lyra* has had some difficulties." He paused as Archon Koning snorted. Swallowing, he continued. "The decoy package broke open. The other one ran too low on power so the failsafes kicked in."

"And?" She tipped her head forward a fraction, and a light source on the far side of Gar's holoscreen caught her silver hair and the jewelled stick that held it up in a soft bun.

"And...the boy is awake. But unresponsive."

"That won't last." She squeezed Gar's shoulder, and Harbin noticed the suppressed wince on the man's face. Her eyes focused on him again, and Harbin pushed back into his seat despite the light-years of space that separated them. "What about the others?"

"The others?"

"The crew of the *Lyra*." She arched a delicate eyebrow, a touch more slate than the grey of her hair. "You don't get to where I am without knowing all the pieces and how you can play them. I told you I have other interests on that ship."

"I..." Harbin tipped his head forward, looking at the plex of his desk rather than the holoscreen. "The mole has not said much of the others."

"And you haven't asked." He glanced up to find her expression flat, except for her blue eyes which sparked with cold fire. Her nostrils flared almost imperceptibly. "Complete the mission, Low."

"That's a little more difficult now." Harbin pressed his lips together, frustrated that he had no backup plan to share.

"Why? It changes nothing."

"We risk harming the bo...the package during retrieval."

She leaned forward and gave him a smile that made his intestines squirm like a nest of Silesian worms. "I'm sure you'll figure out something that doesn't kill *everyone* on board. I want my grandchild back."

The screen blinked out, and Harbin looked out his window to see Delphi Liet, his second, watching him. He cursed himself for not frosting the window.

30: Rebeka

R EBEKA PEERED AT THE child. He stared back at her with wide blue eyes. The skin under them was a bruised lavender. He tore his gaze away, flitting from face to face. The boy's head was hairless, whether because of some genetic anomaly or because someone had shaved it before he went into stasis, she couldn't tell. His skin was a pallid blue-grey, and blue blood vessels were visible underneath. His ashen lips pressed tight together.

Rebeka had sent Tink to continue repairs to the power systems, and Ish had gone back to the bridge. Although she didn't want any surprise visitors, she expected them to arrive at any minute — the ship needed someone on watch. That left her in the cargo bay alongside Severn, Alek and Kandi, who'd returned with her med kit.

Kandi came with her when she stepped forward again. She realized she might be insane, but a part of her had expected a different result than the last few times she'd tried to get closer to the boy. But his response was exactly the same: he flinched and started a toneless, droning scream that went on and on until she stepped away.

"Kandi." Rebeka shook her head. "Leave it for now." Kandi appeared relieved to retreat behind her, coming to stand beside the two men.

The kid sat on the grating in front of the crate, gently rocking, silent and staring now that they'd stepped back. He was dressed in what she could only describe as silver pyjamas, damp after coming out of stasis. He shivered, and she realized he must be cold, waking up on a ship running only the most basic life support. And that was on top of being in shock. It was just another reason why people weren't put into stasis anymore — the shock to the system on emerging was too much. That's if they weren't driven crazy by being in stasis in the first place.

"Are you cold?" Rebeka took a step forward, and the boy pressed back, clawing at the metal of the crate. She stopped then inched forward, the lights dimming in time with her movements. She pressed her lips together in a hard line. "Who are you?" she asked, keeping an edge to her voice. She was tired of this contract and wanted to get it over with stat.

"He's afraid," Alek said, and she felt him creep up behind her. She didn't respond, and instead kept her eyes on the boy, who'd glanced at Alek but stopped the scrabbling.

The boy's eyes flashed back to her, and then he started whispering. Rebeka inched forward, trying to hear what he was saying, but that movement made him stop and press further back.

She slid another few inches closer until she had to tip her head to peer down at him. He glanced around, eyes wild like a trapped animal. She ignored it. He was a threat to her crew that needed to be managed. Or neutralized.

"Captain, maybe he needs some time," Kandi said, placing her hand on Rebeka's arm. "The shock of coming out of stasis...."

Rebeka turned her hard gaze to the other woman, then shrugged her arm away. She returned her attention to the kid. "What...who are you?" she asked, stepping closer to him. "Why were you put into stasis?"

The boy started speaking again, louder this time. Something about the cadence stirred a memory in Rebeka's gut, even though the words still made no sense. The tempo of his rocking increased as he became even louder.

"What's he saying?" Severn asked, his voice slow, though she wasn't sure if it was curiosity or to keep the kid calm.

Rebeka tipped her head sideways, unfocusing her eyes to focus on the sounds. The niggling familiarity bothered her, even though the meaning remained hidden. She glanced over her shoulder at Severn, who'd stayed by the stairs and was casually cleaning under his fingernails. "I have no idea. Cass, translate the boy's words."

It took a few seconds before Cass' voice drifted into the cargo bay. "I cannot, Captain."

Rebeka's eyebrows scrunched together, and the niggle returned: Cass had a thousand languages and countless dialects stored in her data banks. Rebeka turned to Kandi, then Alek. "Do any of you know what he's saying?"

Alek shook his head. "Maybe we should leave him alone for a bit. He's just a scared little kid."

"Not that little," she said. She judged the boy to be about eleven. "Don't you want to figure out what's happening?" she glared at Alek, hands on her hips.

"Captain!" Kandi's tone was sharp.

Rebeka turned to her, then followed her gaze back to the boy, who'd started hitting his head with clenched fists. The flow of sounds got louder, faster, more staccato. She crouched down in front of him, grabbing his hands to stop him from injuring himself. "Stop hurting yourself." Her frustration crept into her voice against her will. His arms strained to pull out of her grip, but she didn't let go. "Why are people trying to kill us?"

He stopped babbling, and his lips rounded as his eyes widened. Rebeka braced herself for another droning scream.

"Iiiii...don't know." The words were spat out of the boy's mouth as his body went rigid. Then his eyes rolled back in his head, and he collapsed in a heap, his wrists still held in Rebeka's hands.

31: Δlek

LIGHTS BLINKED AND SENSORS beeped on the biomonitor, indicating the boy was still alive and sleeping. From the darkened doorway of the medbay, Alek watched Tink's chest rise and fall. She was supposed to be monitoring the boy but clearly had fallen asleep curled up in the seat snugged into the corner. Her mouth hung open and a soft, wuffling snore occasionally escaped, disturbing the stray curl that dangled over her face. With the position she'd ended up in, her head back and to the side, she'd have a crick in her neck when she woke up, if she were at all like him.

I should wake her, he thought. *It's my turn to be on watch.* But he made no move towards her as her eyes flutter under the lids, her freckled cheeks relaxed. However uncomfortable the position, they were all sorely lacking in sleep. And it was only going to get worse soon. He glanced at his wrist patch again, then flicked it, dismissing the coded message.

"Hey buddy," he whispered as Grim twined between his legs. The cat sauntered into the medbay, propelling Alek forward. Stepping fully into the small room, he placed the mug he'd brought for Tink down on the ledge by the door then turned his attention to the boy. Swallowed up by a bed built for adults, he looked younger now than he had in the cargo bay. The shadows under his eyes remained, and the bruise on his cheek was mottled an angry purple and green now that he was out of stasis. It was definitely a bruise, as Ish had suggested, and not a shadow as they'd all hoped.

Alek ran a thumb over the cheek, skirting the bruise. "Who did this to you?" he whispered. Of course, there was no response except the beeps of the sensors. Looking down at the frail form, he realized how easy it would be for someone to end it all — this contract, his mission, the danger to the *Lyra*. When he glanced at Tink, he saw she still slept with her head falling back against the wall. He stepped closer to the bed, leaning over the boy to adjust the pillow under his head. From this perspective, there was something almost familiar about him. But Alek had little experience with kids.

"What are you doing?" a voice froggy with too little sleep said.

Alek spun on his heels to face Tink. "Nothing." He blinked and watched her push out her hands and feet in a full body stretch before bringing her fists in to rub her eyes. "Well, just wondering," he continued as he turned back to examine the boy. "He's a puzzle."

She came to stand beside him. "He's a threat."

Alek lifted his head to look at her, his eyebrows pulling together. Her lips were tight and her jaw tense. She glanced at him as silence hung between them.

"Oh, come on," she said, wrestling her hair into a clip at the nape of her neck. A stubborn curl sprung back out, glinting red from the lights. She blew it out of her eyes. "You're thinking what I am: they're clearly after the kid."

He didn't respond to that speculation, instead nodding at the ledge by the door. "I brought you some coffee."

She stepped over to it and, clutching the mug in both hands, took a sip. Steam from the fresh brew dewed her face. "Thank you."

He shrugged. "It seems warmer in here."

She nodded over her mug. "I got the power to level up."

"You fixed it?" He smiled at her.

"Sure." She tugged the stray curl and stared into her coffee as she took another drink. Her eyes met his over the rim of her mug. "Any update on what's going on outside the asteroid?"

"Bots say the other ship is searching further afield. Ish thinks if we time our exit right, we can make it to that slip point he saw."

She nodded, turning the mug in her hands. "I'll be glad when the *Lyra* is out of this mess. But I still need to finish the fix on the infernal slip drive." She came to stand on the far side of the bed, blowing at the uncooperative curl again as she gazed at the child.

Fiery sparks shot through her hair where the lights of the medbay hit it. He pressed his lips together and nodded slowly, not wanting to comment on what a longshot it all still was. Instead, he turned to small talk. "How do you know the *Lyra* so well? I mean, yeah, you're an engineer. But you're just one person."

She shrugged, her eyes narrowing as she peered at him. "I basically —" She stopped at a gasp between them.

The boy was wide awake, blue eyes flicking between them. Alek put his hand on the boy's wrist and felt the flutter of fear in the pulse.

"It's okay," he said. "It's okay."

Tink put her mug down on the bedside table and crossed the few steps to the dispenser set into the wall. From the drawer beneath it, she pulled out a glass and pressed it against the lever to fill it with water. Coming back, she reached to offer it to the kid. In a whirl of movement, over in a blink, he skittered away. Her mug of coffee went flying, and Tink ended up with water all down her front.

"Aiy." Tink held her arms out and grimaced at her damp jumpsuit.

Grim jumped up onto the bed to escape the mayhem, scowling at Tink before turning his disapproving gaze on Alek.

"Still no sudden movements, I guess." Alek arched an eyebrow, a suppressed laugh playing at the corners of his lips. He turned to the boy, slowly reaching out to take the not-quite-empty glass from Tink. Arms clutching his legs to his chest, the kid's eyes followed his hand. "Water." The boy glanced at him, and Alek drank the last mouthful in the glass. "Water."

Going to the dispenser, he filled another cup. He held it an arm's length from the boy and waited. After a minute, the scar tissue in his shoulder started to protest, but he still kept the glass between them. Meanwhile, Grim sniffed at the kid's toes before rubbing his jaw against one of the arms wrapped around his legs. And slowly, the boy began to move. One hand went to Grim's head while the other reached for the cup.

Being careful not to let his fingers touch mine, Alek thought. *What's he afraid of?*

Grim lifted his nose to sniff the cup, and the kid followed the cat's lead. Seemingly recognizing the non-scent of sterilized water, he tipped it back and stuck his tongue in.

"It's okay," Tink said. "It's just water. Recycled a thousand times. But just H2O."

Staring at her, the boy took a small sip, held it in his mouth for a few seconds then swallowed. Apparently deciding it was acceptable, he gulped down the rest of the glass until a paw reached up to pull it away. The boy giggled and pet Grim's head.

Not exactly a normal boy, Alek thought, *but not something worth killing for*.

"More." The boy held out the glass.

"He speaks." Tink popped up from where she'd been cleaning up the detritus of her mug and spilt coffee with a rag.

"More."

"One word." She grimaced.

"Would you like more?" Alek held a hand out to the boy. "Come on then."

"What are you doing?" Tink asked, dumping the dirty rag and pieces of broken mug in the cycler. Alek looked at her but didn't answer.

Turning his wide eyes from Tink's face to Alek's hand, the boy's lips moved back and forth, like Alek's grandfather did when he was chewing over a problem. When Grim jumped off the bed, the boy's hand followed after him. A flicker of angst passed over the boy's face and his fingers clutched at the sheet on the bed, creeping outwards. After a long minute, their fingers touched, and he allowed his hand to be wrapped in Alek's. Not wanting to startle him, Alek gently closed his fingers, guiding the boy off the bed, away from any remaining shards. Glass in hand, the boy took the few steps towards the dispenser. His herky-jerky limbs seemed unused to movement.

After finishing another glass of water, he turned back to the bed. His stomach burbled loudly.

"Are you hungry?" Alek asked.

Tink's eyes flashed towards him. "He should lie down. At least until Kandi has a chance to examine him."

"He's been lying down for Zeus knows how long. Kandi can come get him in the common room when she's ready to take a look at him." He turned back to the boy, and the sense of something familiar washed over him again. Like a face from his childhood. Maybe the boy was the offspring of one of his very extended family. But, as far as he knew, there weren't any hairless, wan pre-teen boys in silver-blue pyjamas on the family tree.

32: TINK

T HE SLIP DRIVE PURRED. Tink frowned. It was supposed to be silent. Unless they were slipping, then it hummed, almost sounding like a melody. But now it was not harmonious. It whirred, then clunked.

"Poseidon's barnacles!" Tink strained to reach her arms further, without losing her grip on either the split pin or her pliers. Her hand cramped and spasmed. A ping sounded as the pin fell somewhere below the grey water distiller.

"Jacks!" She sighed, blowing a strand of hair from her face, and dropped her arm to the grating. She was small but not small enough. To retrieve the pin and insert it, she'd have to shift the feed pump out of its home. Which meant getting help from Alek or Severn. And Severn was helping Kandi double-check the exterior of the ship.

"Fine, I'll give the difference accelerator some love instead." Tink pulled her contorted limbs out and rolled her shoulders, though the small space where she sat constrained her movements. Glaring at the slip drive, she cracked her neck. "I'll see you again later." She tapped it with her pliers, then froze when it whirred once more, higher pitched this time. Holding her breath, she stroked it with her fingertips, and it quieted down. She exhaled.

Staying in her little cubby hole, she picked up the accelerator. At first, she thought some circuits had been shorted during the last attack, but she'd checked them all. They were fine, same as she'd left them the last time she'd done a strip down and rebuild. But still no juice came out the end. She pulled out her rag and wiped her forehead. After folding her knees into a pretzel that she could rest the accelerator on, she set to work.

A half-hour later and with no progress made, the accelerator sat on the floor again. She loomed over it with the wrench in her hand held over her shoulder, preparing for a downward blow.

"You shouldn't do that."

Tink's head jerked back...right into a metal conduit. "Bleeding Hades." Rubbing the back of her head, she turned to see the boy watching her. He was still in his silver pyjamas, the ship having a dearth of child-sized clothes. Tink was the smallest of the crew, and he'd still swim in her gear. He had a candy bar in one hand that he munched on as he stared placidly at her. The image was completely at odds with the wound-up, babbling kid from earlier. His head still had no hair, and his face was ashen, though not quite as blue as when he'd first woken up.

"No, you're probably right." She put the wrench down, frowning at the accelerator. A chirrup to her right drew her attention. "Grim. Have you been back there the whole time?" The cat swished his tail as he sauntered past her, an iridescent wing sticking out the side of his mouth. She saw no sign of the rest of the cat's dinner — a bakweevil, endemic on most cargo ships, especially those like the *Lyra* that hauled the occasional batch of contraband food stuffs. Tink shivered. Even though she'd grown up around them, she didn't like them dropping in to surprise her when she was working in a tight spot. "Good cat."

Picking up the accelerator, she followed the cat and crawled out of the nook into the engine room. The boy backed up to give her space, the cat twining through his legs.

"So, you're talking now?" She glanced at him as she placed the accelerator on her workbench. The boy followed, coming to stand beside her, though he didn't answer her question. Reaching for the Robertson, she found him examining the accelerator before his gaze travelled over the other bits and bobs of projects on her bench, all while munching on the candy bar. "So that's a no. But it's good to see you're not hungry anymore." She thought back to the meal Alek had made him after he'd woken up in the medbay. Enough to feed the whole crew, and he'd devoured it in minutes. She arched an eyebrow as he looked at her, an innocent expression on his face.

Grim jumped up on the bench, somehow managing to avoid landing on any components. He walked up to the boy and rubbed his face against a hand. The boy laughed. Tink reached over and pet Grim's head, scritching behind his ears. The cat pressed his head into her palm. She drew her hand away and watched the boy mimic her movements, his eyes wide and mouth open.

A scurry sounded over Tink's shoulder, and she sighed as the cat jumped down from the bench and raced off. "The least you could do is kill it." She might not like killing the bugs herself, but she'd be happy if Grim did it for her.

The boy's gaze, having followed the cat, passed over her before returning to the parts scattered on the bench.

"Do you have a name?" Tink picked up a sprocket, and held it up beside the accelerator, then put them both down. Looking sidelong, she saw the boy peering at her. "I'm Tink," she said, a hand to her chest. She reached the hand towards him, palm up. "And your name is...?"

The boy's eyes narrowed as his head tipped to the side and his mouth dropped open. But no sound came out. Tink sighed and reached for another sprocket.

"Ben."

Her gaze returned to the boy, to see him with his hand on his chest.

"Ben," he repeated.

"So, you do talk. Just a man of few words. I like that." She smiled at him, and then went over to the tool chest on the far wall to grab a cog wrench. Turning back, her heart lurched. The boy — Ben — had the accelerator in one hand and was rummaging through the assortment of parts on her workbench with the other. Lunging at him, she grabbed his wrist. He looked at her, his eyes going wide like they had when he'd awoken in the cargo bay.

"Sorry," she said, keeping her voice soothing, or so she hoped, as she let go of his wrist. "It just, well, there's a lot of delicate components on this workbench. And I know where everything is." Tink forced her shoulders to relax, pulling them away from her ears. It appeared that the boy wasn't going to start screaming or babbling again. Instead, he tentatively reached his hands out. One still clutched the accelerator, the other a widget he'd picked up.

"This," he said, bringing his hands together.

Tink's eyebrows pulled together, and she leaned closer to see what he held. A Piezy sensor. "Huh." Reaching out slowly, she took it from his open palm and turned it over in her hand. "Well, I'll be damned." She looked from it to him. "This," she said with a nod, her smile broad, as she took the accelerator from him as well. She put them both on the workbench then sat on her stool. Glancing at him, she nodded towards the chair in the corner. "Pull up a seat."

The boy did as he was told, picking the chair up with a strength she didn't expect him to have in his skinny arms. As she worked, Ben watched over her shoulder, silent except for the occasional grumbling of his tummy. At one point it became so loud, she showed him her secret stash of gummy blue whales and purple octopuses, and they both contentedly munched away.

Finally, Tink hooked up the tester to the accelerator. Lights lit up, and a flutter pulsed through her veins. "Juice in, juice out," she said, reaching over to pat him on the shoulder, before pulling back, unsure of what might set him off. Instead, she gave him a big grin. His eyes were lit up like the tester, and he lifted the widget he held in his small hands.

Tink sat up straight, pondering the widget and the boy's hand for a few long seconds, as she mulled over the thought forming in her head. She glanced back at the nook beside the slip drive then her gaze shifted from his small hands to his small frame to his smiling face. "How would you like to help me with something?"

33: Alek

"**Y**OU'RE SURE WE'RE GOOD to go?" Alek asked again, folding himself into his seat. He glanced over his shoulder at the engineer, buckled into her chair beside the captain.

Tink rolled her eyes. "Yes, for the hundredth time."

"And we're good to slip? Because when we punch out of this asteroid, we're going to light up their sensors. And, no offense to the *Lyra*...." He paused to run his hand over the console to show the ship he meant it "But a ship that can go stealth will have a few more tigers in the engine."

"The *Lyra* has some tricks up her sleeve." Tink looked past him to the viewscreen, which displayed the twilight grey interior of the asteroid.

He glanced over at Ish. The boy sat beside the navigator, clutching Grim in his arms, as Ish showed him the undulating map of space that somehow indicated where the nearby slip points were. The boy stroked the cat's head with long fingers as he watched Ish's hands, wide eyed and mouth agape. He laughed as Ish caused the undulations to ripple with a flick of his fingers.

"Should he be here?" Alek tried to keep the frown from his face. He failed. The boy glanced at him, and his smile fell. "It's not safe," Alek added, softening his tone. "Ish has to fly this bird into the slipstream soon."

"I don't really fly it, I navigate it, but he's probably right."

The boy nodded solemnly and got up from beside Ish, taking the cat with him.

"He can sit by me," Severn said, patting the jump seat beside the Ops console. At the moment, the display beside him showed the locations of the bots crawling around on the outside of the asteroid, like little red spiders. He tapped a button to recall them.

Ish leaned over. "You might want to talk *to* Ben." His eyebrows lifted. "Like he's a person, even if he *is* just a kid." He shifted back and enlarged his holoscreen, zooming in on the slip point. "Slip at phi 50°, rho 6, zeta 4."

"Ben?" Alek asked, the word tugging at something in the base of his skull, causing him to frown again though he didn't know why.

"The boy. His name, apparently, though who would name their kid that, after that medical scam?" Ish shook his head, not looking at Alek. "'Bio-equivalent nutraceuticals'. Bollocks."

"Language," Alek whispered, glancing at Ben. Returning his focus to the viewscreen, his eyebrows pulled together. He recognized the acronym, but it wasn't the itch in his brain. He shook his head and filed away the question of the boy's name to puzzle out later.

Instead, he tapped a switch on his console. The display shifted from the inside of the asteroid to images of the space outside, relayed by the bots skittering back to the *Lyra*. All the panes were empty, showing nothing but the speckled background of the solar system. Cass wasn't reporting any anomalies, but their adversary's ship had this shroud tech the captain mentioned, the ultimate silent running. He sighed, letting the air in his lungs out slowly and pulling his shoulders down. He knew he couldn't trust what the bots were reporting about the space around them. Instead, he'd have to fly by instinct.

I got them into this thing. I need to get them out. "Buckle up, folks. The ride's about to start."

Alek took a large mouthful of starshine, letting the alcohol burn its way down his throat. He usually didn't touch the stuff, but there wasn't much that would calm his nerves right now. The choices were sex or booze. And a vigorous tumble in the bunks was not in the cards. Kandi would kill him with her thumb; Tink would eviscerate him with a wrench; Rebeka would glare him into retreat. And Ish would laugh him off, given that Alek had dissuaded his attentions when they first met.

He tried to convince himself that he'd saved them. He'd gotten them from the asteroid to the slip point, with the enemy only realizing at the last second when the *Lyra* blinked out in front of them. And even though they saw the slip point the *Lyra* had entered, they couldn't easily follow. According to Ish, the slipstream wasn't exactly a conduit. At least, there were many paths through it. Well, many threads that you could followed. Or something like that. They could try to track the ship using...at that point, Alek had stopped trying to follow, and just nodded until Ish realized he'd lost him.

But if he were honest, the hair-raising flight from asteroid to slip point was only part of the reason his nerves were fractious. The other was Ben. *The word, not the boy*, he tried to tell himself. *But the word is the boy*, another voice said.

He pulled his tablet closer and took another sip of the starshine. Stabbing a finger at the screen, he opened a search: BEN. If he'd known what his handlers were messing with when they'd sent him to the *Lyra*, he would never have stepped onto the gangway. For one thing, he'd been trying to save his life, not lose it. His jaw clenched, angry at being kept in the dark by people who said they wanted to help him.

The screen flickered, pinpoints of static dancing across it. Then it displayed a message: Cannot access the Connect.

"Jacks. The slipstream." Another lesson from astrodynamics that he'd forgotten: unless your ship had an ansible ampilifier, the only way to access the Connect while in the stream was *through* the stream. Which right now meant through Ish. "Zeus' bollocks." When Alek lifted the glass of alcohol to his lips, he realized it was empty. He reached over to grab the bottle then dropped his hand with a heavy sigh. There was a reason he never touched the stuff — it went down too easy and didn't bring any clarity.

Sweaty from his small ship workout — run, pull-ups, stairs, planks, repeat ad nauseam — Alek wiped his face with his shirt. The improvised exercise routine had left him thirsty, so when he passed the common room, he popped in for a glass of water. It was dark except for the light over the sink. Even the window to the cargo bay was dark. After downing the first glass in a few quick gulps, he re-filled it.

"What were you doing trying to access the Connect?"

Alek spun around, almost dropping the glass. He swallowed as his eyes started to pick out the captain's shape in the chair in the far corner.

"Bleeding Hades, you scared me." He lifted the glass to his lips and took a sip, forcing his body into a casual stance despite his racing heart. "Not an easy thing to do." He raised his eyebrows, then crossed his free hand over his waist like a shield as he wondered how she knew he'd tried to connect.

"You haven't answered my question."

Alek took another drink and shrugged. "Just looking for some new entertainment."

"Not enough in the ship's banks?"

He let a sneer form. "Nothing to keep me interested."

"What *are* you interested in, Alek *Wa*?" The chair creaked as Rebeka shifted, coming to standing.

Alek didn't like the emphasis she put on his fake family name, but he turned his back to her and put the glass in the sink, forcing his movements to be fluid. "Honestly?" He faced her again. She'd crossed the room to stand by the table. He could see her face better now, and the suspicion written on it. "Sleep."

"So why aren't you in bed?" Her eyes narrowed a fraction as she peered at him.

"Perhaps the same reason you aren't...too much excitement, nerves are a mess," Alek answered honestly. "And I think Kandi would slice me bow to stern if I asked her to join me in calming them," he added, then left the captain to figure out the truth from the lies.

34: Harbin

"THEY'RE GONE." DELPHI GLANCED over her shoulder. Harbin fought the urge to snarl at her for stating the obvious; he knew he'd have a fight on his hands if she decided not to take it. And it wouldn't even vent his frustration. "Should we go after them?" she continued, half turning her head towards him, the long scar on the side of her face visible. Acquaintances often asked why she didn't get it removed. They never asked a second time. The thought made his lips quirk, threatening a smile despite their situation.

He glared at the spot in space that the *Lyra* had slipped through, then turned to watch the navigator and his assistant pluck and poke at wriggling strings on their display, murmuring to each other in sing-song whispers.

"No." He pulled his shoulders back as his nostrils twitched. "Even with my limited knowledge of astrodynamics and this fancy ship, I know that's a fool's errand." *Not without using a set of tracers*, he thought to himself, glad his new ship hadn't come with one of those particular crew members. He'd only encountered a few in his life, and their near-synchronous movements and finishing each other's sentences sent an insect crawling up his spine.

Just then his wrist patch flashed: the Queen expecting an update from her Rook. "I'll be in my ready room if you need me." Harbin spun on his heels, took the stairs up to the command platform in one long step and strode into his office. The door slid shut behind him. He paused to turn on privacy mode then decided against it. He wanted to watch his crew. Instead of going to his desk and pulling up his holodisplay, Harbin went to the dispenser first and got a mug of coffee, searing hot and double-strong. Braced for the conversation ahead, he sat down at his desk.

"They're in the stream?" Gar said, an impeccably groomed eyebrow arching. "How *are* you going to retrieve the package now?"

Harbin wanted to reach through and punch the man in the face. Instead, he sat back in his chair, the hand on his desk relaxed while the other gripped his thigh; the pain of his fingers digging into flesh helped keep his expression neutral. "I've had a message from the ship. The mole says he can protect the package if we attack the *Lyra*." He glanced at his desk, then at the darkness beyond Gar's shoulder. "But I don't trust him anymore. So, it's not guaranteed."

Gar frowned, his head barely moving as he waited for orders. None came. Instead, as Harbin had expected, Archon Halcyon Koning once more emerged from the shadows. She'd taken a personal involvement in this operation. Although he appreciated seeing Gar at the end of someone's leash, the

Archon's intent interest made Harbin's bowels go liquid. And her glacial expression did nothing to put him at ease. He pursed his lips and swallowed to force the bile down.

"I have absolute trust in the operative." Her tone was frosty. "The mole, as you call him, is more my creature than you are. He would die for me." A little warmth came into her voice as she played with one of the rings on her bony hand, peering at it intently. "Would you?"

Harbin didn't speak, hoping the question was rhetorical, and neither did Gar. Out the corner of his eye, he saw Liet repeatedly glancing at him through the window, no doubt waiting for orders.

After a minute, he swallowed and opened his mouth to say something, though he wasn't sure what. One eyebrow on Archon Koning's face twitched, as if she'd heard that little sound across the emptiness of space. And perhaps she had, as her head tilted to the side though she continued to examine her rings.

"I need to know what lengths I can go to. As you say, you have other interests on that ship."

"Any." She looked up at him without lifting her head fully. "Go to any lengths to take that ship down. That is now your prime objective, no matter the cost — their people or yours."

"Even if your mole is lost?" Harbin's forehead wrinkled at the change in orders.

She gave a sharp nod. "Even if the *package* is lost."

Harbin breathed into his chest, the tightness relaxing, the burning abating. That relief was quickly quashed, and just when he thought his day couldn't get any worse, it did.

"But..." Halcyon lifted her head to focus her icy eyes on him. "It's better if it's not." Harbin recognized she meant it was better for him, but he didn't have time to dwell as she continued. "Better that all my interests on that ship are returned to me alive."

Harbin nodded sharply, but the screen had already blinked out.

35: Rebeka

F ROM THE WINDOW IN the common room, Rebeka peered into the cargo bay and watched Ish go through his assigned chores now that the *Lyra* was back in normal space. Or more accurately, she watched Ben mimic everything Ish did. Right down to running his hand through non-existent hair. Despite it being a few days since he'd come out of stasis, there was no sign of stubble growing in.

None of the crew could be specialists, small as they were. At the moment, Ish was tasked with running routine diagnostics. And when he checked something on his tablet, the boy checked something on his hand. When he pressed a button on one of the panels, the boy pressed his finger to the wall. When he furrowed his forehead at some off number, the boy did the same.

Rebeka smiled and took a sip of her coffee as the scene tugged at a thread of memory. The kid reminded her of someone else. Then the smile slipped as she realized who: a girl who couldn't get enough of mimicking everything Rebeka did until — she sighed and stared into her mug, swirling the dregs around — well, until the girl wanted nothing more to do with her. As she looked back at Ish and Ben, she chastised herself. Now was not the time to get lost in nostalgia when they still hadn't decided what to do with the boy. *She* hadn't decided. Although she wasn't a dictator, this was a call she might have to make. All she knew was they needed to get him off the ship if they wanted to get their lives back to normal. Heck, maybe if they wanted their lives to simply continue.

Footsteps sounded behind her, but Rebeka didn't turn around. She knew Alek's footfall well enough. A sound too light for such a muscle-bound man. "Did you finally get some sleep?" she asked before taking another sip of coffee. The footsteps paused, then continued toward the fridge.

"A little," he said. The fridge door opened. "Are you hungry? There's still something green in here." The sound of plastic hitting glass followed as he rummaged inside. "But no bugs." He huffed.

Down below, Ish and Ben left her field of view, and she turned towards Alek. "Intentionally green? We have had some power fluctuations."

He grimaced but nodded. "Yeah, it's meant to be green." He pulled out the package of protein chunks and sniffed them. "Add enough spices and it'll be fine."

A full-throated, feminine laugh echoed down the hall, and they both glanced towards the door. Shortly Ish and Ben tumbled through, the boy giggling about something. They were followed closely by Kandi, who still had a broad smile on her face. As usual, she had a weapon in her hand that apparently needed TLC.

Kandi patted Ben on the back with her free hand. "Have you heard the one about the Lorian and the lady from Adasinga?"

"Kandi!" Rebeka hissed.

"What?" The woman looked at her, eyebrows lifted.

"I don't think that joke is appropriate for a —" Rebeka stopped, realizing she didn't know how old the boy was. "—for a kid."

With flushed cheeks and a wide smile, Ish turned from Kandi to Ben. "Hey, you want to play Kora?" Ish asked the boy, who'd thankfully forgotten the ribald joke Kandi planned to tell. Instead, the boy's attention focused on what Alek was doing. Ben glanced at Ish then up at Alek but didn't move or speak.

Alek turned to the navigator and shrugged.

"Or maybe you want to help Alek cook." Ish smiled, quirking an eyebrow at Alek. "You could do worse than him," he said, winking at the pilot.

Alek flushed. "We had this talk."

"About your cooking? I recall no such conversation." Turning his attention to Ben, he continued. "If you get tired of him bossing you around, I'll be over here." He nodded to the chesterfield, where he proceeded to flop himself, shove the pillow under his head and fling an arm over his eyes.

Rebeka sat down in the armchair, pretending to read the Mintaraen romance on her tablet. Instead, she watched her crew out of the corner of her eye, as the sounds of life washed over her: Alek murmuring instructions to Ben, the sizzle of something hitting the pan, a soft whirr from whatever Kandi was doing to her knife and a snuffling snore from Ish. The ghost of a smile tugged at her lips, and she let it lift the corners.

As time wore on, her head started to nod as the heat from the cooktop filled the room, along with the saliva-inducing aroma of whatever Alek was concocting. More quiet laughter and murmuring chatter served as white noise. Her eyes slid shut, her chin tipping to touch her chest, her tablet coming to rest on her lap.

"Well, isn't this just the picture of a happy family?"

Rebeka's eyes shot open and her head jerked up. The room went quiet, all eyes, including hers, turning to Severn. He leaned against the door jamb, a smile on his face, even though there hadn't been one in his words. He appeared tired, the skin under his eyes the colour of a bruise.

"You look tired," Rebeka said, as she jerked her head towards the armchair. "Why not sit and join us for a bit?"

He turned his gaze to her, and she noted that the smile didn't reach his eyes either. "Sorry, that AI of yours won't fix itself." Rebeka frowned, less from worry about the AI than for Severn.

"Cass?" Ish peered at Severn through half-opened eyes. "What's wrong with Cass?"

"I'm operating within normal parameters, Ishmael. Thank you for asking." The AI's voice grated on Rebeka's nerves...it was too chipper, when her own was ragged from too much coffee and too little sleep over the last 10 days. But she bit her lip; she usually had no problems with the personality algos of the Cass, and after a good night's sleep, she hoped things would be back to normal.

Severn straightened, a frown pulling his face down. "Of course she says that. That's part of the problem." He wiped his hands on a cloth, using a corner to clean under a fingernail. Rebeka didn't understand how comp techs got so dirty. He scanned the room until he got to her. "Well, back to work. No rest for the wicked."

Alek stepped forward, lifting the pan in his hand, as Ben peeked out from behind him. "Are you sure you can't spare a few minutes? Supper's on."

No sooner were the words out of his mouth than Cass started speaking again.

"Warning. Collision imminent."

Whatever she said after that was drowned out by the alarms blaring a proximity alert.

36: ALEK

"THEEERE'S A...AN ANNOMAAALY. SHOULD Iiii nuuullifffy the thhreat?" Alek frowned at the stutter in Cass' voice. And any attempt to 'nullify' whatever ship was out there was a bad idea, whether it was the rebels or Dominion or an unknown wildcard.

"Cass, shut those bloody alarms off," Rebeka shouted as she ran after Ish towards the bridge. The klaxons stopped, leaving blessed silence except for Cass' warbled voice.

"The ship is being boarded. They're jaackiiing into the caaargo bay dooor." Then the sirens resumed, and a thump rocked the ship, almost sending Alek to the floor as he headed into the corridor after Kandi. He threw both arms out to brace himself. At the junction, the captain stopped, hands on her ears.

"Cass, I thought I told you to turn those off. Trigger the EMP." Rebeka tried to raise her voice, but it ended up in a rasping squeak as she struggled to be heard over the sirens, which didn't stop this time. "Cass!"

There was no answer, and the captain pounded a fist into the nearest panel, then turned to Alek. "Help her." She jerked her head toward Kandi. "Try to keep the bay doors closed. I'll get to the EMP."

"Captain." He nodded but didn't move. "I...are you sure EMP is a good idea? It'll leave us dead in the water."

"I suspect if we don't stop them, we'll be plain, old dead." She turned and continued her sprint to the bridge.

"Weapons!" Kandi shouted, pausing at the arms cabinet.

Alek stopped beside her as she swiped it open with her wrist, then he took the blaster she handed him, grabbing a recharge pack and an old-fashioned dagger for good measure. The boy, Ben, reached a hand into the cupboard.

Kandi swatted it away. "Not for you."

The boy drew his hand back as if stung. Alek grabbed Ben's shoulders and peered at him. "Go back to the medbay. Lock yourself in." Ben frowned, and his blue eyes glistened with unshed tears. "It's safer there." The boy pouted but nodded, dragging his feet as he turned away. Alek tucked the blaster into his belt then chased after Kandi, who was already halfway down the stairs into the cargo bay.

Grabbing a rail in each hand, Alek jumped up and slid down to the cargo bay floor. He joined Kandi in taking cover behind one of the broken crates. Out of the corner of his eye, he saw Tink emerge from the corridor leading to the engine room, blaster in one hand and what looked like a bag of marbles in the other. Positioning herself behind the other crate, she glanced at them. Then her mouth dropped open as something over his shoulder drew her attention. Alek turned his head to see what she was gawping at.

"Boll...arnacles!" He reached out and grabbed Ben's wrist as a clunk echoed through the hold. "I thought I told you to go to the medbay." The boy bit his lip but made to get up. The clunk was replaced by a hiss as the air lock beside the cargo bay doors started to open. "Too late now." He pulled the boy down beside him, earning a scathing look from Severn, who'd come downstairs after Ben.

"Too late for EMP," Kandi said into her wrist, as the first of the boarders shouldered through the airlock doors. Kandi peeked her head over the crate and took a shot. But as soon as Alek saw the lacquered black of the figures, he realized their weapons weren't going to do much damage. And he was more worried about puncturing the umbilical that connected them to the other ship's atmosphere.

"They're wearing combat suits." He knew from experience that a blast while wearing a suit still stung and left a nasty bruise, but it didn't kill. Not from their hand-held weapons at least. A blast of return fire rained sparks on them, drawing him out of his memories. Kandi raised her blaster to shoot again, but he brought his hand down on her wrist, causing her to scowl at him. "Save your ammo. You're more likely to damage the ship than the boarders when they're wearing that armour."

"So what do you suggest, mister 'I know combat suits'?" Severn's lips twisted into a sneer. Kandi didn't say anything but arched an eyebrow at Alek.

He shrugged. "I don't know."

"There's not much we can do." Rebeka's voice was soft as steel wool over his shoulder. Alek jerked his head around to face her. Wearing a blaster at each hip and a frown on her face, she flicked her gaze over the others, returning her attention to him as she ducked down beside him. "He's right. Our shots won't get through."

"Smoke 'em if you got 'em," Tink said, and Alek turned his gaze to her. She grinned at something in her hands, bringing dimples to her cheeks.

"What's so fun —" He stopped when she lobbed something from the bag of marbles over the crate, and the ting of metal on metal reverberated through the large space.

"Tink!" The captain's voice was sharp behind him. "Smoke'll blind us more than them."

Alek craned his neck to peer over his impromptu shield. Sure enough, tendrils of smoke rose from whatever Tink had thrown. "And we don't have filter masks," he said as he slumped back down. "Unlike those suits."

Tink frowned then flicked her wrist, and the wisps stopped advancing. "Fine, no smoke."

The thump-thump-thump of well-trained feet on decking rumbled through the cargo bay. Rebeka peeked over the crate. Her eyes narrowed before she ducked back down just as a pulse hit the grating in front of the boxes. Heat from the charge tightened the skin of Alek's cheeks, and he wiped his brow with the back of his hand, making sure the hairs were still there.

"Bleeding Hades. They're Tau," the captain said. Alek swallowed but stayed silent. He'd seen the insignia too: their invaders might be a third-string unit, but they were still Fifth Echelon, the Legion's elite. Rebeka obviously knew her ranks as well as he did. "Special Task Force, specializing in insertion and extraction," she added.

"At least they're not Ki," Severn murmured. Rebeka's sharp eyes flicked to his face, and Alek's eyebrows pulled together. He'd been forced to study the insignia of the Echelons as a child: Ki, Omega, Phi, Tau, Epsilon. It had helped being surrounded by them. But he didn't expect a computer tech to have the same experience. Severn shifted and focused his attention on the invaders.

After a second, the captain continued, turning to Kandi. "Ideas?"

Without answering, Alek stood up and turned to the invaders, hands above his head.

"What are you doing?" Rebeka hissed, wrapping her fingers around his ankle.

"I have a plan."

"As your captain, I order you to abandon this plan." She frowned. "Or at least tell me what it is."

Alek stepped out from behind the crate. He told himself he didn't share his plan because there wasn't time, but in truth, he knew she wouldn't like it. It was simple, really — hand himself over. Maybe then he could have a private conversation with their leader and negotiate with the person who'd sent them.

A figure stepped out from the main body of boarders. The Tau Leader. If his insignia hadn't marked him, the additional tech visible on his gleaming black combat suit set him apart from the rest.

"You." His voice was mechanical through the breather.

"Do I know you, Tau?" Alek kept his tone casual.

"No, but I know you." The response was equally relaxed. "You're famous. Or infamous. Not exactly who I was expecting."

Alek wasn't too keen on his plan anymore — he didn't like that the man knew him by sight, though it wasn't entirely surprising, given his past as an entertainer. Nonetheless, he forged ahead. Maybe there was a way they could all get out of this alive if he served as a distraction while the others came up with a better plan. Though, judging by the tense whispering, it didn't seem they were close to a solution.

"Yet they sent a third-string team to collect me?" He barked a harsh laugh. "I was expecting more."

"I'm not here for you." The snort was audible through the helmet. "As I expect you know. You're just a bonus." Tau stood stock still, not even a shrug of the shoulders visible through the layers of spivex plating. The only movement was the sneer on his face, clear despite the smoky visor which blurred his features.

Alek's blood turned icy hot as he heard the whine of the pulse rifle firing up. But instead of ducking back behind the crate, he charged at the Tau leader with all the strength in his unmodded, worn-out, busted-up legs. The man stood there, his eyes getting bigger for a second. Then all Alek saw was black as his shoulder slammed into a soldier who hadn't been there a moment earlier. Something bit into his arm as he fell. He landed on the grating with the wind knocked out of him and his head ringing.

"Fan out," a woman's voice said as blood dripped from the knife in her hand. The other clutched a pulse rifle. "Kill them all except the target."

Alek expected the rifle to press into his temple any second. Instead, it drifted right and up. He squinted, his head tipping sideways, as he tried to make sense of the sight above him: a black-clad soldier flailed in the air. The thought that a sudden decompression was pulling the soldier out of the cargo bay passed through his mind, but he could still breathe and was getting his wind back. The struggling woman, eyes wide, flew away from him. He shook his head to clear it; the fall must have jostled it harder than he thought — and it had been banged about too many times already in his short life — but the woman was replaced by another black streak then another.

Alek sat up, his head spinning and his ears roaring. He faced the back of the cargo bay, where Ben stood, clenched fists at his sides, staring intently at the flying bodies. His face was white, his lips thin, and dark circles bruised the skin under his eyes. A drop of blood fell from his nose.

A frost spread from Alek's gut and crept up his spine as he realized it was the boy flinging the invaders through the air. Hurling them into the umbilical, back to their own ship, whether they wanted to go or not.

"Oh. Jacks."

37: Rebeka

S ILENCE HUNG HEAVY IN the common room except for the hum of the ship as it coursed through the stream, skimming the boundary with regular space. Rebeka pressed her lips together, unnerved by the sudden quiet.

"We need to get him off this ship," Tink said. "He's dangerous."

"You've already expressed your opinion." Despite her rebuke, Rebeka couldn't disagree with her — whatever else he was, the boy was a threat. He'd proven that, flinging elite legionnaires across the cargo bay as if they were dolls. She shifted her gaze from Tink down to Ben. The boy sat in the cargo bay beside the crate he'd been suspended in and rocked back and forth. An echo of when he'd first awoken. At least he hadn't screamed when Ish and Kandi tried to coax him to join them. Instead, he'd acted like he hadn't heard and shied away as if their touch hurt. So Rebeka watched him from the common room window as he rocked. The blood from his nose was drying on his face, and red droplets marred his silver pyjamas.

"We should have taken him to safety right away." Ish gestured with his arm, knocking the snacking bowl he hadn't touched, sending a few deep-fried jumpers skittering across the table.

"*You* should be on the bridge," Tink said. "We are in the slipstream after all."

"Cass can manage for a bit." Ish drew circles on the tabletop with his finger.

"Didn't you hear what Severn said?" Rebeka turned around, nodding towards Severn as she crossed her arms over her chest. "There's some issue with Cass."

Ish shifted his gaze from his invisible drawing to her. "I don't care what Severn says." He glanced over his shoulder at the man. "Sorry." He returned his focus to her. "Cass is fine."

"No offense taken." Severn opened his mouth to say something more but was interrupted.

"Cass isn't the important issue right now." Alek stood in the door, his arm bandaged. Stepping into the room, he made way for Kandi, who followed close behind.

"Patient will live, despite dumb-ass heroics." She plopped herself into the chair next to Ish.

"Once again, as he says —" Tink nodded at Alek, "— not important."

"Thanks." He quirked an eyebrow at her before taking the empty seat on Ish's other side. "Whatever he did, he's just a boy."

"Actually, we don't know what he is," Severn said, getting up from the chesterfield to approach the table. "No boy can fling Legion marines around as if they're toys."

"Without so much as moving a muscle," Rebeka added, as she turned to look back out the common room window. "Definitely not your normal child."

Ben stopped rocking and glanced up at her, his aqua blue eyes wide and worried. After a few seconds of trying to match his gaze, Rebeka turned away and walked over to the coffee machine. Leaning against the counter, she prodded Ish. "You say we should take him to safety. But we have no idea where safe is."

A hush descended again as the members of the crew glanced at each other. Rebeka watched them — hoping one of them had a suggestion.

"The Sisters." Kandi dropped the words into the room without looking up from the dagger she was honing.

"What?" Severn asked, his tone sharp, though he wasn't the only one with questions.

"The Sisters of Elazir." Kandi stopped working on the weapon in front of her and looked up at them, her chin jutting out and her left eyebrow arched, before returning to her blade. Rebeka's mouth opened then snapped shut.

"I know who you mean." Severn's voice was quiet.

Silence crept around the room, filling the space with a heaviness. For a minute, the only sound was the soft burr-burr-burr of stone on metal.

Finally, Tink broke the oppressive quiet. "My initial suggestion of spacing him might be kinder."

"We're not spacing him." Rebeka glanced around the table, but five pairs of eyes looked past her. She turned to see Ben standing in the doorway, stiff except for a trembling lip. She sighed. "It wasn't a real suggestion. We would never do that."

She stepped up to the boy, who flinched but let her put her hand on his shoulder. "But you are an enigma we need to puzzle out."

"I'm..." His watery blue eyes peered at her. "Ben."

"Well, Ben, I think you should get some sleep. You've had a rough day." She turned him around, gently nudging him. "Go on, back to the medbay."

With a glance over his shoulder, the boy did as he was told, followed shortly by a grey shadow as Grim emerged from behind the chesterfield and sauntered after him, nose up and tail flicking.

"If not the Sisters, then who?" Kandi lifted her knife to examine the edge.

"The rebels?" Severn crossed his arms over his chest and arched an eyebrow.

"We can't take him anywhere without breaking the contract," Rebeka said, more to herself than anyone else.

"I'd say the contract is already broken," Tink said, echoing the thought that crept into Rebeka's own head.

38: TINK

T HEY WERE SLIPPING AGAIN. Tink's stomach always knew when they were in the slipstream, despite Ish's admonishments that she was being ridiculous and there was no such thing as slip sickness. But Ish was happiest in the stream.

Before they'd met, he'd been on the cusp of being forced into a life as a military leader. Until his formidable mother helped him escape those plans. It was a near thing though, despite the Hatari Convention, which mandated that every Dominion planet allow any adult of age to leave their home world. Together, Ish and his mother had stood up to his austere grandfather and domineering father, and the uneasy alliance they'd formed in order to set Ish's future, to see a somber and severe Ish replace his grandfather as head of their House.

Tink shook her head; she couldn't imagine that Ish. He would've been shut away from space and the stream. Forced to fight and politic instead of laugh and create. Unable to play music because it led to dancing, and dancing led to fornication. Dissuaded from loving anyone — male or female — unless it was deemed an advantageous match. Tink was grateful to Ish's mother, and thanked the Spinner she'd found him — an unlicensed navigator — looking for work on Ikari station. But she wished he wasn't so keen to take them into the slipstream, which he was eager to do even though it drained him. She liked things that were solid and followed the laws of foundational physics. Not this fluidic, cosmic hocus pocus.

Glaring at the spiced protein chunk wrap she'd taken from the kitchen back when they were in regular space, she counted the seconds, sure they had to surface soon. Her stomach rumbled while it heaved. It was used to space rations: protein chunks, green bars and rehydrated algal goo smoothies. Not the delicious creations Alek somehow concocted with the same ingredients and a dash of seasoning. Tink frowned, tearing her gaze away from the plate.

"No getting used to this food." She patted her abdomen. "He's not long for this ship." Her stomach fluttered, and she frowned, not sure it was entirely due to hunger. Regardless of his toothy smile and culinary skills, she was still determined to see the obnoxious pilot off at the next port, whatever the captain said.

A chirrup sounded in response to her voice, followed by a low caterwauling. Tink sighed and, grabbing a torch, shimmied under the impulse flux conduit, careful to keep away from the hot metal pipes to her left.

"Grim, where have you gotten yourself into now?" The cat chirred. "Always getting stuck and then refusing a helping hand unless it has food in it," Tink grumbled as she wiggled forward until the light caught two green eyes. She scritched her fingers along the floor, trying to coax the cat out. He just scooted further back. Then Tink's stomach lurched before settling down...they'd finally come out of the stream. One problem solved, but she still needed to figure out how to get a cat out of her engine.

Tink grimaced then crawled back out. Grabbing the wrap, she took a big bite despite her still unsettled stomach, then pulled out a protein chunk. Sliding back under the conduit, careful not to get too close to the searing metal, she offered the piece to the cat. He crept forward, his whiskers twitching as he sniffed the morsel. He started to back away, turning his nose up at her offering.

"Come on," Tink said with a huff. "You were a starving stray until I took you in." She was about to call him names when he streaked past her, leaving her alone under the engine.

"What's got —" The ship shuddered, throwing Tink further forward. She cursed as she hit one of the hot pipes. Luckily it was her back, covered by her jumpsuit. "What in Zeus' bollocks? Cass, what just happened?" she asked as she shimmied back out of the small space.

"The ship has come to a stop."

"Um, thanks." She dusted off the front of her jumpsuit. "Why? Is there something wrong with the engine?" Tink asked the question out of habit; she knew from its purr that the engine wasn't the problem, but the thought of sabotage made her queasy.

"No, the engine is running a-okay."

"A-okay? Are *you* okay, Cass?" Tink scowled but didn't wait for an answer. "The algal generator?" Though that didn't make sense. The ship wouldn't stop suddenly just because the fuel system was acting up; there were reserves in place.

"No. Ish stopped the ship."

"Ish? Where's Alek?" Tink ran down the corridor, intending to give him a piece of her mind. "Abandoning his post." Taking the stairs two at a time, she muttered to herself, not expecting an answer. "Why the hell would Ish stop the ship?"

"There's another ship off our starboard," Cass responded, not getting the concept of a rhetorical question.

Tink stopped short. "A ship? The same one that's been following us? How did it track us?" Ish had told her it was near impossible to track another ship through the slipstream. At least not without a set of tracers. *Near* impossible, not totally.

"This is a different ship."

She started running towards the bridge again. "Captain, what's our status?" Rebeka didn't answer. Tink stumbled onto the bridge, stopping at the face that filled the viewscreen. It wasn't one she recognized but, judging by the captain's expression, she did. A woman with sharp cheekbones and long black hair stared at Rebeka with eyes that glinted like obsidian. Dark liner framed her eyes. Her lips pulled into a sharp frown, were a shocking red.

"What do you want, Gothe?" Rebeka asked, and Tink's mouth dropped open as she flicked her gaze back to the woman onscreen. She might not recognize the face but the name was infamous. Legate Marpo Gothe, rebel leader. Not some piddly regional commander either but the high muckety-muck, the big kahuna. The general at the head of the Hudsonite Brigade, the most successful, most feared rebel faction. Tink had to be honest: the Legate wasn't what she'd expected. Even from the cropped image of the woman on the viewscreen, Tink could tell she was reedy under her black uniform, and she seemed too young to have risen so high. She'd always assumed Gothe was 70 years old and built like a tank.

"You have something I want." Her black eyes were hard as stone, and Tink was left with little hope of them getting out of this without giving her something.

"We've been over this," Rebeka replied, pulling her shoulders back as she took a step forward, placing her hands on the rail between the captain's chair and the cockpit. "I have nothing to give you."

Gothe's lips formed into a vague smile, half sneer, as an eyebrow raised. "I think we both know that's not true. But I'm not here for you...this time." She looked down at her hands, nails painted a red that matched her lips. "You picked up something that belongs to me."

Tink leaned as casually as she could on the railing beside the captain. "You don't know what you're talking about. There was nothing but a worthless plant." As soon as the words were out of her mouth, she wished she'd stayed silent as both the woman's cold eyes and the captain's turned to her.

After a few long seconds of glaring at her, Rebeka turned back at the viewscreen. "As she says, I don't know what you're talking about."

Tink stood up straight as she felt a presence behind her, and the woman's eyes shifted to look over her shoulder. She followed the direction of her gaze. Alek had stepped onto the bridge, followed by Severn.

Returning to peer at Rebeka, the woman's eyes narrowed. "You're sure you have nothing for me?"

"Sure." The captain made the single word hard and crisp.

"Clearly, I've been misinformed."

The screen blinked out, and Tink collapsed into the captain's chair.

"That was easy," she said, her gaze shifting between Rebeka's tense back, Alek's tight jaw and Severn's narrowed eyes.

"Too..." Alek and Rebeka both started.

"...easy," the captain finished, and exhaled sharply before turning to peer at Tink. "Get out of my chair."

Back in her engine room, with her stomach rumbling so loud that Grim danced away from her, Tink finally chowed down on the wrap she'd abandoned in her sprint to the bridge. It was cold but still delicious — not a bad choice for a last meal. As she chewed, the cat stalked off down the corridor, soft and low: he was hunting something. At least he wouldn't get stuck somewhere in her engine this time.

She turned back to examine her latest project: a goo bomb using inedible leftovers from the algal generator that would coat their opponents in slime, clogging air holes and blurring visors. As long as she could contain the blast radius.

"'The smoke will blind us, Tink'." She paused, appreciating her impression of the captain. Putting the wrap on the plate, she flipped her goggles over her eyes and rifled through the tools on her desk for her plasma scalpel. Her hands didn't find it in its usual spot amongst the bits and bobs. She twisted her lips — the mess had morphed into downright chaos. Instead of cleaning, she reached for her laser gun. She was just leaning in to solder the first join when she heard light footsteps behind her.

"What do you want, Ben?" she asked without turning around. When there was only silence in response, she lifted her goggles up and turned to him. The boy stood in the doorway, a slight frown on his face, his eyes wide as always, as if they were sucking up the world. Tink sighed to see the cat clutched in his arms, purring away and rubbing his head against Ben's jaw.

"Come on in." Tink jerked her chin in invitation.

He hesitated a few seconds then stepped over the threshold. When he gently put the cat down, Grim didn't dart off into the maze of the engine room, instead twining through Ben's ankles as the boy took a few careful steps over to the bench. "I can help?"

Tink couldn't decide whether it was a question or a statement, but she answered anyway. "No, you shouldn't help with this." She turned back to her work. "Kids shouldn't make weapons."

"S'not a weapon," he said, the words muffled. "Self-defense."

She glanced at him, curious. Her mouth dropped open. "Are you eating my lunch?"

Biting his lip, Ben looked from her to the remains of the wrap in his hands, then his gaze darted back to her. His lips twisted into a grimace, and his eyes started to glisten.

Tink's stomach went gooey. "It's alright. You're a growing boy." She turned to the workbench. "I was done anyway," she said, despite the quiet rumble in her tummy. She nodded towards the tool chest. "There's some more candy in the bottom drawer. Why don't you bring it over, and we can share?"

Ben did as she suggested, then came back to sit on the floor at her feet. He was quiet, not pressing her to help work on the slime bomb. She glanced at him, thinking it weird that a kid who woke up screaming was so quiet. Her mouth opened again when she realized that he was using her snake scope to play with Grim, flicking it around for the cat to pounce on. It was a delicate instrument of her own making. She breathed in sharply but was distracted from saying anything by a shadow appearing in the doorway.

"Severn." The computer tech's smile grew when he looked at her, his dimples deepening. Tink's stomach felt like she'd swallowed one of those flittering bugs Grim was always catching then letting go so he could catch them again. She returned his smile as the memory of his lips on her neck flickered through her body.

"Tink, am I glad to see you." He stepped into the room, the smile wavering as he noticed Ben and Grim. Slowly, his eyes came back to her, and he jerked his chin, a silent request that she come over there.

Tink's eyebrows quirked in question, but she put her tool down and went to join him by the door.

"Do you think he should really be in here?" Severn said, his voice low. "You know, given what he can do? It's unnatural."

Tink glanced at the boy. If Ben heard him, the boy gave no indication. "I...."

"And I don't think he's telling us everything he knows." Severn peered at the kid. "He might be dangerous...to the engine."

Tink frowned. It didn't feel right to listen without defending the boy, but she also couldn't really disagree. Instead of saying anything on that point, she changed the subject. "What did you need me for?"

Severn glanced up and lowered his voice even further. "I think someone has messed with Cass."

"What?" Tink said; at a normal volume again, it sounded too loud. Severn grabbed her shoulders, as if the weight of his hands would make her voice quieter.

"I found evidence of encrypted messages without a signature. Who else could do that except the ship itself?" He glanced at the boy. "I can unencrypt the content but..." His eyes slid sideways again. "I need to crack her core. And that needs two people to press two buttons."

Tink's head was shaking before he even finished speaking. "No, no. That's a bad idea."

"You know Cass has been having problems." His volume rose, before he dropped it again, glancing up, as if the AI lived above their heads rather than throughout the ship.

Tink's stomach growled, and she used that as an opportunity to put him off. She tipped her head towards Ben. "Kid ate my lunch. I can't think on an empty stomach." Raising her voice, she continued. "Hey, if you're still hungry, I'm going to get some more to eat."

Ben smiled at her and scooped up the cat. His hold on Grim lasted until he got to the door, then the cat took off down the hall, followed more slowly by a subdued Ben and a silent Severn. Tink made sure to slide the engine room door closed, though the cat could find a way in if he wanted to.

The common room was empty except for the three of them. Tink stuck her head in the fridge to see if there was anything left of the lunch Alek had made. With a sigh, she accepted that no matter how long she stood there, it wouldn't magically appear. She popped her head up.

"Chocobug bar?"

Severn grimaced but Ben nodded, his nose pressed against the window overlooking the cargo bay. Tink pulled out a couple of bars and went to stand beside him, handing him one. He tore it open and started munching without removing his head from the glass.

"Whatchalookingat?" she asked through the mastication of her own bug bar. The boy poked the window with a pale finger. She looked in the direction he indicated. Grim walked along the railing at the top of the staircase.

"Seriously, Cat? You're going to break your neck."

Tink jumped sideways, her mouth full of chalky bug meal, at the sound of Alek's voice. She scowled at him, but he was focused on the view through the window as he chewed his own bug bar with gusto.

"You should not be so silent," she said, looking askance at the muscle-bound man, disconcerted she hadn't heard him enter the room.

His shoulder lifted, but whether he was shrugging or working out a kink, she couldn't tell. "What's that?" he said.

Tink followed his gaze to a point beyond the cat. She squinted, trying to make sense of what she was seeing. The bite in her mouth turned chalky, and she swallowed hard, trying to force it down despite the lump in her throat. "Fire!" She coughed the word out, sending flakes of bug bar against the window. She didn't know what fed it, but it had gone from spark to conflagration in a matter of seconds. "Cass! Fire in the cargo bay."

"Locking down the cargo bay. Suppression in 10 seconds."

As Tink flung herself down the corridor to the door leading into the cargo bay, she counted out the seconds. She arrived at the closed door with a second to go. A tick later, nothing happened. "Cass?" she queried as Ben and Alek stepped up beside her, pressing their faces to the window set into the door.

"Suppressors are non-functional." Cass' voice was calm, as always.

"I told you she was having problems," Severn said with a calmness that unnerved her. He leaned against the wall behind her. She scowled at him before turning back to the door. The fire continued to grow.

She slammed her palm against the door as she blinked away the stinging in her eyes. "Cass, vent the cargo bay."

"There's a lifeform in the cargo bay," the AI said, and tears formed in Tink's eyes as she spotted Grim. The cat was climbing the boxes of algal nutrients Tink hadn't gotten around to stowing yet, as he tried to get away from the flames licking through the air. A tear tracked down her cheek.

She felt a hand on her right shoulder. She looked into Alek's eyes, which also glistened in the dim corridor.

"A fire on a ship can't be allowed to burn," he said, giving her shoulder a squeeze. "Cass, vent the cargo bay."

"NO!" The boy's voice seared through the air, the force of it causing Tink to stagger back into Alek and throwing both of them off balance. She landed on top of him as he fell to the floor, then she watched, stunned and unable to move, as Ben placed his hands on the door.

"It's locked," she said, but her voice was drowned out by a sudden roar as the door opened. Ben lunged through before anyone could stop him.

Severn lunged forward, his eyes wide, reaching out his hand. He pulled his arm back just in time to save it from being broken by the door slamming shut again. He stepped up to the door, banging a fist on the glass. "Come back here, you little...."

Standing, Tink went up on tiptoes beside him, craning her neck to get a view of Ben. He stared at them with big eyes and shook his head.

Grabbing the cat, he tucked Grim into his pyjama top, holding him tightly with one hand. When he reached his other hand towards the wall a few feet away, the cover on a switch shattered. Tink knew what it was, and apparently so did he: emergency atmosphere evac. Any hauler worth its snot had one, meant to be used by someone in an atmo suit with grav boots on. She pounded the door with her hand. Whatever he was, he was still a living, breathing person.

Bracing his feet wide, he met her eyes again, then punched his hand towards the distant wall. Tink watched in horror as the button moved without him touching it. Wind whipped at his clothes, but somehow he managed to hold himself in place, like a tree rooted into the cargo hold floor. After a few seconds, he closed his eyes and wrapped his other hand around the cat.

"Cass! Stop the depressurization."

"Manual override in effect. Atmosphere evac complete in 10 seconds."

Tink slammed her hand into the door again. "Bleeding Hades, Cass."

"How long can he survive in there?" Severn asked, horror dripping from his words.

"No idea." Tink turned and slumped against the door, head in her hands, unable to watch it anymore. "If he were a normal boy, he'd be dead already."

"Evac complete. Repressurization commencing."

"How long, Cass?" she asked without looking up.

"30 seconds to safe atmosphere levels."

"Too long." Tink shook her head in her hands.

"We don't know that," Alek said, his voice drifting down from over her head. She felt gentle fingers graze over her hair before pulling away.

"It's just a damn cat," she said, the words hoarse as they tore from her throat. Though, if she were honest, her stomach ached at the thought of Grim being consumed by flame or jettisoned into space.

"Kandi?" Alek said as Tink lifted her head, wiping away her tears.

"Already here. What in Poseidon's barnacles happened?"

"Fire," Severn said, giving her room. Tink shifted, coming to standing.

"Cass, open the door," Kandi said.

"10 seconds to safe atmosphere levels."

"Safe enough. Open the door. Override code nine-one-one-whiskey-tango-foxtrot."

The door slid open. Ben stood on the other side, shivering. Freeze-dried blood tracked from his nose over blue lips, and his teeth chattered. Otherwise, he appeared unharmed. Then Tink noticed streaks of blood across his pyjamas.

Grim's claws, she realized, her eyes watering again as there was no sign of movement from the bundle the boy clutched.

Carefully, Ben extracted a limp cat from underneath his top and handed him to Kandi. "Fix him?"

Kandi nodded, her expression grave. "No promises, but I'll try."

Tink sniffled and wiped her nose on the sleeve of her jumpsuit. Grabbing Ben's shoulders, she shook him then drew him tight to her. "What were you thinking? Risking your life for a cat."

He pulled away from her. "It's not Grim's fault someone started a fire."

39: Rebeka

R EBEKA PEERED AT TINK over the rim of her mug as the other woman twiddled some widget in her fingers. Tink was thinking, which was not always a good thing. Rebeka was sure the engineer had come to her office to give her a piece of her mind, even though she'd only made subdued small talk so far.

"Kandi says Grim'll live." Tink didn't look up.

Rebeka arched an eyebrow — that wasn't what was on Tink's mind. "Really?"

A frown furrowed Tink's forehead. "I know you don't —"

"Spit it out," Rebeka said before taking a mouthful of coffee. Tink's eyes flicked up, then back at her widget; her shoulders slumped. "And get your feet off my desk."

Tink stopped her fidgeting to look at her, then plopped her feet on the floor. "I've been thinking—"

"I can see that."

Tink made a face at her, then shifted her gaze to stare at her widget. "I *think* we should take the boy to the Sisters."

"You trust the Sisters of Elazir as much as I do." Rebeka shifted forward, resting her elbows on the desk. She knew Tink had spent some time at one of the Sisters' orphanages before Emmon found her. "What's changed?"

Tink lifted a shoulder and grimaced. "They're the only power player that hasn't attacked us. Or threatened to. And they do have a mandate to care for the destitute, downtrodden and orphaned." She returned to examining the widget as she flipped it around in her hand.

"I don't think he's an orphan." Rebeka took another sip of coffee, the hot liquid lending a pleasant warmth to her throat and stomach. Tink glanced up from her widget but didn't speak. "And how do you propose we get him to the Sisters?"

Tink's eyebrows pulled together. "We fly the ship to one of their sanctuaries. *The* sanctuary — the Tower of Solitude — and ask them to take care of him."

"That's not what I meant." She carefully placed her mug on her desk before looking back at Tink. "How are we supposed to contact *Emmon Bell* — the owner of the *Lyra* — to get permission to renege on the contract when we're running silent? If we break silence, our hunters will find us and kill us."

"We don't have to break sil—" Tink's eyes narrowed and her lips twisted.

"No one else on this ship knows that —" Rebeka heard a sound outside the open door in the supposedly empty bridge. "Never mind." She picked up her mug again and tilted back in her chair as Severn's head appeared in the doorway.

Tink's gaze slid sideways before returning to Rebeka. "I think if we all agree to break the contract to save a little boy, to hell with what the owner says."

Rebeka arched an eyebrow at Tink before turning her attention to Severn.

Severn stepped into her office. "Hey, I didn't expect anyone to be here."

"Understandable. It is the middle of the night cycle." Rebeka peered at him over her mug. "What are you doing up and about?"

"Couldn't sleep." He nodded at her mug. "Too much of that stuff lately." He turned back towards the door, and Rebeka watched him. At the threshold, he paused, shifting to face them again as he clasped the door frame with both hands. "Sorry, I couldn't help but overhear. Are you really considering taking him to the Sisters then?"

"Do you have a reason we shouldn't?"

He shook his head. "No, might be the best place for him. If we take him to their home base, as Tink suggested, it's beyond the Wall. Technically outside the Empire. And even the rebels aren't stupid enough to attack the Sisters." He stared at his palms. "Though there is the disease factor," he added, shrugging as he looked back at her. "I'll just be glad when this is all over."

"You and me both." She took another sip of coffee before continuing. "But before we do this, we need to get the others on board."

40: HΛRBIN

"WE'RE GOING TO THE Sisters of Elazir." The voice on the other end was tight, as if the man didn't relish the thought. Harbin understood the sentiment. The Sisters might be able to treat diseases others couldn't, but they also took care of those they couldn't cure — the incurable and decrepit from across the Empire and beyond. The Empire. The rebels. The cartels. They all depended on the Sisters for the services they provided, even as they envied the Sisters' power.

Though not all of them were sisters nowadays. The majority were still female, but some were male, and a fair few landed somewhere else on the web. The stories said all of them were diseased themselves. Harbin didn't believe that even though he'd only been to a sanctuary once, when he was a child and his grandmother was dying. The dim lights, the droning chants, the smell of incense not quite covering the antiseptic and astringent concoctions. He vowed never to return, trusting his health to the medicines of Dominion doctors rather than the Sisters' melding of magic and tech. But the people tending to his grandmother had all seemed hale and hearty.

Harbin sniffed. Archon Halcyon Koning would not be pleased. The Sisters were a faction to be reckoned with. They had amassed a dragon's hoard of wealth, though what they hoarded most was secrets. And that was where their power lay. Well, that and the rumours of necromancy and clandestine missions into the Desolation to unearth more secrets.

"Which sanctuary?" Harbin finally thought to ask.

"Which do you think? The mothership."

A tense smile crept onto Harbin's lips. "Across the Wall."

"Across the Wall." He almost heard the smile reflected in the other man's voice. The Wall had no other name; it didn't need one. It separated the worlds of the living from the ghosts of the dead. The Dominion from the Desolation. Few outliers lived beyond the Wall, just madmen and edge cases too far gone even for the Badlands. And, of course, the Sisters. Their headquarters, when it appeared at all, appeared outside the wall. Harbin returned to the present, realizing the man was speaking again. "...slip ahead. Intercept us at the Wall."

"Ship comms are still down?" Harbin asked. The Wall had fallen into disrepair, suffering from benign neglect, until recently. Most didn't know the Empire had begun repairing the gaps, testing the mesh. Now it was fully functional, and he could turn it on at a signal, after which the portals were the only way through. And the only way through a portal was to enter a unique access code given solely into the care of the owner of each ship commissioned in the empire: the Dominion liked to keep track of who had business across the Wall. And the owner of the *Lyra* never left his villa on Passalida.

"Yes."

"So, there's no way through unless they light up their comms, which might also tell us where you are since you're not capable of that."

Harbin tapped his desk, and the connection cut off. He kept tapping as he thought about his options. He hated what he was going to do next. But he still did it. Flicking his finger, he brought up the screen again and called Ellis Gar.

"I need reinforcements," he said before Gar even had a chance to spew a greeting.

"Why?" Gar's voice was hard.

"They're going to the Wall. With a couple more ships, we can trap them against it." Harbin didn't mention the Sisters, not yet, though he imagined Gar could guess if he spared a brain cell to consider it. Or if he hadn't found all the bugs in his ready room. Harbin glanced at the ceiling then back at Gar. The pursed lips and narrowed eyes revealed the man knew the stakes: they were all screwed if the *Lyra* delivered the boy to the Sisters. Even the Emperor himself didn't mess with the Sisters of Death.

41: TINK

"**B**LEEDING HADES."

Tink's head lifted, shocked enough at hearing those words in Rebeka's voice to be dragged away from tweaking settings on the flux condenser. Her eyes homing in on the captain. Rebeka rarely swore, and if she did, it was the softer curses: jacks, barnacles and the like. But returning her gaze to the viewscreen, Tink had the urge to swear herself.

The Wall was up. Gossamer strands of light reached out from the portal, still a pinpoint speck in the black. They dissipated into flecks of silver before strengthening again as they neared an accelerator on their way to the next port. More like a web than a wall, it stretched for uncountable klicks, creating a mesh of lines that could slice a ship apart. And she recalled Ish saying it was replicated in the slipstream: the portals appeared as points of light, like bioluminescent plankton in a dark sea, while the lines made a net that sliced through the currents, leaving inky black.

"When did *this* happen?" Kandi said. The Wall was old, older than the Dominion some said, and it had fallen out of use, full of gaps and tears. And there was no purpose to it anyway: no one wanted to go into the Desolation.

"Can you get us through?" Rebeka asked.

Kandi shook her head. "The Sisters could. Or Emmon Bell, if we could contact either of them, but our comms are still down. Should we light them up?" Rebeka gave a sharp nod of her head, and Tink's finger hovered over the tablet beside her, ready to send a response to Kandi's message, one that would be bounced from ansible to ansible, unable to be traced back to her. Then Kandi's hand hit her console, making Tink jump. "Jacks!"

"What?" The captain stood and stepped towards the Tac station.

"Something's jamming the comms." Kandi turned to the station beside her. "Severn?"

"Busy. Sharks closing fast." Severn didn't turn as he pronounced what they already knew. A shiver of Sharks pursued them, sleek and matte grey and bristling with weaponry. They'd already scorched the *Lyra*'s port flank, despite Alek's piloting. Tink's gaze slid towards the pilot. Noting the tension in his neck and the straining muscles of his forearms, he certainly seemed to be trying to get them out of this in spite of the ship's protests. Severn's voice interrupted her contemplation. "How did they know we'd be here?" He punched something on the console in front of him with his knuckle.

"Can you get the comms up?" Tink asked.

"Comms or weapons, your choice." Kandi stabbed her console with her fingers.

"Can we slip through?" the captain asked, her voice back to neutral, as she sat back down.

Ish shook his head. "Not without a slip point, and I don't see one. Besides..." He plucked at his holoscreen, squinting as if that would make a point appear. "Navigator lore says the Wall exists in the stream."

Tink felt useless, unable to help her crewmates. Her friends. She couldn't manufacture a slip point. She couldn't make the engines go faster than they were. She was just glad she'd installed the plasma booster the captain had bought, otherwise the Sharks would have caught them already. All she could do was fix the comms, or at least pretend to. As she reached for her console, their portside was strafed by a pulse cannon blast, and she was forced to grab her armrests.

"The portals are the only way." The words were rough coming out of Alek's tight jaw. "There isn't a gap big enough to get this ship through."

"But they're all closed, as far as the sensors can read," Kandi said, shaking her head. Her fingers moved almost as fast as Ish's when she flicked through the screens on her display. "I don't see any way through the portals."

"Not without the owner's access code," Severn added, his tone almost casual despite the situation. "Maybe we surrender...."

Tink glanced at the captain, who'd looked sideways at her. Another blast rocked their stern, starboard this time. Tink watched as Ben's hand clutched the arm of the jump seat he was strapped into beside Severn. Tink opened her mouth as the ship slid sideways.

"Were we hit?" Rebeka said.

Alek shook his head slightly, the muscles in his jaw tight. "Just making us a harder target."

"If we get out of this, we're retrofitting the *Lyra* with pulse cannons." Rebeka looked entirely serious, even though she'd always argued most ship-mounted weapons cost more than they were worth.

The ship shuddered from another glancing blow. "That was *not* me," Alek said.

"How far to that portal?" Tink asked, and Rebeka's hand grabbed hers and squeezed. She looked into the captain's deep brown eyes as the woman shook her head ever so slightly. "Do you have another plan?" Tink's voice was almost a whisper, as she grasped at a wild hope that the captain had a card she hadn't played. Tink had kept her secret for ten years...they both had.

"Life or death situations are not the time to make critical decisions." Rebeka's eyes held hers.

"Next portal is 15000 klicks away," Cass said, the AI apparently realizing Alek was too busy evading Sharks to answer. "Sharks at 16000 klicks and closing."

Tink pulled her console in front of her, punching in an access code that unlocked advanced admin systems.

The captain grasped her hand again. "Tink. You don't have to."

Four sets of eyes turned to stare at her. Only Alek — who was busy — and the boy — whose face was nestled into the cat's head — didn't turn her way. Recovered from his recent lack of atmo, Grim looked disgruntled but resigned.

"Sharks at 11000 klicks."

Scanning the faces, the ache in her gut disappeared, taking her doubt with it. "Yeah, I do." Turning to her display, she pulled up a screen that stayed hidden except in the privacy of her own quarters with the door locked. "Alek, head towards the portal."

Alek spared a glance at her, confusion written on his face. "Are you insane? We'll be scattered across space if we fly into a closed portal."

"It won't be closed." Tink started to punch in a series of letters and numbers and seemingly random symbols.

"Sharks at 7000." Cass counted down the distance between them and their pursuers. "6000."

"Do it!" the captain ordered. "Now." The ship slued sideways, towards the energized mesh and the shut iris that filled the viewscreen.

"Impact with portal in 5000 klicks."

Tink slammed her palm to the display to be scanned.

"4000."

Slowly, too slowly, the iris opened.

"Impact in 10...9..." Cass continued her countdown, her voice calm, as if she were counting the remaining protein packs in storage.

"Shark coming in hot on our stern," Kandi said.

"5...4..."

The *Lyra* turned sharply, the ship moaning in protest. At the same time, the port side tipped up while the starboard tipped down. After a lifetime spent on a ship, Tink felt space sick for the first time outside the slipstream.

"One."

Tink held her breath as the ship slid through the half-open iris.

"We made it." Her voice was a whisper. "We made it," she added louder, as if that would make her believe it.

The ship shivered as a shot from a pulse cannon grazed their tail.

"Some of the Sharks are heading through after us." Kandi focused on the display in front of her as the viewscreen shifted to the rear view. Through the iris, Tink could see the Shark that had fired at them, followed closely by its cohorts.

"No, they're not," Ben said as he curled his fingers into a fist. Tink's mouth dropped open as the iris snapped shut. Sparks and shrapnel shot through the air on the far side of the portal.

"Ha." Tink felt a brightness in her chest and a lightness in her head at the fact that they'd survived. Everyone else looked so grim, except Ben, who returned her smile. "Cheer up," she said, scanning the room. "We're alive." Then she arrived at Ish, and her smile dropped.

"How do you have the owner's codes?" His tone was flat, his eyes revealing a mix of confusion and hurt as realization dawned. She struggled to undo the uncooperative buckles of her seat then stepped forward, opening her mouth to answer, even though she didn't know what to say. Faced with his angry expression, she turned to stare at the floor, to try to come up with some explanation for why she'd have the owner's codes. Failing, she returned her gaze to meet his, but he looked away.

42: ΔLΘK

T HE WALL SPARKED AND pulsed as debris from the Shark hit its glistening lines of concentrated light. Alek eyed it in the second before the viewscreen shifted to show the space ahead of them.

"The last known location of the Tower of Solitude is 251 megaklicks away." Cass' calm voice was tempered by the heavy silence that filled the bridge. Alek did a quick calculation: two days in regular space...if they couldn't find a slip point. Enough time to sort out the puzzle of the *Lyra*, her owner, and the package.

"Thank you, Cass," he said when no one else responded. Then he spun around to face the others.

"The next portal is 10 minutes away at a Shark's max speed." Cass' tone seemed downright chipper.

There was no response to that pronouncement, and Alek was sure the others were doing what he was: calculating their odds. And they weren't good; the Sharks would be on them well before they reached the Sisters.

"Thank you, Cass," the captain finally said from behind the hand she rubbed over her face.

"Which means they will be here in 20 minutes."

"Thank you—" Alek and Rebeka started at the same time. He saw her lips quirk in a small smile that reflected his own, but it did little to relieve the tensions that flowed like Ish's stream lines through the bridge.

"Why didn't you tell me? I thought I was your best friend." Ish's voice was quiet as he stared at his display, but there was a bite to his tone. Alek edged away, even though the navigator's ire wasn't directed at him. Ish turned to glare at Tink, whose arms were crossed over her chest. He stood up and started towards the door. Looking between Ish and Tink, Alek tried to work out why Ish was so angry. As he replayed their encounter with the Sharks and their approach to the portal, his eyes went wide, then narrowed as they homed in on Tink: she didn't have the Wall code because the owner gave it to her. She had it because she *was* the owner of the *Lyra*.

"Stop." Rebeka imbued that one word with the weight of command, making Alek wonder again at her background. "Sit." Ish obeyed, though he stared daggers at Tink as he returned to his post and slumped into his seat. "We can hash this out later," the captain continued as she glanced at Tink before returning to Ish's back. "Right now, we need to get the hell out of here. How long until we can slip?"

Alek watched Ish in profile. His jaw clenched and his Adam's apple bobbed as he swallowed.

"Ish!" Rebeka repeated.

"I don't know. Why don't you ask our owner?" Ish pulled up his display but otherwise didn't move. Alek glanced at Tink, who stared at Ish's back, her shoulders hunched and a frown pulling her face down.

The captain's sigh drew Alek's attention. "Because it's a technical question. Can we slip? Deep, to evade their sensors?"

Ish lifted a hand to pluck at his screen, becoming more animated as he did so. After half a minute, he nodded. "There's a point at phi 80°, rho 9, zeta 3. But there's some damage to the exterior."

"Do it."

"But...."

Alek watched Ish in the half light, as his face shifted from anger to something else, which caused Alek's eyebrows to wrinkle in concern. *Fear.*

"Do. It." The captain barely glanced sideways as she continued. "Tink, go check on the engines."

"But—" Tink started.

"Go." Rebeka's dark gaze turned to Tink, and her voice dropped. "Make yourself scarce."

Rebeka knew, Alek realized. She was in on Tink's secret, which he'd only just puzzled out. That bit of intel certainly hadn't been in the brief his handlers gave him.

Tink frowned, but uncrossed her arms and did as Rebeka asked, leaving the bridge. Ben followed, still clutching the cat. Grim hissed and spat at everyone they passed.

Once Tink was off the bridge, the rest of the crew glanced around at each other. Alek saw that Mino was the *only* one who'd known. Kandi's grim expression made it clear it was news to her, and he reckoned she had some words saved up for Tink. Severn's eyes were narrowed, and his nostrils flared. Cass must have known, but no one had ever thought to ask.

"I can't believe she didn't tell us," Severn said with a surprising venom in his voice as he peered at Ish.

Ish shook his head. "I know."

Alek could see his eyes glistening. "I'm sure she had her reasons," he said, leaning closer to Ish.

"What reason could she have for lying?" Severn turned his rancour on Alek, making him wonder at its source. Severn had only been on the ship as long as he had. Too short to feel a deep, personal sense of betrayal. Unless Tink and Severn had gotten closer than he realized. Alek's lips pressed into a grimace at the thought.

"Enough." Rebeka shifted her attention to Kandi and Severn. "You two, check the damage to the ship. See what we can fix from the inside. And I don't think it needs saying, but until we're in the clear, we're running silent. Which means no arguing."

Severn looked as if he wanted to rebel, but Kandi turned to do as ordered. Since he stood between her and the exit, he either had to face her down or go ahead of her. He chose the same option Alek would have, but as he spun around, his gaze slid to Ish again. His sudden interest in the navigator was another mystery to puzzle out.

Alek's eyes flicked to Ish, who grasped at ribbons of light in his holodisplay. Alek's stomach churned, and he tried to tell himself it was because they'd just entered the stream.

Here Be Monsters

43: Rebeka

R EBEKA'S LIPS THINNED AND her eyes narrowed
when Alek started to head after Kandi and Severn,
despite not receiving orders. She knew she shouldn't be angry
at him for taking initiative, but her skin almost itched with
tension. As she opened her mouth to say something, she saw
him pause as his gaze fell on Ish. She turned her own attention
to the navigator. His shoulders were rigid, his tendons strung
like wire. His skin shone with a sheen of sweat and had taken
on a sickly green hue.

"Sit down, Alek," Rebeka said softly, and the pilot gave her
a sharp nod; she kept forgetting that he'd been trained by
someone. His eyebrows pulled together, and a frown tugged at
his lips as he sat down at his post, glancing from her to the
navigator. "I need you to help Ish. He's going to be busy."

"What she means is she told me to go deep," Ish said
without taking his eyes off his display. The wavy lines had
shifted from their normal teal and rose hues to muted purples
and navy blues. His jaw twitched in time with his fingers.

"I don't..." Alek started, then stopped, his mouth hanging open as he looked to her for an explanation.

"And I don't know where we're coming out yet," Ish added.

"Usually, he has exit points mapped by now," Rebeka explained, wondering how pilots could know so little about the slipstream. Though honestly, she knew barely more than was required herself. If they survived, she'd sign them both up for a remedial course in the astrodynamics of stream mechanics.

"Why not this time?" Alek asked.

"Because we don't know yet where to find the elusive Sisters of Elazir." Rebeka pulled up her display. "I'm going to see if I can suss out their location."

"How exactly? If we send a signal out, can't they figure out where we are?"

"Carefully. One ping at a time."

"And what should I do?" Alek asked.

"Watch our back while Ish rides the current."

"I thought the deeper we go, the less likely we are to be detected." He spun his seat around and started scans of their nebulous environment.

She looked up at him. "But we still might cast a shadow on their scanners. Especially if I'm sending up flares as I search for the Sisters."

"And it's dangerous down here." The words were strangled as they came out of Ish's tight throat. "It's not just the physics that gets warped."

Rebeka opened her mouth to say something about not scaring the newbies when the ship quivered. She grasped the armrest. "Alek?"

He turned to his display and punched a series of icons, shaking his head as the data scrolled. The ship shuddered, and Ish's fingers clenched.

"They can't have found us that quickly." Alek zoomed into an area on his display and cast it to the viewscreen. An amoeboid haze pulsated against the darkness.

"It's not the Sharks." Ish's shoulders pulled back as he reached for a squiggle of light over his head. "Here be monsters," he said, his voice almost as deep as Alek's.

A screech emanated from somewhere on the ship, and a shiver crawled along Rebeka's spine. Her mind told her it was metal-on-metal strain caused by warped physics. But her heart argued that it was biological.

"There's...nothing on the scanners. Just shadows." Alek flicked through a series of wavy lines. "Oh. But Cass has found the Sisters."

"Cass?" Rebeka asked. She clutched her armrest as the *Lyra* hiccoughed. A ripple pulsed on Ish's display, where the undulations were now almost blue-black. She didn't know how he could see what he needed to. But then he didn't really seem to be *looking* at all, with his eyes unfocused.

"Exit point in 30 seconds," Cass announced.

"More warning next time, Cass." Alek glanced over at Ish, and Rebeka followed his gaze. The navigator's limbs locked in place as he fought to pull the *Lyra* out of the stream.

"I'm sorry, Alek. The Sisters' sanctuary became visible on subspace scanners without warning."

"Perhaps *they* found us," Rebeka said. The ship jerked forward as if hit from behind, distracting her from the thought. "Ish?" she asked, an edge to her voice she didn't like. There was no response from the navigator, whose unfocused gaze travelled over his display. She forced herself to breathe slowly, lower her heart rate. "Alek? What was that?"

The pilot shook his head, furiously flicking through screens.

Ish fell back into his chair, his muscles going slack. Rebeka had a moment of terror thinking the navigator had passed out until she saw the stars of normal space appear on the viewscreen.

"I told you, there are monsters in the deep," he said, his voice sounding tired. "But we're safe now."

"Won't the Sharks find us?" Alek shifted in his seat to face both her and Ish.

"I think the Sisters have a say in who gets to visit them and who doesn't." Ish nodded towards the screen, where a pale blue dot stood out from the surrounding stars. "And there are the Sisters."

Rebeka squinted and realized he was right. The dot was a space station. "Cass, how long to the station under impulse?"

"Three hours ten minutes fifty-three seconds and —"

"Close enough, Cass." She got up from her chair, the stiffness of her muscles surprising her. "I suppose I should go find the boy and prepare him for life with the Sisters." She scratched her neck as her head shook. It was life, but it might not be a life Ben wanted.

"I can help you find him," Alek said, getting up from his chair.

"You need to get us to the station and plot our course through their maze."

"Maze." His tone was flat. "They have a maze?"

"Their station moves around, popping in and out of scan, through some tech no one understands. Just to keep their privacy and security." Rebeka gazed at him, an eyebrow cocked.

"Of course they have a maze." He nodded, his eyes tensing and his lips almost smiling, as if he embraced the challenge of piloting through one.

Ish reached out a limp hand and patted Alek's forearm. "Go. It's a while until we reach the maze. Cass and I can hold the bridge for a bit." He tipped his chair back, seemingly content where he was.

Rebeka squinted at the top of his head for a minute. "No. Call Kandi. She can keep watch while Cass keeps us pointed in the right direction. You need your beauty sleep." She patted his shoulder then returned her attention to Alek. "I go high, you go low?" She didn't wait for him to reply before heading out the door.

44: Tink

TINK BANGED HER WRENCH a little too hard against the piece of metal, and the ping echoed down the corridor. She'd given up her secret to save their lives, and now *she* was the bad guy. Even the ship seemed angry, resistant to her efforts to futz with it.

She wrenched the lever with her bare hand, ignoring the heat, while watching the sensor on the outside of the converter. *So I kept a secret.* Tink yanked harder. She'd done it to protect herself and her clan, people who'd almost been wiped out by the Dominion in its pursuit of hegemony. It wanted a monopoly on the kinds of knowledge Tinkers held dear and distrusted their nonconformist tendencies. She'd done it to protect other Tinkers. *Liar*, a voice in her head said.

"Shut up," she muttered to herself. She'd kept it a secret because one lone Tinker working on a pissant starship was an entirely different thing from a Tinker *owning* said pissant starship. Tinkers didn't own starships. Her uncle hadn't kept his ownership a secret, but then he'd been a rebel, much more daring than she was. And now he was dead, along with the rest of her family, and the ship was hers.

Again, the word liar echoed in her brain. She sighed. Maybe she'd been a little motivated by wanting to have an ordinary life with her crewmates — who'd never be friends with the owner.

She stared hard at the sensor, which showed everything operating within spec. A frown pulled at the corners of her lips. When she placed her hand on the side of the converter, it felt normal. All systems were normal. The algal converter should have shut down as soon as it sensed a problem. There was no longer any trace of doubt: someone had messed with her ship.

"But who would do that?" She ran her hand over the warm casing before removing it. Severn's spying hadn't uncovered anything. "We weren't even involved in this mess yet."

"Is it still broken?"

Tink spun around in the small space to face Ben, who clutched the cat in his arms. Grim stared at her with his green eyes as he purred.

"No," she said, wiping her hands off and detaching the sensor. Nudging past him, she headed down the hall back to the engine room. "It's purring like a kitten," she added over her shoulder. Dropping the sensor on her workbench, she reached into her toolbox and pulled out a bag of candy — supernova blasts this time — and held it out in offering, as she popped one in her own mouth.

"But it's still not right." It was a statement, as if he could sense her questions. He took a sweet, unwrapped it and started chewing as he slid down to the floor. Grim turned a few circles then nestled into his lap.

"No, it's not." Tink chewed on the sour candy, her mouth puckering, as silence settled around them, each mulling over their own thoughts. She sank to the floor and leaned against the transformer behind her, feeling its gentle hum and warmth relax the muscles of her back. After a minute, she was drawn out of her own head as she watched the boy's frown deepen, the cat's tail flicking sharply back and forth. "Gummy spider for your thoughts." He lifted his head and gave her a questioning look. "It's a figure of speech...what's on your mind? Whatcha thinking?"

Ben's lips scrunched and pursed and pulled into a grimace as he pet the cat, looking down at him. Finally, he returned his gaze to her. "What are the Sisters like?"

Tink's mouth opened, but she didn't have a ready answer for that question. She sucked hard on the candy as she considered her words. "They take care of the ones that have no one else to take care of them." He looked at the bag of sweets but didn't take another one. His eyes glistened. "What's wrong?"

He shook his head, pressing his lips together. Then he pulled his shoulders back and looked at her. "I'm sure the Sisters will be fine if they take in orphans."

Tink rubbed a spot of goo on her palm with her opposite thumb. "We could ask the captain if you could stay." His eyes grew wider. "I have some sway, you know."

For a few long moments, Ben stroked the cat as he regarded her. Then he shook his head. "No. It's not safe for you if I stay. It sounds like the Sisters can hold their own against whoever is after me." He nodded. "It's best if I stay with them."

Tink knew he was probably right, even if she didn't love the plan despite agreeing with it. She reached for her probe again. "I should probably get back to work."

"Can I help?" he asked.

"No, probably not, unless you know something about algal converters."

The boy shook his head as he reached for the candy, grabbing one and tucking it into his pocket, then carefully removing the wrapping from another.

Tink reset the probe's tuning, her eyebrows pulling together as she puzzled through the thoughts in her head. "No, the only other person on the ship who knows anything about them is Alek. He pointed out the clogged manifold before—" She squinted. "Before the sabotage."

"You're wrong," Ben said around a jaw full of candy as he stroked Grim's back. "The captain knows."

"Why do you say that?" Tink put the probe down and unwrapped another candy, tucking it into her cheek to work away at.

He looked up at her, his eyes wide as always — as if the world were full of wonders — then he shrugged. "She's the captain. It's her job." He scritched Grim's chin as he spoke. "And Severn."

"Severn?" Tink cocked her head to the side.

The boy nodded slowly as he kept stroking the cat. "He knows a lot of things. Not just computers." Ben took another sweet from the bag. "Like how to tweak a plasma scalpel to be a makeshift dagger. Or how to communicate via subspace while in the stream without being detected." He popped the candy in his mouth.

"What do you mean?" Tink asked, but Ben had gone quiet, his eyes big and glistening. The only sounds were the munching of candy and the purring of Grim as Ben stared at the entry to the little alcove they were in. Then footsteps echoed in the corridor. Footsteps Tink recognized.

"Severn." Who'd recognized a Mean Green in the dark engine room on the Leviathan. Her stomach sank as she reached for something to use as a weapon — her goo bombs or at least a hammer — but all her hand found was her new chain ratchet.

45: Alek

INSTEAD OF SEARCHING THE lower deck for Ben, as the captain ordered, Alek inched along the habitation hallway. As he did, he listened for footsteps, either the captain's or Severn's. At the third door on his left, he stopped. Glancing both ways, he made sure he was alone. Then he jimmied the door with the thin piece of magnetize flexiplex he'd brought on board. A twitter coursed through his stomach as he realized there was no way to hide what he'd done if his suspicions turned out to be baseless.

Entering Severn's dark room, the sparseness surprised Alek. His own digs were spartan, but that's because he'd fled the Haggishi cartel with his life, a bum knee, and little else. He'd always presumed Severn was more high maintenance.

Because that's how he wanted to appear. Alek hated being played, and he'd most definitely been played, as had everyone on the ship. But Severn had also come onto the *Lyra* with more luggage than Alek. *If it wasn't stuff to make himself at home, what was in there?*

He searched all the usual places for some hidden item that might reveal Severn's true identity, or who had sent him. He peered into the small cupboard behind the mirror set in the wall. He flicked on the tablet sitting on the tiny desk that folded down beside the bed. His eyebrows tugged together in surprise on finding it had no security — no passcode, no retina scan, no request to swipe his wrist patch. It didn't take him long to realize that was because there was nothing on it. An unusual amount of nothing, unless the two ancient Cygnian space operas were some massive cipher. But they looked legit to Alek, and he'd been exposed to more than his fair share of culture.

He lifted the mattress on the pristinely made bed...it was like the man didn't sleep. There was nothing but an extra pair of shoes and the two travel cases. Alek opened them both. Again, no security. In the first one, he found only T-shirts, underwear and a picture of some man in a hideous frame. The face was vaguely familiar, and for a second, Alek thought the man might be Severn's father, but he bore little resemblance. Though that wasn't much of an indication of biological kinship with all the mods available these days. In the second case were pants and a flight jacket, as well as a perfectly legal blaster. Nothing else.

Alek squatted back and rubbed his face, trying to think of other places *he'd* hide nefarious orders or a secret comms unit. Light glinted off the frame, and he picked it up again, moving it back and forth. The image inside moved, and Alek startled, dropping his free hand behind him to keep himself upright. Hitting something soft, he glanced down; his hand had landed in Severn's box full of clothes. Looking back at the image, he realized it was a vid on a loop, not a live display. The man smiled at the camera, and his blue eyes lit up. Aqua eyes, with a touch of green Severn's lacked. A wave of nausea ripple through Alek as he realized where he'd seen eyes that shade before. It was such a rare colour. *Like Ben's.*

He didn't want to believe it, and turned the image over, hunting for some other explanation but half expecting a super-miniature subspace comms unit on the back. Then his forehead furrowed and his head tipped sideways as he looked at his other arm. The one buried wrist deep in the crate, palm resting on the bottom yet inches from floor level.

"What are you doing?"

Alek spun around in his crouch to face the door, wishing he'd thought to pick up Severn's blaster. But seeing the captain, he forced his face to neutral as he tried to come up with a believable story. "Captain."

"I asked you a question." Rebeka peered down her nose at him, her jaw set and hands on her hips. "Why are you in Severn's quarters when you should be below looking for Ben?"

Alek took a deep breath, then realized there was nothing he could do but tell the truth. Or at least part of it. "I've suspected for a while that we have a saboteur."

She gave him a hard stare then nodded crisply, as if she'd thought the same, but stayed silent and waited for him to continue.

"And I think it's Severn." He handed Rebeka the picture.

She arched an eyebrow. "I know you don't like him, but sabotage?"

He shrugged. "It's either him or me." He nodded at the picture in her hands. "Who does it remind you of?"

Her eyes narrowed, then she turned her attention to the picture. She stared at it for a second before her lips rounded and her eyes widened. "Ben." Her eyes flashed to Alek, her voice hard. "Is this the boy's father?"

He held up his hands. "I don't know. I found it in Severn's case." He tipped his head towards the small, open crate.

"How do I know it's not yours?" she asked.

"Do you agree this is his luggage?" He waved a hand at the case.

She glanced at it then nodded.

"Take a close look at it." His stomach flipped and his hand dropped to the floor as it suddenly felt like the ship was moving through syrup. The expression on Rebeka's face told him she felt it too.

"What's that?" she asked, her eyebrows pulling together.

"I was hoping you could tell me." The ship returned to normal, the sick feeling in his stomach passing. When she shook her head, he continued, "So back to this then." He waved his hand at the luggage in question.

"It looks like a case."

He shrugged. "You might need to get nearer to it. Pay special attention to its dimensions. Outside versus in."

Cautiously, Rebeka knelt by the case, pushing her hand through the man's underwear. "A false bottom." Her eyes flicked to meet his. "Have you opened it?"

He shook his head. "I just realized it was there when you stopped by."

"You make it sound like a social call." The captain started throwing Severn's clothes on the floor. "Do you have your combat knife?" He hesitated as he debated how to respond, since he knew his knife would reveal a glimpse of his secrets: only soldiers in the King's Guard, the Aspidas, had combat knives with the royal crest. Rebeka lifted her eyes up to peg him with a hard stare. "Don't try to bullshit me. I know you have one, and if you're the type of person I think you are, you have it on you. I promise to give it back."

"I don't..." he started, then stopped. He pulled it out and handed it over. To his surprise, her gaze barely paused at the insignia on the hilt. Instead, she unsheathed it and used it to pry out the false bottom.

She whistled. Even though he couldn't see into the depths of the crate, he was pretty sure his suspicions were correct by the way her eyes narrowed and her jaw clenched.

"A personal comms unit. Ansible enabled."

"That's an expensive piece of tech."

"Beyond even an Aspidan's pay?" Rebeka cocked an eyebrow even as she stared at the offending equipment. She yanked it out with a hard tug and threw it against the wall, breaking it into pieces. Standing up, she turned her fiery eyes to him, clenching his knife in her hand. "I'm going to kill him."

"Um, maybe not with my knife." He nodded at her hand. She looked down, flipped the hilt towards him and handed it back.

"No, that would be too easy given what he's done to my crew."

46: Tink

"Severn," Tink said as the computer tech's head popped around the corner. She tried to plaster a smile on her face while swallowing her too-big piece of candy. A coughing fit ensued.

"Hey, Kandi and I are doing a survey of the ship, making sure nothing's too broken." He stepped in and squatted beside them, making himself comfortable. "How's everything in here?"

"Fine. We're just doing some routine checks on the engine, aren't we, Ben?" The boy nodded but stayed silent. Tink stood and Severn joined her but kept his eyes on Ben.

"Oooh, supernova blasts!" With a broad smile, Severn nodded towards the bag Ben clutched in one hand. The other rested on top of the cat, who sat in his lap. "Those used to be my favourite. I loved how they sizzled on your tongue." He stepped forward, tipping his chin to the boy. "But I haven't had one in years."

Ben continued to stroke Grim in silence as he glanced between Tink and Severn. The cat started to mrowl deep in his belly.

Severn leaned in towards Tink. "I hope I didn't say anything wrong."

"He's quiet. You know that." She tipped her head, as she tucked her chain ratchet into her toolbelt then stuffed her hands into her pockets, which she discovered were empty except for an oily rag poking out of one. Her voice was barely a whisper when she continued. "And now that I think about it, Grim has never liked you." She kept an eye on him as she inched open her tool chest.

Severn shifted closer to Ben. "Can I have one?"

"Sure," the boy said quietly as he proffered the bag to Severn, upsetting Grim. The cat hissed, then scurried into the snarl of wires and conduits. Ben moved to stop him, but Severn's hand snatched the boy's wrist.

"I don't think so." His voice became hard, holding none of the warmth he'd used speaking to her. He hauled Ben to him as he pulled out a tiny blaster — small but still deadly — and pointed at the boy's temple. "You're not getting away again." He jerked his chin at Tink, peering at her over Ben's head. "Hands where I can see them."

Tink paused her rooting around. She turned to stare at him through narrowed eyes, but otherwise she didn't move. Only when the whine of the blaster charging filled the air did she raise her hands, abandoning her quest for some sonic snaps.

"Over here, slowly."

She did as he asked, ignoring the nuts and bolts that started to vibrate on her workbench. Releasing Ben's wrist, he reached behind his back and pulled out a circlet of pulsing lights and handed it to her.

"Put that around his head."

Tink fumbled with the loop. "What are you going to do with us?" she asked, trying to distract Severn from the rattling rising around them. In front of her, Ben's lips were pressed thin and the skin around his eyes tight. Out of the corner of her eye, she noticed a pair of pincers hovering above the grating they'd been lying on a second before.

"I'm going to take *him* back where he belongs. To the people he belongs to." Severn's words were clipped. "So they can put him back in his cage. With you? Nothing if you turn this ship around right now and head back to the Dominion proper."

Tink snorted, pausing in her movement to lower the circlet over Ben's head so she could scowl at Severn. "And why would I believe that?"

He ignored her, instead jerking his chin at the loop. "Hurry up."

"Or what?" Tink didn't move.

"Or I kill you and everyone else on board before I take the boy anyway." Severn's voice rose, echoing in the engine room. "My ride is already on its way. Having you take me back is just a convenience. And frankly, I'm tired of this ship and everyone on it." A smile, lopsided and lecherous, formed on his face. "Except you. I had fun with you."

Her checks flushed with anger as a memory of his fingers on her hips flashed through her brain. Instead, she focused on his comment about killing them. "And how would you explain that away, a ship full of dead people?" She looked down at Ben without moving her head as a couple of rivets rattled past her feet.

"You have a Cass AI." His lips arched in a sneer. "I don't need to explain it." As he finished, he seemed to realize what was happening around him. He paused just as a tool flew through the air and struck the back of his head. Unfortunately, it was one of the soft mallets used for delicate hammering — Tink didn't even know why she had it, other than that it had belonged to her uncle — but it was enough to throw him off balance and release his grip on Ben.

Tink grabbed the boy's wrist and hauled him into the jungle of cables, conduits and machinery that filled the engine room, hitting the main light switch as she passed to plunge the space into a starry night of emergency lights and status beacons.

Crouching between the processed fuel conduit and the cycler housing, Tink felt a warm droplet fall on her hand. It was hard to see in the dim light, but glancing at Ben's ghostly face, she knew what it was. She took the oily rag out of her back pocket and dabbed the blood from his lip and chin, placing her other hand on his shoulder. Despite the heat from the surrounding machinery, the boy was shaking, clearly drained by the effort of moving tools around the engine room.

"Sorry," he said, his voice thin.

Tink shook her head and touched her finger to her lips. "We have to be quiet," she mouthed, even though he was barely audible above the sounds of the engine.

He leaned close as if to speak but stopped when a new sound emerged.

Clunk. Clink. Clunk. She recognized the noise instantly. Boots against the honeycomb grating of the floor.

"Tink. I know you're still in here." Severn's words echoed through the canyons of metal and plex and silicone created by the machinery. "I could take you with me...keep you as my little secret."

Tink was on the verge of telling him she'd rather be dead when his next words stunned her into silence.

"Come out into the light, come out into the night, under the stars, into my arms." His warbled rendition of an atrocious love ballad filled her engine room, breaking her concentration. He stopped singing but continued his monologue. "Do you think your friends are going to come to your rescue? After you lied to them?"

Tink shuffled forward a little, ignoring Ben's grasping hand. A whistling started, and it took her a few seconds to realize what it was: the ballad without words. A circle of light swept back and forth along the aisle. Severn had picked up a torch...her torch. She clenched her jaw as she grasped in the dark for ideas.

"Besides, I've already taken care of Ish."

She paused, her stomach clenching, but forced herself to not respond.

"He won't be waking up for a while. If he wakes up at all."

Tink looked up, wondering if Cass would hear her if she whispered to ask after Ish.

"And Alek. Well, let's just say he has secrets he needs to keep."

Tink pursed her lips, keeping them tightly shut, and pushed herself back to Ben. Looking at her with his eyes large in the dark, he pressed his palm to the grating. Tink's stomach heaved as the ship suddenly felt sluggish, like it was moving through atmo thick as molasses.

"What are you doing?" Severn's voice was harsh as it bounced off the walls. She didn't know what Ben was doing, but she knew it was big. And big meant bad for him, it seemed. She placed her hand on his — it was ice cold — and shook her head.

"No." When she spoke, the word came out as hardly more than a sigh. Still, she felt it when he stopped and the ship returned to normal.

A buzzing sound reached Tink's ears. It was familiar, but she couldn't quite place it. She frowned and popped her head up, her eyes just above the cycler housing as she tried to get eyes on what Severn was doing. She couldn't see him. Instead, her gaze fell upon the axial stabilizer. She dropped back down, her cheeks hot as a plan started to form in her mind. If she could disable it, it would send the ship into a spin. It might be enough to throw him off balance long enough that Ben could run to safety.

Casting her hands around, she looked for a tool to use to disable the stabilizer. A screwdriver, even a shim. But there was nothing. All she had in her belt was her new chain ratchet.

She collapsed against the housing.

Ben came to sit beside her. "I can help," he said, his hand — no longer ice cold — coming to rest on top of hers, his face serious.

She placed her other hand over his. "I know you can. But not this time. Find something to hold on to. Tight. And be ready to run." She held his eyes until he nodded, then she started to shimmy under the conduits and pipes between her and the stabilizer.

A pop punctuated the buzzing. The ship shivered.

"One little circuit." Severn said, then continued as the ship shuddered again. "Two little circuits." The buzzing turned to a whirr. "Three little circuits, four." Severn's voice got louder as he continued his chant.

An acrid smell filled the air, and Tink's stomach clenched as she realized what the buzzing was: he was taking a laser cutter to her ship. Her whole body flushed with anger. As she finally cleared the equipment, she rose into a sprint.

"Stop."

She didn't listen. A sparkler of light ahead of her told her he'd fired his blaster, hitting metal.

"That was a warning. If you don't stop, I will kill you...after I destroy your ship."

Tink reached the stabilizer and smashed her ratchet into its spinner with all the momentum of her sprint.

47: Rebeka

A S REBEKA STALKED DOWN the corridor towards the bridge, she opened her mouth to ask Cass where Severn was. "Cass —"

That was all she managed before she was thrown against the bulkhead as the ship rocked.

"What the —?" The ship rolled the other way, and she fell to her knees. She hissed as the rough floor grated against the scar of an old injury. Her eyes squinted then widened as she noticed red splotches on the floor ahead. "Where's Ish?"

"You sent him to bed while we search for the boy?" Alek winced as he pulled himself up the wall on the other side of the corridor.

"While *I* searched for the boy." She peered at him as she pushed herself up. Turning her attention to the red spots, she quickly lost hope they might be something other than blood. "Cass, where's Ish?"

"Ishmael is in his quarters."

Rebeka's stomach clenched. Right where the trail of crimson drops led. She jogged the short distance to the navigator's room. The ship juddered again, forcing her to brace herself on the doorjamb. Alek wasn't so lucky, and he grimaced as he hip-checked the wall.

"Cass, open Ish's door."

"The door is locked, Captain."

"Override it. Code alpha-beta-kappa-gamma-yada-yada."

"Is yada-yada actually part of the code?"

She scowled at Alek then shimmied through as the door slid open. Ish lay on the floor. She dropped down beside him, trying to remember her battlefield first aid. Blood seeped from a gash on his side, but she was more worried about the wound on the back of his head, and she thought she should lift his head up to slow the bleeding. *But maybe I shouldn't move him.* She bit her lip, unable to recall the head trauma instructions, so she placed a couple of fingers on his neck. There was a pulse, but she didn't know if it was strong or not.

"Kandi, get to Ish's room now."

"Little busy right now. Trying to figure out why the ship is going catawampus."

Rebeka turned her gaze to Alek. "Relieve her. Send her here." Alek made to stand just as the ship slipped sideways again. He grimaced as he landed hard on his right knee. She grabbed his wrist. "With her kit."

He nodded and headed out of the room, bracing himself on the walls as he went.

A groan drew her attention back to Ish. His eyes fluttered but didn't open. Dried blood covered the shaved side of his scalp where fresh blood, bright red, still seeped from the wound. She pulled off her long-sleeved shirt and pressed it against his head.

Running a hand over his forehead, she frowned. "I'm sorry. You were happy to stay on the bridge, and I treated you like a child." She blinked rapidly. "And after I promised your actual mother that I'd take care of you."

Footsteps sounded in the corridor, and by the time Rebeka turned around, Kandi was in the room. Dropping down beside the navigator, the part-time medic set to work with a fierce intensity. Wrinkles formed at the corners of her eyes as she examined Ish.

After a minute, Kandi lifted her head and blinked. "Why are you here?" She jerked her hand, which held a disinfectant wand. "Go. Help Alek. Figure out what the hell is wrong with this ship before we all end up with our heads bashed in."

Rebeka stood, pausing for a second, then did as she was told and jogged to the bridge as fast as she dared.

48: Tink

A HORRID SCREECH FILLED the engine room as the axial stabilizer reacted to a chain ratchet being tossed into it. The sound pierced Tink's heart. The *Lyra* seemed to hold its breath, and time paused. Then the ship juddered, and the stern slipped sideways. The movement threw her into the solid metal of the inner hull just as another blaster shot hit the ceiling above her head, sending down a cascade of sparks.

The wild shot told her that Severn had been unprepared for the ship's spin. She shook her head to clear it, and tried to grab onto something, anything, to keep herself steady. Pain seared through her right shoulder when she moved, but her hand landed on a pipe carrying coolant to the engine. The cold seeped through the metal to sting her skin. As the ship shifted wildly again, she heard a curse. Peeking over the unhappy stabilizer, she saw Severn shaking a red hand. Glancing up, she smiled at the expellant pipe above his head.

"Serves you right for messing with my ship." A flash and ball of heat over her left shoulder suggested she'd be wiser to stay silent.

"This could have been easy. I told the truth when I said I'd take you with me. But, no, you had to be stubborn." The ship rolled again, but she didn't hear any stumbling or swearing, only the steady clunk of boots on grating. "What kind of Tinker damages their own ship? No wonder the empire purged the rest of your insane clan. Now you can join your uncle."

Tink's blood pounded in her ears as her anger flared again. But fury had an upside — it drowned the nausea of the bucking ship. She bit back her retort and crawled to the far side of the stabilizer, where a lever was attached to the edge of the cycler amendment tank...ready to be put into use to lift the lid manually if need be. Or bash treacherous brains in. Twisting the lever free, she fell back against the stabilizer, the metal warm on her back.

"You've made a big misstep, haven't you?" she said, which resulted in another spray of blaster-induced sparks too close to her head. The footsteps neared as she did some quick math on her fingers: *four shots spent.* "First, thinking I cared more about my ship than my friends. And second, what will your employers do when they discovered you've failed?"

"I haven't failed yet." She could hear the sneer in his voice as he fired another shot. A spark singed her skin. The footsteps stopped.

"And that's five," she said as she popped up to standing, the lever at her side. Severn smirked at her, leveling the blaster at her head. He pulled the trigger, then his eyes opened wide and his nostrils flared as the weapon whined. Tink stepped forward, swinging the lever. "Those wee weapons are convenient for hiding," she said as Severn staggered back, dodging just out of her range. "But their charge only holds five shots."

She followed through on her momentum and jabbed Severn in the stomach with the pointy end of the lever. It forced the air out of his lungs and made him stumble and fall backward onto the decking. Unfortunately, the lever didn't draw blood. She strode over to him, ready to bring the bar down on his head if need be. Standing over him, she hesitated...she'd never killed a person. She didn't even kill the bugs that lived in the ship's nooks and crannies. She left that to Grim.

Instead, she dropped her knee into his abdomen, using her body weight to add force to the impact. She pushed the bar across his throat in an attempt to cut off his air until he blacked out. Then the ship spun again, and she tumbled sideways, landing on her already bruised right side. Pulling herself up onto hands and knees, she coughed, trying to orient herself. The lever twisted from her grasp as Severn wrested it from her. A second later, he was sitting astride her back, forcing her to the floor. The bar ended up across her throat.

Severn pulled back hard, and stars filled her vision. "You know one benefit of being a Omega division agent?" His voice whispered in her ear, his tone flat. "Extensive training in all the deadly arts where they break us." He pulled the bar tighter, not budging as the ship heaved once more. "And break us again." Black started to creep across Tink's eyes as he pulled the rod tighter. She clawed at the bar, her mouth moving but unable to draw enough air into her lungs. "And they keep breaking us until we die or we can't be broken anymore. Then they mould the survivors into killers who can fight anywhere."

Stars speckled Tink's vision, telling her she was close to passing out, when she noticed a grey blur in amongst the stars. For a moment, she thought it was only a fuzzy spot created by her oxygen-starved brain, then it resolved into a four-legged form. She tried to shake her head, but the bar across her throat prevented her. Hissing like an Andoran asp, Grim skidded to a halt at Severn's side, challenging him with all his sharp, pointy bits exposed.

Severn seemed to accept the cat's challenge because the pressure eased from Tink's neck. She coughed as she clutched her throat where the bar had been. Then she watched in horror as Severn swung it at Grim, making contact across the side of the cat's abdomen. A sob escaped her tight throat as his small form flew through the air and struck the bulkhead. Grim slid to the floor, where he lay unmoving.

Her fingers grasped at the grating, trying to pull herself towards the cat as Severn advanced on him.

"No," she said, but it was barely more than a whisper through her battered throat.

"No," a louder voice said. Tink closed her eyes as tears formed in the corners. *Ben*. He hadn't listened. He hadn't run. She watched, unable to do anything as Severn turned slowly to the boy, a sneer forming on his lips.

"They certainly didn't breed you for intelligence, did they?" He jerked his chin toward the cat then looked back at the boy. "After I kill that creature, you're next." He spit the words out as he turned back to Grim.

Tink pushed herself up on all fours and started crawling towards Severn. *If I can just....* But another erratic turn of the ship flung her sideways, and what little air she had was knocked out of her. Her back would be as bruised as her side after this. If she survived at all.

Through star-filled eyes, she saw that Severn hadn't yet hit the cat with the lever he clutched over his head. In fact, he was moving as if through a vat of bearing grease, even though every muscle in his body was tense.

"I. Said. No." Ben's fists clenched at his sides, tension holding him stiff. Glancing at him, she realized the boy held Severn frozen in place. Blood dripped in a steady stream from Ben's nose, and purple bruises marred the skin under his eyes. He took plodding steps towards Severn, and Tink pulled herself after him, trying to grasp at his clothes to stop him. But her fingers caught only air.

She watched Ben reach out an open palm to the back of Severn's head. But then Ben fell to his knees, and Severn was able to move again. He turned, pulled the lever back, and prepared to strike.

"No." Tink closed her eyes, not wanting to watch, but unable to stop it. But what she heard next forced her to look. It wasn't the sound of a boy's skull being crushed, or even of a cat being hit. It was the sound of Severn babbling in a language she didn't understand.

Opening her eyes, she saw Severn fall to his knees in front of Ben, cheeks flushed, the forgotten lever falling from his fingers with a clatter. The man's eyes were wide as he gesticulated towards Ben. Unintelligible words spat from his mouth, and the more he babbled, the wilder his eyes became.

Tink mustered all her strength and, ignoring the muscles and tendons that cried out in protest, dragged herself to Ben. "What..." she started but stopped when an angry juddered coursed through the *Lyra*.

"I scrambled him." Ben's eyes peered at her, glistening. His mouth twitched. Tink wrapped her arms around him and the unconscious Grim, steadying them as the ship swung wildly again.

49: ∆lek

THE SHIP MOANED ITS unhappiness as Alek tried to force it to do his bidding. The control stick juddered in his hands. The *Lyra* was going to fight him to the end. Which might be soon given the increasing frequency of the chaotic spins that hampered his attempts at navigating the maze deployed around the Sisters' station. Barely visible blips of light marked the 'walls' made up of a matrix of mines. The fact that Alek had to squint to make out the pinpoints of light and matte grey against the black meant they were armed...and the *Lyra* hadn't been invited in.

He had no choice but to attempt to fly it by sight since Cass hadn't yet answered any of his requests to overlay a map on the viewscreen.

"Cass, what y'at?" His jaw clenched tight as he spoke. The AI remained ominously silent.

"Any idea what's going on?" Rebeka asked from over his shoulder, as Kandi tumbled into the bridge and flopped at her station.

"Maybe not crashing us, that's an idea," Kandi said. The ship shuddered in response.

"I meant why we're slip-sliding all over the place."

Alek shook his head, trying to find space to think while keeping the ship from spinning out again. "It feels like the axial stabilizer is gone. But that makes no sense."

"Why?" A weak voice filtered in from the doorway.

"Ish!" Kandi jumped up, but her exclamation cut short by a grunt when the ship slipped sideways. A muttered curse followed.

"I didn't clear you to get out of bed."

"I'm fine."

Out of the corner of his eye, Alek saw Ish push against Kandi as she tried to get him to sit in Severn's seat beside hers.

"You're in your pyjamas," she said as the ship shimmied, struck by a bit of space junk. "But now that you're here, sit." She tried to push him down but gave up when he struggled too much.

"Sit down, both of you, and latch in." The captain's tone brooked no argument, and Ish stumbled into his seat beside Alek. Alek heard the click of a latching harness and nodded his approval.

"We're starting to hit some debris." Alek's jaw clenched. "It's like the Sisters haven't cleaned out the remains of previous interlopers from their maze." He tugged at the stick, nudging the ship away. "Buckle up."

"Back to Ish's question, why?" Rebeka asked. "Why can't the axial stabilizer be malfunctioning?"

"It's such an easy piece of equipment to keep ticking." Alek pressed a pedal at his foot as the ship tugged sideways. He gave the portside engine a little more juice. "You'd malign Tink's engineering to say it's malfunctioning." He tapped left as the ship shimmied again.

"It's not a..." Ish took a laboured breath in. "...malfunction." Alek spared a quick glance at his co-pilot. Instead of the usual slipstream ripples and waves, his display showed lines of code in varied colours. "Bastard!" Ish said with more oomph that Alek thought him capable of right now.

"So, what is it then?" Alek's gaze slid sideways as he struggled to keep the ship from sliding into a mine.

"Severn."

"Severn." Rebeka's voice was sharp as a laser.

Ish nodded. "When he bashed me over the head, he said..."

Glancing right again, Alek saw a flush on the navigator's cheeks.

Ish huffed out a breath. "He said he'd make sure there was another Cassandra event." He plucked at his display, flicking his fingers through letters and numbers. "He's definitely messed with her." Ish shook his head. "I'll see if I can sort her out, but it'll take time."

Alek swore he heard a growl behind him before the captain spoke. "Maybe he took out the stabilizer too."

Ish didn't say anything as he glanced from his display to the viewscreen. "Um, station." Alek returned his focus forward to the station looming large on the screen. The maze had...disappeared. There was no sign of the mines that had blocked their way a few seconds ago.

"Can you dock the ship like this?" Rebeka asked.

Alek didn't answer, using all his strength to help keep the nose of the *Lyra* pointed in the right direction, the ship still fighting him. The scar tissue in his shoulder seared in pain, but he ignored it. After a minute, the ship gave a little.

"Good ship," he whispered as he shrugged his shoulders. The sweat on his back caused his shirt to stick to his skin. "If it *is* the stabilizer, I can correct by adjusting the —" He reached over to the far end of his console as another judder nearly tore the stick from his grasp. "...the...."

He was forced to abandon his quest and grip the stick with both hands. A thump sounded beside him, and he glanced sidelong to see the captain jab a button on the console.

"Adjusting off the inertial dampers on the starboard side," she said, rubbing her left side as the ship settled into an unhappy path toward the station, shivering with displeasure every now and then but otherwise behaving.

Alek nodded sharply then breathed in deeply, willing his muscles to relax. For the most part they complied, except for the one shoulder. Maybe the Sisters of Elazir could give him some poison...potion. If he managed to get the ship and its crew through this last part alive.

50: TINK

T INK GAZED OUT AT the *Lyra*, sparkling bright in the inky sky outside the station, showing few signs of their recent escapades. She hadn't let the Sisters touch her engines. She'd fixed the axial stabilizer herself, all the while apologizing to the *Lyra*.

She'd only allowed the Sisters to patch the outsides of both the ship and herself. Watching them the whole time. Tapping her long fingers on her leg, she waited for the rest of the crew to join her. She hadn't talked to them much since arriving, preferring to stay with her ship, overseeing the Sisters' mechanists work, while the others explored the station. She didn't know if they were still angry that she'd kept her status as owner of the *Lyra* a secret.

Gazing out at the ship, her back faced the Tiered Gardens of Elazir, one of the 1000 Wonders of the Universe. Right up there with the Sisters' station itself, with its ability to disappear from normal space, presumably into the slipstream, even though the next largest thing to navigate the stream was...well, the Leviathan.

But to Tink the marvel was that the *Lyra* was in one piece and looked almost new. She sighed, taken by a sudden wave of melancholy. At what point would the *Lyra* cease to be the ship she'd grown up on? Quit being the ship her uncle had given her a home on after her parents abandoned her? Stop being the ship he'd left her in his will?

Prodding her side with her fingers, she barely felt the bruising from being bashed around the engine room. The Sisters' healing prowess was legendary for a reason. And somehow it hadn't cost them a single chit. Her eyebrows tugged together. A flicker in the glass caught her eye. She turned to peer at the person who'd come to stand beside her. *Ish*.

"I..." they both said at the same time. Ish fell silent, looking out at the *Lyra*.

"I'm sorry," Tink said. "For not telling you about, you know, the ship being mine."

He shook his head, bringing his hand to her elbow. "It's okay. We'd only just met. I get why you kept it a secret." He turned to meet her gaze. "I would've treated you differently, and we wouldn't be the friends we are." Dropping his hand, clasping it behind his back, he returned to look out the window. Tink followed his lead. "And once you keep a secret, it's hard to unkeep. But now, I think we can still be friends, despite you being the boss."

Tink scoffed, glancing over her shoulder as she heard steps behind them. "I think we both know the captain is the boss of both of us."

"True." He tipped his head then turned away from the window, leaning against the buttress, arms crossed over his chest.

Tink turned to the others, smiling at Ben. She swore he'd grown taller in the few days they'd been with the Sisters, his head almost the height of her shoulder. Though he still had no hair.

"Are you sure you won't come with us?"

He nodded. "This is the best place for me to stay." He turned his big, sea-blue eyes on her. "For all of us." She wrapped him in a powerful hug, like the ones her uncle used to give when he was being very avuncular, which caused the cat in his arms to grumble. She pulled away and ruffled the fur on Grim's head. The cat stared daggers at her, but she didn't care. The smile on her face started to falter.

"You should keep him," she said, looking from the cat to Ben. "He's taken a shine to you. He can keep you company as you settle in."

Ben returned her smile, then the smile fell. He shook his head. "I can't protect him." His voice dropped lower. "I don't have the same powers here."

Tink inhaled sharply — it was the first time he'd acknowledged he was different somehow. "How will you protect yourself then?"

He straightened, standing even taller. "I can take care of myself. I escaped, didn't I?"

"No, you...." She realized she had no idea how he'd ended up in a crate on the Leviathan.

He sunk his face into the spot between the cat's ears then lifted his head, his smile back, more subdued. "No, a ship cat belongs on a ship." As if to punctuate his words, Grim jumped out of his arms and sauntered over to the door leading to the docks, where he proceeded to lift his leg and start cleaning himself. It seemed the Sisters had worked their magic on him too.

"Thanks." Tink turned back to Ben with a half-smile, half-grimace. "If you need anything...."

"I'm not the one who will need help," the boy said. His gaze shifted over her shoulder and became unfocused as he peered out at space, his eyebrows twitching. "Be careful of the sea serpent. There's a kraken in the deep that will try to kill the lion."

Tink squinted and shifted from one foot to the other, then opened her mouth to speak, but Ben shook his head then looked at her again, a grin on his face. Hearing footsteps behind them, she turned.

Rebeka walked towards them, the Sister Prime at her side. The Sister wore no makeup, and her headdress dug into the skin at the side of her face. Despite her placid smile, the woman's sharp eyes flicked from Tink to Ish to Ben. She even examined the cat in a split second as she and the captain came to a stop.

"You're sure you're okay taking care of Severn Lynch?" Rebeka asked. "We can't pay you to tend to him." It was probably the tenth time Tink heard her ask the question in the few times she'd seen Rebeka on the station. But the Sister just smiled serenely behind her gauzy headscarf.

"We do have some capacity to care for those who cannot pay. It's our sworn duty, in fact." Her voice lilted through the humid, flower-scented air. The purveyors of culture thought the gardens beautiful. Tink found them cloying. The Sister's tone deepened as she continued, her head shaking softly. "And we have much experience caring for those whose minds are broken. And his is a very broken mind." Her gaze slid to Ben.

"And the boy..." the captain paused. "After our next contract, we can give you some money for his keep. And the repairs too."

A tinkling laugh that grated on Tink emanated from behind the fabric swathing the Sister's mouth. "Nonsense. Part of our mission is to care for orphans as well. And as for the ship, it's not every day we see a ship with a CASS-ANDRA AI. Besides, we're happy to help friends of Kandira." The woman's gaze slid to said friend, and though she couldn't be sure, Tink thought the *Lyra*'s medic-security officer flinched slightly. The Sister reached out her hand, palm up.

"Thank you." Rebeka nodded sharply, placing her own hand on the outstretched one. "If there's anything —"

"We should probably be going soon." Alek muscled between the Sister and the captain with his shoulder bag. "We do really appreciate the hospitality, but if there's one thing my mother taught me, it's to leave as a happy memory rather than as a rotten guest."

The Sister's eyes shifted to Alek's face, focusing sharply. "Your mother taught you well, Alek Wa," she said, the serene smile back on her lips. Then she slowly turned her body to Kandi. "Kandira, I hope you had a good visit." Kandi nodded, shuffling from one foot to the other as she looked down at her shoes. The Sister placed one hand on Kandi's head. "I'm sure it heartened him to see you."

Kandi lifted her head to look the woman in the eyes. "Yes." She nodded sharply. "I was surprised to find you elevated to Prime."

The Sister shrugged, though Tink noted a tightening at the corners of her smile. "I live to serve. And I do my duty." An eyebrow quirked, almost as if she hadn't meant it to, and she held her other hand out to Kandi in the small space between them. Tink caught sight of a cylinder in the palm. "Be well," the woman said, her voice low.

"I will." Kandi snatched the object from the Sister and slid her hand into her jacket pocket.

The Sister Prime returned her attention to Rebeka. Flicking her hand, the door behind them slid open. "Fare well amongst the stars." She bowed her head slightly and took a sliding step back. "Go through the jump gate. It will take you past your hunters."

The question of what jump gate formed on Tink's lips as she turned to the door. But it died and withered in her dry mouth, a trill of fear rippling through her veins, as she watched a patch of dark space beyond the window shimmer into a circle of blue waves.

51: Rebeka

R EBEKA BLINKED AT THE spot where the jump gate had rippled out of existence a second ago, blue fading into black.

"Well," Rebeka said when no other words came to her brain. Stars flickered into being where the gate had been, leaving no hint that space had just been distorted. The Sisters had called it out of nothingness — it wasn't there, then it was, and now just as quickly it was gone. The Dominion's jump gates were monstrous constructions, and it took the materials of a planet and the energy of a sun to construct and maintain the bridges to other gates.

"Those Sisters have some mad skills," Ish said, his mouth agape as he gazed at the viewscreen.

"Mad tech," Tink added, absentmindedly stroking Grim who kneaded her lap, as she squinted at the screen. Rebeka didn't disagree with either of them.

"They do at that," Alek said, shifting in his seat. He didn't sound impressed, and Rebeka didn't disagree with that sentiment either. She watched his jaw clench as he turned to his display.

"Are you sure the Sisters will take care of Ben?" Tink asked, tipping her head to Kandi.

Kandi nodded, keeping her eyes focused on her console. "You saw their station. It's not like the Sisters need the money from selling him, even if they could. But they swear unbreakable vows, and whatever else they do, they take those vows very seriously." She stopped fiddling with the buttons and sliders in front of her, and Rebeka heard her swallowing.

"What about this new Sister Prime?" Rebeka asked, her eyes narrowing.

Kandi's ponytail swished as she shook her head. "No one told me the previous Prime had died since I last visited. But it doesn't matter. The vow is the vow."

"Did the old woman's death have something to do with whatever the new Prime gave you?" Tink asked, and Kandi's head spun around, her eyes wide.

She shook her head after a few seconds and reached into her pocket. When she pulled out her hand and opened the palm, it held a small cylinder. Wrapping her fingers around it, she flicked her wrist. In a blur, the cylinder morphed into a staff as long as Kandi was tall. "A piece of my battle armour. Hard earned." She looked down at the staff with an expression akin to reverence, and Rebeka could understand why. It was beautifully crafted and exquisitely balanced. And an Antaran would never let her armour out of her possession. Not until death, and even then, it was often buried with them if there were no daughters to claim it.

"Why —" Ish started.

Kandi's sharp look stopped him. "I needed their help, and they needed payment."

Swallowing the tightness in her throat, Rebeka vowed to learn more about the business of the Sisters of Elazir beyond medicine. She was glad that Alek had stopped her from offering a favour in return for them taking care of the boy.

"Any idea where we are?" she asked the room instead, forestalling any more questions.

Alek flicked his fingers over his console and a holographic projection appeared in front of the viewscreen, showing a map of the surrounding space.

"The Green Zone," he said, his tone flat.

Rebeka gave him a caustic look, even though she could see for herself that he wasn't lying. She sighed. She'd already spent more of her life than she cared to in the lawless sector of space nestled between rigid Dominion security and the rules of the cartels.

52: Harbin

H ARBIN LOW HELD HIS head high and his shoulders back, even though he expected he was marching to his death. Always look death in the eye, his mother had said. In fact, she said it right before she left to fly a suicide mission into rebel territory when he was only eleven. His jaw clenched, but he kept moving.

His ship had just docked. As he'd left it, Delphi Liet had held his gaze, her expression unreadable. Perhaps calculating how she'd take control of the ship when he didn't come back. They had a berth in the belly of Halcyon Koning's station orbiting Metropolis — the mother planet of the Dominion. Despite being so close to the absolute centre of ultimate power, despite technically being a soldier of the empire, he knew he belonged to her. She'd been his Archon since she'd plucked him out of the orphanage he'd been sent to following his mother's death. At the time, Halcyon had been its patron, only a Consul then, and came to survey its wards. Always on the lookout for talent. Perhaps she'd seen his potential after he'd stabbed that other boy in the hand for stealing his bread.

And now his potential would come to naught, all because of that pissant ship and her derelict crew. Harbin huffed out a breath of air, his nostrils flaring. Something prodded the tight muscles of his back, and he realized he'd come to a stop.

He refocused his gaze on the present. Before him, doors the height of five men rose. Made of real wood gilt with real gold, they each must have weighed as much as ten men. But they opened smoothly to admit him, with no indication of how. His minders stayed outside as the doors swiftly but silently closed behind him. The breath of the massive doors closing whispered at his heels and propelled him forward. His boots clicked as he crossed the tile floor, towards the woman who stood beside a fireplace filled with pyroplasmic flames, her back to him. On either side of the fireplace, large windows set in delicate, upside-down wishbone frames looked out onto the stars. The top panels of each held a snake-like creature rendered in tinted plex and gemstones. In the hearth, the purple hue of the flames contrasted with the green and gold tile that framed the fireplace.

But that was nothing compared to the shimmer of silver and gold that was Halcyon Koning. She wasn't a young woman, and she was one of the few who was happy to let the world see that. A headdress topped her silver hair, the delicate gold shivering even though she stood marble still. A gold and diamond tunic hung from her narrow shoulders, skimming over a slight figure. She wore loose pants with sandals seemingly made of filaments of light on her feet. Even as a child, he'd been dumbstruck by the casual way she carried opulence and power. On her unmodded face, lines crinkled at the corner of the sharp eyes she flicked his way.

Harbin dropped to his knee before her, and his eyes focused on her feet. For a long few minutes, they didn't move. Then the shimmer shifted slightly, and he felt the woman's hand fall lightly on the top of his head.

"You've disappointed me, Harbin." Her tone was even, a whisper almost, soon lost in the vast space. The pressure in her grip increased, the fingernails biting into his scalp, and he was again surprised that such a slight frame could hold so much power. She forced his head around, though he didn't resist, until he was looking into the flames. Out of the corner of his eye he noticed a flick of movement, then the fire changed to an image.

The *Lyra*.

"I gave you a simple task." Her voice grew louder, an edge to the words. "Find this ship and retrieve my property." Harbin felt blood trickle through his hair, almost tickling, as her grip grew tighter. Quiet again, she continued. "I had faith in you, but you failed me." There was silence, and Harbin's face flushed as the fire shifted again to a series of faces.

"Do you see the faces, Harbin?" Harbin didn't answer. "Not rhetorical." Her voice was hard and glacial. "Do you see them?"

Harbin tried to nod despite the grip on his scalp. "Yes." The word came out as a hoarse whisper.

"Can you remember them?"

"Yes," he hissed, his tone injected with venom as he forced it through his dry mouth.

She leaned down so her words whispered over his ear. "That is the crew of the *Lyra*." Grasping his head tighter, she turned it again so he faced her. Bringing her hand, slick with his own blood, to his chin, she lifted his head up, almost gently, until he was looking in her black eyes. Lined with age at the corners, they reflected the hues of the fire. Her face was serene except for the sharpness of her gaze and the hard line of her mouth. "Do you know what you need to do?"

"Yes," he said, his voice stronger. Apparently, he wasn't going to die today.

"Tell me."

"Find the *Lyra*. Kill her crew. Painfully, if possible."

"Yes." A smile crept into her lips, and Harbin's heart tightened. The Archon Halcyon Koning was most beautiful when she was contemplating death.

Did you enjoy a Dead Ship in the Deep Black?

I WOULD APPRECIATE IT if you'd leave a review – it lets me know people enjoy what I'm putting out there and helps more people discover the book. If you want to know what happens next, check out a sample of Book 2 – *A Lost Ship in a Dark Grave* – after the glossary.

And if you want to keep up on the series, have early access to side stories, and get special peeks behind the scenes, sign up for my newsletter at reneastle.com.

People, Places and Events

Ansibles: Communication stations that relay signals across the vast distances of the Dominion near instantaneously. Origins of ansible tech unknown.

Antillia: Planet home to some creepy crawlies...salesmen and insects.

Archon: Ruler of an imperial clan in the Emperor's name. Technically reports to Taxarchon.

Argent, The: A ship, Barracuda class, under the command of Harbin Low, a leader in the Tau division.

Aspidas, The: The Emperor's Own guard. Must be a member of imperial family to join. They might be privileged but they're also brutal and efficient. As a concept: the Aspida. Individual member: Aspidan.

Badlands, The: Area of space at the edge of the Dominion, nestled between the core empire and the Desolation. Home to the desperate and the destitute.

Bakweevil: Large beetle endemic to cargo ships that haul provisions.

Barnacles: Mild swear word, similar in intensity to Jacks.

Bleeding Hades: Swear word, stronger that Barnacles.

Cartels: Organized crime conglomerates. Some of the most prominent are Mantas, Kraits, Haggishi and Bullheads.

Cassandra event: Destruction of spaceship and station, put down to a fault in a CASS-ANDRA AI. Afterwards, most Cass AIs were decommissioned.

Centauri Convention: Law that restricted human bioengineering and banned the use of non-human genetic material in humans. Not to say it doesn't happen — it's just illegal.

Chit: Slang for official digital currency common of the Dominion.

Clan Koning: Prominent imperial clan, currently ruled by Archon Halcyon Koning.

Clan Erregina: Prominent imperial clan, currently ruled by Archon Tyre Erregina.

Connect, The: Interstellar information network spanning the Dominion. Reliant on ansibles.

Custard Bug: Insect. Larval stage is plump with creamy insides. Used to create scrambles as well as desserts.

Desolation, The: Area of space, location of an ancient cataclysm. Few dare to tread there, fearing ghosts or aliens...or both. Home only those too far gone for even the Badlands and to the Sisters of Elazir. Separated from the Dominion by the Wall.

Dominion, The: The empire that controls most of the known universe, both a spatial and political entity. The power of the known universe, spanning all the way from the Desolation to the no-man's land claimed by the cartels. Ruled by the Emperor, supported by the imperial clans. Peace and stability are maintained by the Legion and SIPS.

Emperor: Reclusive ruler of the Dominion. The Emperor's power is absolute.

Euko Station: Third-tier space station that only exists because it is the anchor station for a third-tier jump gate.

Fifth Echelon: Elite divisions of the Legion, with extra-special training and skills: Ki, Omega, Phi, Tau, Epsilon.

Green Zone, The: Area of space between core Dominion and the regions claimed by the cartels. Despite nominal Legion patrols, lawlessness is the norm.

Guilds: Corporations that drive the economy. Some say they control it.

Hail Hecate: Invocation of thanks to the goddess of magic, doorways, crossroads and jump gates.

Hatari Convention: Law requiring every Dominion planet to allow any adult of legal age to leave their home world. People must be free to find another planet more suitable, or find no home and wander the black.

Hauer Gate: One of the oldest jump gates, site of a huge battle where the Dominion consumed that last holdouts of the Coalition of Independent Planets ("the Coalition").

Hera Wept: Curse, an utterance of exasperation.

Hudsonite Brigade: Under the leadership of Marpo Gothe, the most powerful faction of the loose, fractious organization of rebel groups. Fighting for the abrogation of the Dominion and divestiture of the Emperor.

Jacks: Mild swear word, similar in intensity to Barnacles.

Jump gates: Shortcuts between two points in space built and run by the Dominion. Alternative to the slipstream —

cheaper and don't require an navigator, human or AI. But the Dominion knows your business.

Klicks: Measure of distance (also kiloklicks and megaklicks).

Legion, The: Main imperial armed forces supposedly loyal to the Emperor, and tangentially the imperial family. But loyalty can be bought as well as earned. Organized into divisions named from Alpha to Omega, each with special skills and training.

Lyra, The: Jack-of-all cargo ship, trying to stay on the invisible side of the law.

Mantadae Gate: Jump gate and its station, where the *Lyra* picked up Grim — or Grim picked the *Lyra*, depending on your point of view.

Mean Green: Algal converter. Turns algae into fuel.

Passalida: Hedonistic planet of villas and eternal sunshine.

PhiRoZeta: Spatial coordinate system to indicate where something is in relation to another object; for example, where your attackers are in relation to your ship.

Port Nyx: Spaceport between Metropolis and the Badlands. Also called Nyx.

Secretariat of Interplanetary Peace and Stability (SIPS): Local constabulary, keeping order maintained on planet and station. Sometimes they're overzealous.

Silesian Worms: Giant, multi-legged arthropod. Adults are as long as your average cat with the girth of a cat's tail. They live in great nests. You don't want to stumble across one unawares, as you're as likely to be their dinner as they are yours.

Sisters of Elazir (The Sisters): Nominally charitable association that tends to the sick in hospitals across the Dominion. Secretive about their treatment methods, cures can appear magical. The Sisters have amassed wealth and power but are always on the lookout for more.

Slipstream: Methods of subspace travel. Alternative to the Dominion-controlled jump gates. Requires a navigator or sophisticated AI; best to have both — there are monsters in the deep.

Solace: Environmentally controlled planet with managed weather systems; popular vacation destination.

Spivex: Synthetic spider silk woven and shellacked into plating resistant to blaster strikes and other impacts.

Takeshi Blue: Type of impulse drive engine.

Tartarus: Planet in the Badlands.

Tau: One of the divisions of the Legion. Known for incursion skills and never backing down. Also, leader of the division.

Taxarchon: Archon of Archons. Second most powerful office in the Dominion, after the Emperor. Selected from the Archons of the great clans (currently clan Ayaba).

Tiger Ants: Reddish striped ant with a painful sting that can leave limbs swollen and aching. Dried and crushed, can be used as a numbing, peppery seasoning...just don't add too much.

Tower of Solitude: Home base of the Sisters of Elazir, stationed across the Wall. Marvel of technology, it appears and disappears from regular space.

Vulcan V: Jump gate station closest to the Badlands.

Wall, The: Ancient mesh spread across the space to protect the Dominion from the Desolation. When active, it can slice ships into pieces, but it's assumed to be non-functional.

Zeus' Bollocks: a swear word, stronger than Jacks.

Book 2 Excerpt: A Lost Ship in a Dark Grave

1: Alek

"**A**RGH!" ALEK WA YANKED on the control stick, trying to pull the *Lyra* in a sharp loop away from whatever danger had caused the ship to buck and the sirens to blare. The ship moaned its displeasure with what he was doing, and the stick shook in his grip. His shoulder muscles strained, and an old injury threatened to surface. Alek clenched his jaw, fighting the ship.

Despite being able to conjure a gate out of empty space, the Sisters of Elazir apparently couldn't check that the space it dropped them into was clear. Or didn't care enough to check. His lips pressed together and his nostrils flared.

"What the hell is that sound?" Captain Rebeka Mino loomed beside him, peering at the view screen, but it just showed the empty black in front of them. "Cass, a 360 sweep please."

"Rear cameras offline." The AI's calm voice drifted down from over their heads.

"Can you turn the bloody sirens off?" Kandi shouted as she punched a finger into her console. In an instant, an unnatural quiet fell on the bridge. "Here's the last image from the rear...," she started, her voice too loud for the sudden silence.

A slice of a space appeared on the view screen. In the distance, Alek could make out an object, like a doughnut around a post. A flutter rippled through his gut.

"Magnify." Rebeka stepped towards the screen, blocking his view. But he'd already seen all he needed to.

"Bleeding Hades."

A hand fell on his shoulder, and he turned his head to see Tink staring at the viewscreen. Her sentiment echoed his exactly, and tension wrinkled the space between her amber eyes. Alek pulled his gaze away before she caught him looking at her and resumed her usual standoffish demeanor.

"What is it?" Ish said, squinting at the screen.

"A Dominion station." Kandi tapped at her console. "We've been marked. They're sending ships."

"Can you get us out of here, flyboy?" Mino turned to peg him with a hard stare.

"Strap in." He arched an eyebrow. "It's going to be hairy." Rebeka and Tink both did as he said without argument, and he turned back to the controls. "Kandi, is there somewhere nearby we can hide?"

"Working on it." Her voice was tense, her words clipped.

"Looking for slip points." Ish's fingers moved over the holographic ripples in front of him.

"Can someone tell me where we are?" Rebeka's voice filled the bridge, edged with anger. "Besides just the Green Zone. You'd think with the tech to create a jump gate out of empty space, the Sister's could have dropped us somewhere *not* next to a Dominion station."

Alek's eyebrow quirked to hear her echo his thoughts. Even after minimal interaction with the Sisters in their Tower of Solitude, he got the sense that they had their own agenda. The Sisters at the Tower were the upper echelon of power in a powerful faction. They were different from those who served at the local sanctuaries, like the one near where he'd grown up. For one thing, the Sisters at that old sanctuary wouldn't have known him as Alek Wa. A flicker coursed through his intestines: maybe the Sisters at the Tower knew his real name.

"We're inside a solar system..." Tink voice came from behind him.

"Not a lot of help, Tink."

"I'm looking." Although he couldn't see her, he heard her fingers clicking furiously over her console.

"We're next to a gas giant," Kandi said. "There's a series of moons around it. We might be able to hide in there."

Alek didn't say anything as he pushed and pulled the stick, forcing the *Lyra* onto the course Kandi plotted. Something whined as the ship expressed its unhappiness.

"Don't break my ship." Tink's voice was quiet but her tone serious. The whine petered out as the giant blue-green marble appeared on-screen.

"Ship's incoming," Cass said just before sirens started sounding again. "They're sending a message: stand down and prepare to be boarded."

"Not too happy at having a ship pop into being out of empty space, I imagine." Ish sounded way too pleased at that thought given their current predicament.

Alek shoved the stick forward, maxing out the ship's impulse engines, pointing its nose towards a rocky moon that looked like a promising hiding spot. "Hold onto your lunches." He twisted the ship into a roll around the icy moon to their left, hoping the plumes shooting from it would scramble the signal from their pursuers' marks. Without damaging the *Lyra* or her crew.

"Rear cameras back up," Kandi said as a new slice of space appeared on the viewscreen. "They're *Hogfish*." Her smile infused her words. "Slow. Not very maneuverable. The dregs of the Dominion fleet."

"So easy for a hot shot pilot to outrun," Tink said.

When Alek turned to scowl at her, he saw she was smiling. The captain, however, scowled at him. He turned back around to focus on flying.

"There's a slip point outside the orbit of this gas giant. At phi -35°, rho 12, zeta 7."

Alek made a quick calculation. He waited until they were past the rocky moon, and into the shadow of the gas giant, then he tacked, changing course to head towards Ish's slip point.

The silent seconds ticked by and they watched the *Hogfish* recede into the distance.

"I think I know where we are." Ish's tone was subdued as he reached for the holographic map in front of him. With a flick of his fingers, the wavy lines of his slip chart morphed into a star grid. As he rotated it, lines appeared, bisecting the three-dimensional image. The flutter in Alek's stomach turned to icy rock.

"Canacus." The anger in Mino's voice turned cold. A blue blip showed their location near the edge of Dominion-patrolled space. At the far reaches of the Green Zone. Beyond that, the law of the Cartels ruled. But in between the two there was no law at all. And that's where Canacus sat.

"Why the Green Zone? And Canacus, right next to the last Dominion station." Alek stared at the coffee machine. At a sound overhead, he glanced up. Grim peered down at him, his jaws moving as he consumed something crunchy. Other than the cat, it was just him, Tink and Rebeka in the common room. Kandi had taken food and drink to Ish, who was on the bridge navigating them through the slipstream.

"What are we going to do?" Tink asked. "In the Green Zone?"

Alek understood the engineer's misgivings. A quadrant of space between Dominion hegemony and Cartel control, the Green Zone was a quagmire where anything was permissible, as long as you had the power to back it up. It certainly wasn't a place where honest people found honest work. In fact, honest people tended to live short lives out here.

Glass full, he turned to face the room. Rebeka stood opposite, leaning back against the glass overlooking the cargo bay, while Tink sat at the table, fiddling with something he couldn't see. Both women scowled. Alek walked over to the captain and handed her the coffee.

"Ta." Rebeka nodded at him, then took a big gulp of the hot liquid. Her eyes squinted at him over the rim of the mug, though he couldn't tell if it was the tension or that she still didn't trust him, even though he hadn't been their saboteur, and had, in fact, helped save the *Lyra*. She shifted her gaze to Tink. "What we always do," she said as he returned to the kitchenette to make another drink. "Find enough work to keep the ship running and ourselves fed. And maybe a little bit more."

Tink shook her head. "You think they could have dropped us somewhere safer." She slapped a metal tool down on the table. "Do you think the Sisters knew where we'd end up when they sent us through their gate?"

Alek recalled the shimmer of blue and lavender the Sisters of Elazir had conjured up out of empty space. Jump gates required a solar system's worth of energy to build and maintain, and theirs had popped into being in front of them. He opened his mouth, but it was the captain who answered.

"What do *you* think? They made a gate appear out of nothing." She took another swig of coffee.

"They knew exactly where they were dropping us." He leaned against the counter, wrapping his fingers around his warm mug as he took a sip.

Rebeka straightened and downed the rest of her mug. "At least they could have dumped us somewhere closer to a job." She strode over to him and placed her mug in the sink. She didn't look up when she spoke, but her hands went to her hips and her frown deepened. "But I might know someone in the neighbourhood who needs some odd jobs done."

Alek glanced between her and Tink. His stomach went cold despite the warm coffee. He was sure he wouldn't like this odd job, since the last one nearly got him killed.

2: Rebeka

T HE HEAT AND HUMIDITY pressed down on Rebeka from all directions. With each breath, the heavy air squeezed her chest like a giant snake. Sweat sheened her face and crept along her stubbly scalp, making it itch. The pinpoint light of the distant sun made her wonder how it could be so oppressively hot.

A chittering noise brought her attention back to the cargo in front of her. She frowned then shifted her glare from the rattling crates to Sera Fox. Her old comrade-in-arms looked as cool and crisp as if she'd just stepped out of a chiller, which just made Rebeka more cranky. "It's illegal."

"It's not illegal." The statuesque blonde tore her predatory gaze from Alek, who peered out over the rippling swamp grass. She sighed theatrically in Rebeka's direction, tossing her hair over her shoulder. "They're just bugs."

"Smuggled bugs." Rebeka brought her hands to her hips, and a breeze caressed her armpits. She sighed at the slight cooling sensation, then the breeze disappeared. Her shoulders slumped.

"Bugs that can make you hallucinate," Tink mumbled as she checked the seal on one of the crates, jumping a step back when it rocked towards her. "Alive bugs."

"The gourmands want them alive. It's just good business. Besides, what harm can bugs do? As long as you don't eat them. Or lick them." Her mouth opened then snapped shut before she spoke again. "Maybe avoid touching them." Sera's gaze shifted over Rebeka's shoulder, squinting as she homed in on something. "You really do travel well these days, Mino."

Rebeka turned to see what had caught Sera's attention. Kandi strode down the gangplank, weapons strapped to hips, arms and thighs. "Sera, we could get in trouble if we're stopped."

"I have a permit."

"A clearly forged permit."

"I have an official in my pocket." Sera shrugged a shoulder. "In my pants actually." Her voice dropped to a purr. "He quite likes it there. Call him if you run into any trouble." She flicked her attention from Kandi back to Rebeka, arching an eyebrow as she held out a tablet. "Do you want the job?"

Rebeka's jaw clenched, and she stared hard at her former troopmate. A skimmer flew overhead, causing them both to look up. She squinted but couldn't tell if the sleek, unmanned craft bore Dominion markings or none. And she couldn't decide which was worse.

Sera's lips quirked into an almost smile. "Some habits never die." She jerked her chin and the hand holding the waybill towards Rebeka.

Rebeka grimaced but swiped the tablet from her. "You swear we don't have to open the crates?"

"As long as you deliver them within the fortnight, they'll be fine. The tablet contains care instructions, though they don't need much. They're alive but dormant."

A crate almost jumped at Alek as he reached down to load it onto the hover cart. "You call that dormant?" He straightened up and stepped back.

Sera's predatory gaze came back, joined by a wolfish grin. "You should see them when they're wide awake. If there's a swarm of them, *you* become dinner." Her eyebrows twitched.

Alek's eyes slid from her to Rebeka, clearly unimpressed. Rebeka couldn't disagree with his assessment, but they didn't have much choice. They needed food and fuel to get them the hell out of the Green Zone and back into the oppressive but orderly Dominion-controlled sphere.

She gave Alek a sharp nod. He stepped back up to the crate, giving Tink a lopsided smile as she joined him.

"Let's get 'er done." Tink took hold of her side. "Sooner we load them, sooner we're rid of them."

"You're sure you can trust her?" Alek asked, nodding towards the closing cargo bay doors. A clank sounded, shutting out the sweltering haze of the moon. Though now the cargo bay felt like a swamp, stuffy and damp and smelling slightly of rotten vegetable matter.

Rebeka slid her gaze from the door to the pilot. "No." She turned around to the overstuffed bay. "But she loves profit more than plotting. And there's no profit in turning us over to Dominion customs officers."

"You're sure about that?" Tink came to stand on her other side. A crate rattled and chirped. Something dropped from above them, landing with a thud. Grim's weight bore down on the crate, his eyes fixed on it as he made a chirruping sound.

"She'd lose her cargo and gain notice of the authorities." Rebeka tried to make her voice sound more certain than she felt. "Shoo, not for you." She waved her hand at the cat. "There's plenty of bugs already on the *Lyra* to keep you busy." Grim's green eyes peered at her as he waggled his rump before settling onto the pile of boxes.

About the Author

Rene Astle is the scifi pen name of C. Rene Astle.

She gained a love of fiction, fantasy in particular, and a voracious appetite for story literally at her mother's knee, being read The Hobbit and Chronicles of Narnia – because those are the types of stories her mom wanted to read.

From her father, she got an enduring curiosity about the universe, earned shivering in the dark beside a telescope on cold, Canadian winter nights waiting to witness some celestial event.

Now she fits in writing between her day job, gardening and getting out to enjoy supernatural British Columbia.

As C. Rene Astle, she's the author of the Bloodborne Pathogens dark fantasy series, as well as a number of short stories.